Love on the Island

Jo Lyons

Gekko Press

Book Cover by Canva

First edition 2024

Also By

Benidorm, *actually*

Benidorm, *again*

Your Place or Mine?

The Coach Trip

Lovely Reviews

"Jo Lyons has written a book and it's hilarious!"

Jenny Colgan, The Summer Skies

"So, so funny. Really great characters.
Warm and friendly and funny."

Suzy K Quinn, The Bad Mother's Series

"Couldn't put it down!"

"I stayed up half the night to finish it."

"So warm-hearted and uplifting."

"Best debut I've read in a long time."

If you have enjoyed reading this novel, please leave me a review on Amazon or on your social media. I love to hear your thoughts and it helps new readers discover my books.

Happy Reading!

To my amazing niece Gabs,
I'm a lucky aunty.

Chapter 1

When *the* major achievement of your day is not having a substantial meltdown, and you can't even manage that, you have to wonder if teaching is all it is cracked up to be. And when you turn to your boyfriend for a shoulder to cry on, and he more or less says he'd rather rot in prison than continue the relationship a second longer, questions need to be asked, soul-searching needs to occur.

I drive straight home from school, relieved to see my twin, Lois, is waiting for me on the sofa, remote control in hand.

'How come you're so late?' she asks. I take one look at her kind, concerned face and burst into tears.

She leaps up, drawing me into a warm hug. 'I knew it! They've done it again, haven't they? You've been stuck in that dead-end school on a zero-hours contract for years, and now they're letting you go, just so they don't have to pay you over the summer. It's outrageous!' She is livid. She holds me at arm's length. 'I forbid you to go back to that hideous Victorian workhouse, ever again.'

'But what about the poor kids?' I say, wiping my cheeks with the palms of my hands. 'They'll be devastated if –'

'FUCK THE KIDS!' she bellows. 'Who cares about the FUCKING kids?'

We take a beat to let this land. Lois is a paediatric nurse; caring about kids is pretty much her bread and butter.

'Libby, I hate to see you slaving away night after night. They're always giving you extra classes, extra responsibilities, all without extra pay or a permanent contract. You need to learn how to stand up for yourself.'

'But that's not the only reason I'm upset.'

She sighs knowingly. 'It's Arrogant bloody Josh, isn't it?'

For a caregiver, her attitude to people can be a little brusque, but unfortunately, she is spot on. I show her the text he sent me earlier.

'I think we should put a pin in the relationship,' Lois reads aloud. 'Circle back in a few months maybe?'

The words scrape across my heart.

'Maybe?' she gasps, staring at me. 'Maybe? Like he's only willing to get back with you *if* he's desperate and can't find anyone else. He's such an arrogant prick. I knew this was coming.'

I nod glumly as a fresh stream of tears dampen my cheeks. A tingle of fear crawls up my spine as I read between the lines. 'Is this because he thinks I'm boring? Is that it?'

'No! Of course not.'

'It is, isn't it?' I check my phone to see if Josh has sent me another message. He hasn't.

'No,' Lois warns. 'Do not keep checking to see if he has messaged you. Don't give him any more of your precious time or headspace, or you'll end up with high blood pressure.'

Living with a health professional has its drawbacks; you are constantly measured against World Health Organisation parameters.

'Libby, you are far too good for him anyway. Let him go. He's never been right for you. Do not reply.'

Living with a health professional who is also your overly protective twin sister, conversely, has its benefits. She is the best cheerleader anyone could hope for.

'I know it hurts now, Libs, but perhaps this break up is exactly what you need. Between Josh and the school, you had what you *wanted*,' she says, pausing dramatically, 'but not what you *needed*. You've been stuck in reverse.'

I take a moment to process.

'Is that Coldplay?' I ask. 'Are you Chris Martin, right now? Are you trying to fix me?'

'Yes. Yes, I am.' There's a twinkle in her eye as she does namaste hands. She knows I've always carried a torch for nice, kind-hearted global superstars. 'You have the whole summer to explore what life has to offer. Travel. Be spontaneous. Date men who aren't self-obsessed and married to their own reflections.'

'I'm hardly much of a catch. I'm single, unemployed and when you get married next year, I'll be homeless,' I say, sniffing up the rest of my tears. 'Besides, you know the most adventurous thing I've done this year is buy an air fryer. I'm hardly the spontaneous type.'

'You're not unemployed, you're between jobs and you're not soon-to-be homeless because you can stay here for as long as you want.' She sweeps a hand casually round the cosy living room and its homely sage green walls and handmade colourful furnishings. 'But you're right, it wouldn't hurt you to be more spontaneous once in a while.'

'Maybe this is why Josh wants to take a break. He thinks I'm not spontaneous or exciting. Maybe what we actually need is *more* time together, not apart.' My mind begins whirring with possibilities of a romantic reunion. This whole thing could even be a cry for help. A last attempt from Josh to get my full attention. Like an over-looked middle child constantly singing 'Somewhere Over the Rainbow' while simultaneously tap dancing on the dining room table and doing magic tricks, desperate for parental affection. From his point of view my job is very demanding. My marking piles are very high.

'No, please. I'm begging you. Have nothing more to do with him. He really doesn't deserve someone as lovely as you.'

'Maybe the text wasn't actually meant for me,' I say, grasping at straws. 'Perhaps he was breaking up with his... his personal trainer or his...?'

'It was definitely for you, Libs.' She looks away pretending to pick at some fluff on the sofa.

I screw my eyes at her. 'What are you not telling me?'

'I'm sorry,' Lois says with a sad look. 'I found out today that he's on Tinder.'

'Eh? Tinder?' I'm instantly confused. 'You've got Tyrone, what do you need a dating app for?'

Tyrone is my sister's fiancé, and he is adorable. The three of us hang out all of the time. *All* of the time. Probably too much now that I come to think of it. He often jokes that he is in a committed relationship with conjoined twins.

Lois gives me a wide-eyed stare. 'What? God, no. I love Ty to the moon and back. He's my rock. My soulmate. You know that. I'd never cheat on him. Never. He's my dream man.'

'Thank goodness,' I say. I love Tyrone. 'So, why are you on Tinder?'

'I'm not.'

'So, how do you know about Josh?'

Lois guides me to sit back down and clears her throat noisily. 'Clever Amy at work asked me and Booby Julie what we thought of this guy who'd just uploaded his profile this morning. I recognised Josh straight away.'

Her words hardly seem real. 'This morning? Before he'd even broken up with me?'

Lois looks sorry for me. 'Clever Amy was asking if he sounded weird because… well, it doesn't matter why, the main thing is he is back on the prowl, and you need to forget all about him.'

'What does Josh's profile say?' My heart is hammering in my chest. I trust her implicitly. I would give my life for her in a single heartbeat. We always tell each other the truth.

She reluctantly swipes at her phone and turns the screenshot towards me. I take in Josh's handsome profile pic and try to ignore the stabbing pain as I flick over the description of what sort of new lady he is after. He is looking for glamorous, party-loving, adventurous women who throw caution to the wind and are partial to a no-strings relationship. In glaring capital letters, he has written NO TEACHERS.

Chapter 2

'I think he was sick of me always talking about work and staying in with my marking piles,' I say, trying not to sound so hurt. 'But he obviously thinks I'm not sexy enough or glam –'

My sister's cheeks go pink with outrage. 'Nope. Do not start self-doubting and putting the blame on yourself.' She flicks her glorious long brown curls over her shoulder, her big brown eyes wide with compassion. 'We are eleven out of ten stunners. He's the fool that can't see it. He's the dickhead with the problem. Not you.'

I love her sense of self-worth and confidence. It oozes from her.

'He's moving on very fast considering we were together for nearly four months,' I say, a batch of fresh tears pooling in my eyes.

'You have to move on too,' Lois says gently. 'Forget him. Don't dwell in the past.'

Is barely one hour ago considered 'the past'? *Is it?*

I ignore her and carry on. 'Do you think it's a cry for help?' I sound very desperate. Very needy. This is not my finest hour.

'Even if it was, would you really take him back after the way he is carrying on?'

I shake my head, barely able to look her in the eye.

'Libby, he is not right for you,' Lois sighs. 'If you want to get back at him, then make him jealous by moving on and never looking back. Your pride has been dented but come on, you were never in love with him, were you?'

What a question to ask at a time like this. All I can do is shrug. Everything around me is imploding at the same time, my relationship, my career, my confidence. Everyone around me is moving forward while I seem to be going backwards at full steam.

'Listen, I've got some news that will take your mind off him,' she says, her eyes shining. 'You'll never guess what. You know how I've always wanted to go on *Love on the Island*?'

'Yes, of course. You're obsessed.'

It's that programme on TV where extroverts go to live semi-naked in a luxury villa, surrounded by potential lovers. Lois has been infatuated with the show since it began.

'I'm not watching the new series with you if that's what you're asking. It's Tyrone's turn this year.' I hate it. She knows this.

'I finally got accepted,' Lois laughs.

I have misheard her.

'Sorry, what?'

She sucks in her lips and raises her eyebrows. 'I've been picked as a contestant!'

I continue to stare at her. It's like looking in a mirror, except her features are expertly highlighted and contoured. She looks sophisticated while, with my drab work clothes and tangled hair, I look like a woman who gave up long ago.

'What do you mean? When did you apply? What about Tyrone?'

'I applied to go on the show last year before I met Ty. Then I fell head over heels and forgot all about it.' Lois practically has sparkles coming out of her eyes every time she mentions Tyrone's name. I've never seen a couple more in love.

'They emailed me out of the blue to see if I was still interested, saying I'd signed some contract. You know I always click the terms and conditions without reading. Who has time to read the small print?'

'Hmmm.' I do. I always read the small print. But now is not the time to remind her. 'So, have you replied? What did they say?'

'Not yet. I'll do it tomorrow when...'

At that moment, the door opens, and Tyrone fills the frame. He may as well live with us the amount of time he spends here.

'Have you told her the good news?' he says chirpily.

'You know about *Love on the Island*?' I say surprised.

'*Love on the Island*? No. I mean me moving in. Yikes. All three of us cramped into this poky flat.' He laughs. 'Living the dream, eh?'

I look at his bags. He has two massive holdalls. 'You're moving in... today?' I glance over at Lois.

'Sorry, I meant to tell you but with everything going on...'

Tyrone drops the bags at the door, takes two giant steps towards us and swoops my sister up into a loving embrace. He is huge compared to her petite frame. He collapses onto the sofa, pulling her down to sit on his knee before giving her an adoring look.

'So, what's this about *Love on the Island*?' he asks.

Lois is lit up like a Christmas tree in his arms. 'Just that the producers of *Love on the Island* reached out to me today.

They want me on the show. Because I'm crazy hot and gorgeous.'

Tyrone is visibly distraught. 'Babe, no way. I don't want to see you kiss some random muscle-mountain. They'll be all over you. I couldn't take it.'

He's right. He is insanely in love with my sister. It would crucify him to see her flirting up a storm with other guys.

'Oh, God, no, honey. I wouldn't dream of going on the show. I did the video entry before we even met. You're the only muscle-mountain for me. I don't have eyes for anyone but you.'

They exchange the same dreamy expression. It causes me to look away as a brief pang of longing jabs at me. I've never had that with any of my previous boyfriends. Never.

'Just because I signed a contract doesn't mean I *have* to go on the show,' Lois tells him.

'You've signed a contract,' he says in a worried voice because he is an up-and-coming lawyer. 'Seriously? You haven't signed an agreement, have you? Those things with TV companies can be watertight.'

She nods meekly and hugs him tight. 'But I don't want to go on the show. They can't force me.'

'What if you're contractually obliged?' I ask. This would be awful for them.

'I'll withdraw. If the worst comes to the worst, they can sue me.' Lois gazes up at Ty. 'There's no way I'm leaving you for the whole summer. I couldn't bear it.'

He lifts her chin towards him and places a gentle, reassuring kiss on her lips.

They could really do with me out of their way so they can live as a proper couple. Stroking each other's cheeks, foot-massaging and having sex on the kitchen table whenever the mood strikes, without me always there as a third wheel.

I pinch the bridge of my nose to stop feeling faint. I knew this day would come. Trust it to be this day.

My mind flashes back to the horrors of earlier. After a long day of doing mock Ofsted curriculum deep dives (not as interesting as it sounds) and ploughing through children's texts describing why resilience and challenging yourself is the key to success in life, the last thing I had expected was the headteacher to pop his head around my classroom door to casually inform me that I'll not be needed the following term.

I was so gutted. And to make matters worse, I rang Josh for a shoulder to cry on but instead of answering, he sent me the 'put a pin in it' text back. And now, Tyrone has officially moved in, meaning I should really start searching for a new job and somewhere new to live. It's all a bit overwhelming. I can feel my soul disintegrating. I belong nowhere, I have no one. Perhaps Lois is right. I need to escape for the summer, have fun, do something spontaneous for once.

'Did you know your signatures are virtually identical?' says Tyrone to Lois, snapping me out of my misery. He is checking the small print on the contract. 'Don't worry, babe. There's got to be a way to get you out of it without them taking legal action.'

Lois is stroking his face and looking at him with a doe-eyed expression, as though it will help him find the get-out clause that he's after.

Suddenly an idea comes to me.

A solution to everything. For both me and for Lois.

I slap on a bright smile to hide how I'm feeling. 'I'll do it!' I hear my voice catch. 'I'll go on the show instead of you.'

Lois's head whips round. 'Wait. What? No way! You hate that show.'

'It beats teaching summer camps and being surrounded by nothing but wine and piles of exam marking. And it might be nice for the two of you to spend some quality time together... without me always hanging around.'

Lois gasps. 'No, Libs,' she says, leaping up. 'Don't make this about me and Tyrone needing our own space. We'd never do that to you. We love having you around. Don't we?' She is so astute.

Tyrone is nodding emphatically. He is very emotionally literate for a man. He is also very good at doing what he is told.

'It's not about that,' I lie.

'Well then, it's about winning Arrogant Josh back. That's not a good reason to go on the show either. He doesn't deserve you after the way he dumped you like that.'

'He dumped you. When?' Tyrone asks softly.

'Today. By text,' Lois explains before turning to take my hands in hers. 'I want to see you being happy, but you'd be doing the show for the wrong reasons.'

She's one hundred per cent right but the more I think about Josh dumping me by text, the school dumping me right before the holidays, and the fact that I haven't done anything remotely interesting in years, the more my misery is growing. I think maybe this opportunity is fate.

'No, really,' I tell her. 'What have I got to lose?'

I'd simply be leaping with both feet from one pile of shite into another.

'You said every episode is like one long, tedious never-ending TikTok make-up tutorial.'

'Did I?'

I totally did.

'And when was the last time you got dolled up to go anywhere, Libs?' Lois says, defending her favourite programme. 'You are not cut out to appear on such a bloodthirsty, over-the-top, reality TV show. Imagine all the drama and back-stabbing. You said the temper tantrums and hissy fits were worse than your school nursery.'

I did.

'And you might struggle to get employed by a primary school afterwards.'

That's a good point but I'm past caring.

'Look, I'm sorry I forgot to mention Tyrone was moving in, but I think you're just overwhelmed by everything that has happened today, and you're making panic-fuelled decisions.'

She's totally right.

I've developed a deep-rooted fear of body oil, protruding six-packs and Turkey teeth but to be fair, she did make me binge watch the entire series with her. And everyone's teeth were blindingly white to a seizure-inducing degree.

'Listen,' I say, trying to sound convincing. 'You said yourself I should do something spontaneous.'

'The US show would cast a wider net for her.' Tyrone is clearly Team Libby and has been desperately trying to come up with positives while he searches for a way to keep Lois from having to go on the show. 'It will give her a more global reach. Cover all bases. Target an expansive range of territories.'

He's making my potential search for a new mate sound like a difficult product launch. I can feel a panic setting in. It would be way too out of my comfort zone.

'Thanks Tyrone. I'm sure *someone* on the island will find me attractive.' My voice is rising a full octave with each sentence, as all my insecurities about life, where I'm going and what I'm doing bubble to the surface. I have as much sex appeal as a rotting banana. Maybe Josh was right. I haven't got what it takes to be sexy and adventurous. I'm a joyless husk. They'll see right through me.

Tyrone looks like a man at a tribunal hearing who is about to choose his words very carefully. He looks from my sister to me and back again. Me and my sister are practically identical. He has to be complimentary without being *too* complimentary. He will be forever caught between a rock and a hard place. He can't find us both sexy. It's almost painful to watch.

All of a sudden, the exhaustion of losing my job and my boyfriend in the same day, sweeps through me. 'No worries. Forget it. It was just a stupid thought. They won't force you to go on the show, sis. They'd have to prise you from my dead arms. I'll leave you two to your film. I'm off to bed. See you in the morning.'

Lois jumps up to hug me. 'I'm sorry. I'm sure once you sleep on it, you'll realise it's not a good idea.' She holds me at arm's length. 'Someone deserving will come along when you least expect it and sweep you right off your feet.'

Her phone suddenly bursts to life, startling us all. A face is video calling her. A man's face. Lois thrusts it at me, her eyes wide. 'Oh my God. It's them! It's *Love on the Island*. What will I do?'

'Simple. You accept the call and explain that you aren't going to do the show,' says Tyrone firmly as the phone continues to trill.

We're all looking at each other as though we're playing tennis with our eyeballs while we wait for Lois to move. It looks as though her body has frozen in time. Her eyes flick to mine. And before I quite know what I'm doing, I grab the phone from her and, in one swift movement, I release my hair from its bun and glide over to the fireplace so he can't see Lois or Tyrone in the background, and press accept.

'Hello. Thanks for calling,' I say with a smile, as I make what could be the worst decision of my life.

Chapter 3

I sit down slowly in the pretty armchair next to the fire. Rows of books are crammed into the white shelving in the nook behind me, and a charming Edwardian sash window provides a flattering glow from the streetlamp outside, as I hold Lois's phone in front of me.

'Hi there, it's Cam. Cameron, one of the producers from LoveIt TV,' he says, giving me a friendly, reassuring smile.

As if this wasn't already daunting enough to get my head around, I squint to get a clearer picture. I am looking at the most attractive man I have ever seen in my entire life. He sweeps soft brown hair from his forehead as though to give me a clearer view of his incredible blue-green eyes. His smile is lighting up his entire face and drawing me in.

He's American. An *actual* American TV producer.

What am I doing?

'We spoke briefly last summer during your VT.'

I stare blankly at him.

'Your video audition?'

We most certainly did not.I would have remembered interacting with such a genetically superior and well-sculptured member of the species. And I would have gone completely to pieces. Rather like I am doing right now.

How did Lois not reveal this one tiny but significant detail?

He holds my gaze as though he is used to women turning beetroot red and severely mute in his presence, and carries on. 'I'm calling to go over the schedules and confirm the press releases that need to be carried out before you fly out to us.'

I stare at the screen nodding, my hand trembling slightly as I lift it up to capture a more becoming angle, less nostril and more forehead. Tyrone and Lois are gesturing wildly for me to end the conversation.

I should say something.

He waits patiently for me to respond.

I should explain that I'm Lois's near-identical twin sister and I'm about to fraudulently pass myself off as her, all so that I can get off with somebody, anybody, just to make my very recent ex-boyfriend jealous. And so that she can spend some well-earned alone time with her lovely fiancé, instead of being dragged through the courts by his TV company.

'Fly out to you? To the island?' I manage.

He is heart-stoppingly gorgeous. And that accent! He sounds like a film star.

'Yes, that's correct.'

'Which island would that be?' Images of me surrounded by a tropical paradise, drinking from coconuts and bathing in waterfalls, far, far from any marking piles, swim pleasingly into my mind causing pangs of excitement.

'Mexico.'

Call me old-fashioned, but as far as land masses go, that is not an island.

'Does Mexico have actual islands though?'

'Yes, but we're not allowed to go on them.'

'So, it's more like *Love near the Island*?'

He doesn't look a bit flustered by my interrogation. He gives me an amused smile. 'We thought about it but *Love similar-to-but-not-quite on the Island* just hasn't got the same ring.'

He's funny.

'Can I check what name you've decided on? I believe you mentioned Lulu, Lala and Lolo to our researcher.'

Lois has always regretted not having a more exotic name. She has the good grace to look sheepish.

I watch Cam efficiently flipping through papers on a clipboard. He must have quite a few contestants to get through. 'To be honest, I can't find your real name on here.'

'Erm, Olivia Jackson. But I'd like to be called Libby on the show.'

'Are you a big fan of the show, Libby?' he asks smiling encouragingly at me.

I'm completely thrown by his easy confident manner and extreme good looks and in a panic, I say the first honest thing that springs to mind. 'No, absolutely not.'

His eyes widen in surprise.

'I mean, yes. Absolutely, yes. It's the best show that's ever been made.' My voice breaks halfway through because I am so rubbish at lying. In my peripheral vision, Lois is mouthing, 'Do not do this' to me.

Too late.

I laugh nervously. 'So, Cam, whereabouts in America are you from?'

'Canada.'

Touché.

'But I live in California,' he says. 'That's on the west coast of America.'

It sounds so sophisticated.

'Ah, yes. California.' My recent Year Three Geography project springs suddenly to mind. 'The Golden State. It's the third largest and most biologically diverse of all the states.' I say, nervously trotting out some impressive stats. 'It's the pistachio capital of the world.'

Lois is shaking her head.

'Someone has done their homework,' Cam says in a playful tone, even though his eyes are wondering if he's made a huge mistake. 'Although, I think you'll find California is the *avocado* capital of the world.'

Cripes. He's correcting me. Me, the teacher. But he's so ridiculously good looking I'm going to have to let it go.

'And the show?' he says. 'Any last-minute reservations about taking part?'

Here it is. My get-out-of-jail card.

Am I in or out?

It's decision time. I'm known in primary education circles as being impressively decisive, yet here I am, beating about the bush, all because he is as handsome as fudge.

'Are you absolutely sure about the avocado situation? Because I did do an extensive Google search.'

He smiles and repeats the question. His voice is so soft and warm. I could listen to his accent all day. He's got an intelligent manner about him that makes me want to talk to him all night.

'Who wouldn't have last-minute reservations?' I say.

'It's not the easiest of shows to go on,' he says. 'It's a lot of pressure. It's not for the faint-hearted, that's for sure.'

'I can imagine.'

A strange giddy feeling in my stomach is compelling me to use long and overly complicated words.

'Nearly every episode is one random smorgasbord of haphazard snogging and *she said, he said* tit-for-tat,' I say as though I'm writing a review for The Guardian. I don't know what is coming over me but it's borderline horrific.

'Interesting. Interesting,' he says, beginning to frown. 'Some might view it like that, I suppose.'

'You could even say it's a social satire of reductive, trepidatious twentysomething behaviour. Almost toxic and playgroundy, if you will.'

God help me. Make it stop.

I watch his face fall and instantly regret trying to show off. Tyrone and Lois are staring at me open-mouthed.

Why? Why am I like this?

'Playgroundy?' Cam asks, giving me a quizzical look. 'Oh, like in the school yard?'

'I'm sorry. I shouldn't have said that,' I blurt, backtracking like mad. 'I'm sure a lot of work goes into producing the show. I just meant that it tends to reveal how childish we can all be at times.'

'No worries. We edit the show that way. We take out all the boring chit chat about war, poverty and saving the planet, and keep the focus squarely on what really matters to today's discerning, globally literate audience,' he flashes me a huge grin. 'Which is of course, who fancies who.'

His eyes are sparkling. There's a hint of a smirk going on which causes me to giggle. I'm in way over my head but relieved he is willing to overlook every crackpot word I've just said. I emit a nasally laugh that causes Lois to put her head back in her hands.

To me, this is the very definition of flirtatious patronising banter. My favourite kind.

'That's very reassuring,' I say playing along, after all, no one does patronising banter quite like teachers. 'But I think you'll find it's who fancies whom.'

There's a small silence where we stare at one another. Perhaps he is wondering if my flirting is too much. Then to my relief he starts chuckling. It transforms his whole face. 'Funny. So, Libby, do you want to be on the show?'

My heart is in my mouth. *What am I doing?* 'Yes. Yes, I do. One hundred per cent. Sign me up.'

'Are you sure? Not too reductive or trepidatious for you?' he says, grinning.

I shake my head slowly. I am so up for this. It feels like the best decision I've ever made in my entire life.

He checks his notes, unaware of the turmoil I'm in. 'You'll be the only British woman to appear on the show. We're taking a bit of a gamble that you'll fit in.'

Of course, I won't fit in. Because Americans don't understand sarcasm or know how to make a proper cup of tea and because we are baffled by your incessant over-the-top friendliness, but mostly because we are deeply ashamed of our terrible yellow teeth.

'We're hoping you'll connect with our British audience and increase our overseas viewers.'

'We British are famed for our strength of character, our superior intellect, and our moral fibre. As long as you don't make out that I'm a desperate, slutty villain, I should be fine,' I joke as though I'm going to be the star of the show, right across the planet.

Cam tugs at his collar. I've clearly caught him off guard. He seems unsure of how to handle a British woman telling him how to do his job. It feels rather empowering. I can see Lois and Tyrone rolling their eyes at one another. I shift away so that I can't see them.

Cam recovers himself quickly. 'Well, of course, we don't script this show. Not like we script other reality shows. We prefer a more natural take.'

He is very charming and believable. But I suppose all Canadians are.

'I have to say, Libby, you're a lot different to how you were last year.'

I slide my eyes over to my sister.

'I'm sure I am.'

And I'm sure my sister did a much better job of enthralling him during her interview. She will have flicked her long shiny hair, licked her plump, glossy lips and batted her lashes. Men find her kind of energy enticing. I'm what you might call borderline unkempt. Like most committed workaholics. The opposite of what LoveIt TV are looking for.

'I'm sure if I go in there and be kind and courteous, people will connect with my vibe.' *I have no idea what I'm saying.* 'After all, at the end of the day they are the qualities that matter. We can't all be glamorous super models.'

Cam is giving me a curious look. 'I agree. And sure, while you're stunningly gorgeous and beautiful, it's great to see that you also have a naturally wicked sense of humour. And I love that you're so self-deprecating, and you aren't afraid to tell your truth. I think you'll do extremely well on the show. I can see you getting a lot of airtime.'

Wait. What? He thinks I'm gorgeous.

And stunningly beautiful.

He literally just said gorgeous and stunningly beautiful in the same sentence.

Professionally, I should correct his semantics, the wasteful use of cumulative adjectives that mean the same thing. But unfortunately for me, I respond depressingly well to praise of any kind. I sit up tall and give him a bashful smile. 'Really?'

'Yes. Really.' Cam has incredibly thick lashes for a guy. They're very appealing. He blinks slowly as if to show them off, making my heart flutter. His eyes have flecks of gold in them. And that accent of his is mesmerising.

'Okay. That's great. So, I have questions,' he looks briefly down at his notes. 'How are you in relationships?' he asks gently.

I take a second to swallow the hurt of Josh's very recent rejection.

'Unbearable,' I say, causing him to laugh.

'Any relationship complications to declare before going into the villa?' he asks grinning. 'It's the sort of thing the press love. Disgruntled ex-boyfriends coming out of the woodwork.'

I hardly want to admit I've just been dumped by a 'put a pin in it' text. Besides, Josh has probably forgotten about my very existence by now.

'Erm, I guess the only complicated relationship I have at the moment is...' I say, my mind blank. '... is with bread.'

'Bread?' Cam throws his head back and roars with laughter. 'Huh. I did not expect that. You are full of surprises.'

Full of surprises? No one has ever said that about me.

'Sorry,' he says eventually calming. 'That must be a pain. Are you allergic to it?' He sounds so invested, so attentive.

'It's the wheat. It bloats me,' I announce in a sudden knee-jerk reaction to the question.

For the love of God why? Why?

'Okay. I'll put no wheat products down on the form,' Cam says kindly.

'And you?' I ask, my adrenaline levels are sky high right now. 'What's your most complicated relationship, Cameron from Canada?'

'Meat,' he explains, grinning. 'Specifically, cheeseburgers and fried bacon. Because I'm supposed to be vegan.'

Who doesn't like a quick-witted, mostly vegan, fast-food loving TV producer? And now we have something in common. Our dietary struggles. I start giggling. He finds me funny and gorgeous. He has a very nice smile and kind eyes. And he's obviously a man of good taste because he thinks I'm gorgeous. Gorgeous, even with my complicated relationship and sensitive bowel.

I suddenly feel shy in front of him. I can feel a heat rising from my neck as I become unusually tongue-tied. I watch him scribbling down notes. He looks back up expectantly. We lock eyes, unsure of who should talk next.

'Anything else that disagrees with you?' His voice is so warm and caring, rather like a friendly GP lulling you to offload. I am spellbound. I'll say anything.

'Dairy,' I say, my voice almost a whisper. 'It runs straight through me.'

My sister is shaking her head in disbelief. I've gone too far.

'Right, right,' Cam says in a concerned voice. I have instantly turned the atmosphere awkward. 'Well, I have about twenty other potential contestants to get through today so, how about I send you the schedules now,' Cam says quickly, keen to get me off the call before I reveal any other bowel-related mishaps. 'And a guide to our allergens policy.

You look them over, and we'll talk in a couple of days, okay? I'm sure you have questions.'

Why yes, I do. I have questions for myself. Questions such as where is my filter?

I've lost my words. I'm dying of embarrassment. I literally can't speak.

He gives me a quick friendly wave before clicking off the call.

I take in a deep breath, glad it's over. Common sense gets the better of me as realisation dawns that being on TV might be a truly terrible idea. I will forget this phone call ever happened. Erase it from history.

Lois turns to me, astounded. 'What sort of bollocks was that?'

'Whatever do you mean?'

Lois starts laughing. 'Oh, my God. I can't believe it!'

'What? What are you talking about?'

'You! You're crushing on him.'

'On who?'

'On the producer guy. Cameron.'

'No, I'm not.'

'Yes, you one hundred per cent are.'

'He's not even my type.'

'You don't have a type. It takes you over a year to admit that you like someone even just a tiny bit and by then, well, the less said about your dating history, the better. This is different. You totally fancy him. I can tell. Look at your face! Ty, honey. Doesn't Libby fancy Cam?'

We both turn to Tyrone. He has a silly grin spreading across his face. 'Did you see the way she was playing with her necklace while she spoke to him? And she was twiddling with her hair.'

Like Lois, Ty is very astute. Too astute.

'I don't think I was.'

I totally was.

'I'm just amazed you forgot to tell him about the time you went for pizza and shat it out before the bill came,' Lois says, her shoulders shaking as she tries not to laugh.

'He'll probably not want me on the show now anyway. I have red flag written all over me. He's probably tearing up the contract as we speak.'

What a thing to say to him. I'm so cringe. No wonder I'm not in a relationship.

As though she is reading my mind, Lois stares at me.

'What?' I say.

'Libby, I haven't seen you light up like this in... well, never. I mean, if ever you were going to develop a type, it's him.'

As a twenty-six-year-old woman I do feel I should have at least developed a type by now. A spark of excitement flickers deep inside me. 'Wait. Lois, are you now saying I *should* go on the show?'

'Yes. You deserve to be happy. Some would consider it adventurous, romantic and a free holiday,' says Lois.

Tyrone lets out a massive sigh, shaking his head. His moral compass has kicked in and he has completely changed his tune. 'Some would also consider it fraudulent, time-wasting and immoral,' says Tyrone looking at each of us in turn. 'The poor man. He's just trying to do his job.'

We both give him the same look. It's as though the fact that Cameron is an unholy level of handsome has flown straight over his head. Women have killed for less.

'Okay. I'll do it. It's time for me to be spontaneous and step right out of my comfort zone.'

'Exactly. Go for it, Libs, what have you got to lose?'

For the first time in years, I feel genuinely excited.

Chapter 4

I am jolted awake to the sound of the captain announcing in a thick Spanish accent that we are about to make our descent into Meh-hee-co. I blink myself fully awake. This is probably the third time I've woken during the flight in a cold sweat. The first time, I woke yelling, 'I'VE GOT A TEXT!' which seemed to confuse a lot of people and the cabin crew came running over to make sure my phone was in flight mode.

'This is happening,' I mutter. 'This is really happening.'

The past week has felt like a bizarre dream. One minute I'm moping around feeling sorry for myself over Arrogant Josh, and the next, I've all but forgotten about him as images of Cameron fill my every waking thought. And when I found myself in London posing in a series of awkward angles. Hands on hips, twisting this way and that, pretending to laugh, pretending to look seductive, pretending to care about something meaningful, all I could think was,

'What will Cameron think of these pictures?'. Even when they said, 'Can you look less dreamy, as though you have something really, really important on your mind?'

I answered, 'No problem.' After all, my generation has literally *everything* to worry about, but it was still a struggle not to think about Cam and his kind eyes and lovely smile.

'I'm anxious about global warming, never owning my own home and my massive brand-new credit card bill because of all the outfits you want me to bring,' I told them. To which they looked confused and said, 'No. We meant just like what sandals are you going to wear tonight.'

In the end, they got fed up and told me to think about my moustache. Then they ordered me to go to 'Faces *R* Us' beauty salon nearby as a matter of urgency to get my lip threaded. They also advised me to get my roots touched up, my nails done, some Tatti lashes glued on, and my eyebrows shaped before they could go any further.

'Will that salon do all of those things?' I asked.

They sniggered as though I'd asked the most ridiculous question. 'You'll have to make appointments at lots of different salons, but tell them LoveIT sent you and they'll squeeze you in. But tip big or they'll do a crap job on you.'

They handed me a pile of fliers with salon after salon offering to transform my hair, nails and ability to lure men.

It took a dark-haired, ponytailed lothario all of twenty seconds to chop off a third of my hair and snip, snip, snip into it. He fanned it out over my shoulders, making cooing noises as he admired his handiwork and then clicked his fingers for someone else to come and finish it off. I had little time to feel bereft at the clumps of hair lying around my feet because I was wheeled over to the sink and plonked on a vibrating *chaise longue* to have my head yanked back, massaged and conditioned. All for only three hundred pounds and thirty-six pence, which included a tiny paper bag, plus a tiny thirty-pound bottle of hair rescue serum to put in the tiny paper bag plus a forty-pound tip. Poor, poor credit card.

So here I am, hurtling through the Northern Hemisphere on my way to see Cameron IN REAL LIFE. All waxed, plucked and with a brand-new haircut (a long choppy bob enhanced with the eye-wateringly expensive beach waves and highlights). My stomach is full of butterflies and for the entire flight I have been imagining there will be an attraction between us. A bond. A special thing.

I am also hoping that Arrogant Josh will see me on TV and regret treating me so badly and I will be forever his 'the one that got away'.

I bring up the list of information Cameron has sent through. Even just saying his name in my head is making me feel excited and mortified all at the same time. The thought of us together on a stretch of deserted white sand, turquoise water, warm sea breeze making our sarongs flap, cocktails in hand, is sending quivers up my spine.

I scroll past the information telling me that this year, the *Love on the Island* experience will take place deep in the sweltering rainforests of Mexico. I try not to think about dense tropical jungles, man-eating snakes, spiders the size of my own face and permanently damp sweaty hair. Because on the positive side, Mexico is the hummus capital of the world.

I find the information telling me that prior to the show, all potential contestants will temporarily stay in a holding villa on arrival. We will each have a chaperone to keep us company while we acclimatise to the hot weather. In bold letters there is a reminder that even though we have been selected, there is no guarantee that we will be picked to start the show as part of the original line up. It all sounds very uncertain. But even if I only get to meet Cam face to face so that I can make a good second impression, the trip will be worth it. Whatever happens after that, I suppose, is down to fate.

As the plane shakes its way down to the ground through a series of air pockets and light feathery clouds, the lush expanse of tropical forest comes sharply into view. The coastline is striking because there's barely any difference between the vivid cobalt blue of the sea and the sky. They are separated by a thin strip of sand and what look like high-rise hotels. Then the sheer size of Cancun city appears below me and it is breathtakingly enormous. We swing out to sea and circle back around, flying low above the white beaches and dark green forest. There are perfect circles of vibrant turquoise waters dotted across the landscape that look otherworldly. The country is vast. Simply vast. As we touch down on the runway, the captain says something rapidly in both English and Spanish and before I know it, passengers are jostling to get out of their seats.

Once the jet bridge is fitted to the plane and people start to get off, I ease myself out of my seat and reach up for my travel case. Lois insisted I take some hand luggage, in addition to my two massive suitcases crammed full of clothes and impractical, sky-scraping sandals. It is all far too excessive, but she was adamant that I go prepared for any eventuality. At the thought of our teary goodbye, my soul splinters. We have not been separated like this since she was sent to Leeds for a nursing post, and I was shipped off to Durham on a teaching placement, during our university days.

I follow the crowd along the narrow bridge into the main terminal, tracking the signs to Immigration and Passport Control, down an escalator and across a large concourse that is rapidly filling with people making their way over to join the incredibly long queues. It takes me nearly an hour to get through to the baggage claim area where I look for the carousel with my flight from England on it. Every carousel is packed with people grabbing at luggage. I cast my eye around for a trolley and spot one in the far corner. It has been abandoned for a good reason, wonky wheels, but there doesn't seem to be another one available. I half drag, and half push the trolley over to the carousel. Suitcase after suitcase spills out onto the conveyor belt. Soon, everyone has claimed their luggage but me.

I am hot. I am sticky. I am tired and I am on the verge of a substantial meltdown. I need those cases. They have all of the clothes, the sandals and the make-up I need to make myself look *Love on the Island* ready. I cannot go on the show without them. A message pings into my phone. It is from my chaperone, CHAP 3, saying the driver is waiting for me at the exit and can I please hurry up or he will leave without me as he has another pickup to do, and I am making him late.

I explain to CHAP 3 that my bags have not arrived yet, and they reply to say that always happens, and that they will arrange for my suitcases to be delivered to the villa if they turn up.

If? If? IF?

This is doing nothing for my sky-rocketing blood pressure. CHAP 3 says the main thing is that I do not miss my lift and become stranded at the airport. The holding villa is in a secret location and only my driver knows how to get there.

OH. MY. WORD.

I swallow a lump of panic and clutch my carry-on case tightly. Thank goodness Lois insisted I take one. I make my way through the 'Nothing to Declare' doors where I am greeted by a serious-looking officer. He takes one look at my upset face and beckons me over.

'You have things to declare?' he says sharply.

I shake my head. I am struggling to hold back my tears as they pool in my eye sockets, ready to spill out. 'I don't even have any luggage to declare,' I say mournfully. 'My two suitcases, with everything I need to survive, have not turned up. I waited and waited and now my driver is going to leave without me. What will I do? I have nothing to wear. I *need* my suitcases.'

He is not interested in my lost luggage or the imminent lack of day into nightwear options. Not in the slightest. In fact, it is almost as though I'd not even mentioned lost luggage.

'Open,' he barks.

I hump the carry-on onto the desk and open it up. I'm as surprised as he is to see a huge first aid kit lying on top. Lois. He lifts it out to discover a mountain of bacterial wipes, rubber gloves, packets of clinical NHS-badged adult paper knickers, a surgical gown, tape, a packet of plasters, extreme jungle anti-mosquito sprays, small bottles of Dettol, a year's supply of Imodium and face masks. Everything a serial murderer would need to take their victims apart limb from limb, deposit them deep in the jungle and tidy up neatly afterwards.

'Ah, you doctor?' he asks.

'No.'

'You nurse? You no have visa. You here working illegally? Take our jobs?'

'No. Absolutely not. I'm a Love-on-the-Islander,' I say without thinking.

He looks at me confused.

'I'm here for a TV show,' I explain. 'LoveIt Television? *Love on the Island*?'

I have never seen anyone look so disappointed in my life. He shakes his head. 'My children watch this show. Is terrible.'

I have to agree. 'Yes, it is. I'm very sorry. It's going to be even worse this year because I am on it.'

He looks at me for a few seconds as he discernibly translates what I am saying in his head before he breaks into a wry grin. 'You take selfie?'

'You want me to take a selfie?'

'Yes. For my many daughters. They think I'm not cool, but I show them.' He chuckles to himself while he holds up his phone.

If it will get me out of here, why not? So, I take a selfie with him and within seconds he repacks my case for me and sends me on my way with a promise to investigate the whereabouts of my missing luggage. I hurry towards the exit, hoping and praying my driver is still there. To my delight there is a drinks machine selling cold cans of pop.

My phone pings again as a gulp of delicious cold liquid is running down my throat. It's my chaperone.

'Do not get stopped by the people in the airport asking who your transfer is with!' it says.

What?

Then another text. 'They are time-share bandits. They rent the space in the airport to trick people into going with them to talk about buying time-shares. Do not stop. Keep walking all the way through the concourse to the exit. DO NOT STOP!'

If I wasn't nervous before, then I am bloody nervous now. At the far side of the concourse, I can see a whole line of people almost blocking the path to the exit. They have clipboards. They are wearing suits. They look very officious. They have stopped people to talk to them.

Just as I am feet away from the sliding exit doors, a man pounces causing me to spill the rest of the pop down the front of my cream top. 'Hello. You are from England, right? Who is your transfer with? Let me see if I have you on my list.'

He sounds so convincing. He is checking his clipboard and smiling broadly at me. It feels rude not to acknowledge him as I desperately try to dab myself down. I'm soaked through. I have a huge orange stain spreading outwards across the material.

'No thank you,' I say firmly, as he follows me along without a word of apology for causing me to spill my drink.

Dab, dab, dab.

'Wait just a moment,' he says, still smiling. 'I have you on my list.'

'Oh. You're my driver?'

Dab, dab, dab.

He raises his eyebrows as though in answer. 'Yes. What is your name please and where are you staying?' he asks.

Good job I have no idea. But he's answered my question and that's all that matters. 'You would know my name if you were my driver,' I say firmly as I dab at the awful stain and push past him. I head out through the exit to see a small sweaty man wearing a shirt and tie with socks *and* sandals. He is waving a large card with my name on it.

'Please don't be a conman,' I plead silently as I make my way over.

'You very late, Senora Jackson,' he says by way of greeting. 'Where are your suitcases?'

I shrug and he appears to know instantly that they are still sitting on the tarmac back in Manchester.

'Let's go!' He hurries me over to a waiting limo and screeches away at high speed, through the spaghetti-like mass of roads and roundabouts, onto a near-empty highway, then through a jungle abyss. Dense, impenetrable walls of tropical forest, tangled with shrubs and compacted vegetation, line the narrow track. They loom above us blocking out the fading light. Even if another car was coming towards us, I fail to see how we'd be able to pull over to let them pass.

My heart is racing, and not in a good way. The time has come to dig deep for that resilience within.

I have no idea where I am going.

I have no luggage.

I have a huge orange stain down the front of my cream shirt and because I have nothing but a hospital gown to wear, I will look like a patient fresh from surgery for the foreseeable future, until my suitcases arrive.

I also failed to brush up on the language on the flight over, because I was daydreaming about Cam and what he would say when he sees my new beach wave highlights and glossy nails, and now, regretfully, I can't understand a word that the taxi driver is saying.

Deep breaths.

I am living the dream. Living the dream.

Chapter 5

Thirty-five minutes later, we arrive at the holding villa. It is such a relief, that I climb out of the car and stumble over to the door dragging my carry-on behind me as though the driver has been holding me hostage. In all fairness, that is exactly how it felt. CHAP 3 my chaperone did not reply to a single one of my texts. Not even when I said that I had been successfully picked up but was unsure if it was by the right person, as he was not forthcoming with his information, and would they kindly confirm that I have not been accidentally abducted.

Nothing. Not one word. My nerves are already shot to bits what with the stress of travelling alone to the other side of the planet, only to navigate my way through a hall full of aggressive time-share and car-hire touts. I hammer on the door until an unimpressed Mexican woman answers.

'Hello, I'm Libby,' I say exhausted. 'Are you my chaperone?'

She says, 'Oh, you're here.' Almost as though she's forgotten that her ward, her top-secret person of importance, her one and only job, has arrived.

Oh, you're here? Is that it?

'I thought you'd be longer,' she says, looking past me. 'Did you tip the driver?'

'Do I need to tip the driver? The TV company have paid him already.'

'Yeah, of course. Otherwise, he'll refuse to drive you anywhere ever again. Tipping is a huge part of our culture. Since the Americans started coming.'

'That would have been nice to have known.'

I don't mean to bicker, but I am jetlagged and hungry and ready for a shower then bed. I'm not really in the mood for some social commentary.

'All Americans know about tipping, don't they?'

'I don't.'

'Why not?'

'I'm from England.'

'Oh, yeah. You're the British one. That's right. Well, you have to tip. Just give him ten dollars or something.'

I dig around in my bag and pull out some coins. 'Will one pound fifty do?'

She rolls her eyes. 'Leave it to me.' She marches over to the poor driver who is watching our heated exchange, motor running, anxious to get to his next fare.

'You owe me twenty dollars,' she says, walking past me into the villa.

'I thought you said ten,' I say, following her in.

'That was before he told me that you spent the whole trip ignoring him.'

I have no words. We have gotten off to a bad start and I simply do not care because I am too tired.

'Give me your phone,' she barks, holding out her hand.

'Can I just call my sister to let her know I'm okay? She was worried about me getting kidnapped.'

'No. Hand it over or you'll be in breach of contract. I don't make the rules.'

For Fudges Sake. I bash out a quick text and hand it over. The level of secrecy surrounding the show is baffling. If one word is leaked on social media about you before the show is aired, then apparently you are booted off. She rushes over to a safe and quickly keys in a number and slings it inside.

She shouts over her shoulder. 'I'm in the middle of Elder Scrolls and my dragon is about to give birth any second.' She looks furious with me as though I'm keeping her from a once in a lifetime opportunity. Trust me to end up with a gamer.

'Erm, how long will I be staying in this villa? When will I meet the other contestants? When do we go into the actual *Love on the Island* villa?'

'No idea,' she says with an unhelpful shrug. 'Could be days, could be weeks. There's food for you in the fridge. I made it myself, which is over and above what I'm being paid to do. I may be Mexican, but I am not your waiter. I am your Emotional Support and Well-being Official.'

CHAP 3 reels off a list of dos and don'ts as she races me round the villa, pointing things out. 'You do your own washing and cleaning. There's a utility off there. Don't expect me to tidy up after you. There's a cleaner once a week. Occasionally, I will have to go to the office or into town, so you will be left alone. I am not here for your entertainment. I do not have to listen to your opinions or views. This is the shared bathroom. Shared.' She stops to draw breath and look me up and down. 'I do not have to help you with your beauty rituals, hair, fake tan or waxing. And I definitely will not comment on any questions you have about *Love on the Island*, their plans, how long you will be here or whether I think any of the Islanders are hot. Understand? And by the way, you can cook tomorrow, seeing as I did all the cooking today. Right. That's everything, I'm off.'

I shake my head wearily and pull open the enormous American-style fridge. All the shelves are empty bar one. There is a bowl of suspicious-looking yellow gloop with lumps that look like wet bread in it, next to a sorry-looking sandwich lying curled on a plate. I peel the top slice up to see a thick layer of congealed mayonnaise is hiding a thin slice of cheese which appears to be hiding one leaf of yellowing lettuce.

My whole being sinks. This can't be right. I am going to complain so badly tomorrow. So, so badly. That doesn't even make grammatical sense. That's how tired I am. I slam the fridge door shut.

'There's no way I'm eating that,' I yell after her. It looks disgusting.

'That is my Mexican family speciality. Bread soup,' she calls over her shoulder.

'Bread is literally the only thing I can't eat. Is there any salad I could have?'

'No. It's the soup or nothing.'

I am left gawping after her as she disappears into her room and slams the door shut. I assume the only other bedroom in the villa is for me. I drag my carry-on over to it and flop down on the bed. I don't even have a nightie to change into for bed or for lounging around. I open the case and pull out the hospital gown that my sister packed in case of an emergency. She must have been thinking of that really common scenario where I get rushed into hospital only to find they are clean out of gowns. It will flap open at the back, but it will just have to do.

Once I've showered and put on my hospital gown, I climb into bed, thankful that it is at least comfortable and the aircon is working to keep the room at a bearable temperature. It is too dark now to see outside so I'm happy to fall straight to sleep and forget all about this nightmare journey of self-discovery that I have unwisely embarked on. There has to be a simpler way to make my ex jealous and meet the new love of my life.

I wake early the following morning to brilliant sunshine streaming through my window. I had forgotten to put the shutters down. The view is spectacular. The window is actually a patio door. I slide it open to reveal an elegant, paved swimming pool area right outside. It is beautifully kept, and surrounded by a wide border of tropical plants and palm trees while a high white wall provides security all the way round the villa. I look at the plush sun loungers and table and chairs under a thick white parasol, perfect for al fresco dining. The pool is meticulously clean, and the dazzling water looks very inviting in the already oppressive heat of the early morning sun.

I rummage about in the carry-on to see if by some miracle Lois has packed a spare bikini in there and to my delight she has. Although it looks more like a pair of shoelaces, it will have to do. My sister has thought of everything, including the need to have an all-over tan. There's a toiletry bag with all the essentials in, and a ton of insect repellent. There's a clean pair of knickers and a hairbrush.

My stomach rumbles, letting me know I haven't eaten for almost twenty-four hours. I make my way back into the kitchen and open the fridge looking for some water. I see the sandwich on the plate has been half-eaten and put back. Likewise, the bowl of gloop is empty but has been left in the fridge. I grab the bottle of unopened water to take back to my room. I also spot a fruit bowl on the dining table and grab up what looks like a papaya, but I have no idea how to eat one. I rummage around and find an apple instead.

Just as I shut the door, I hear an unholy sound coming from the chaperone's room. Then I see it bang open revealing lots of winking lights and gaming monitors before she races into the bathroom slamming it closed behind her. There proceeds a series of honking and parping sounds as I scuttle away.

I still have yet to learn her name never mind become familiar with her toilet habits, but if I had to take an educated guess, I'd say my chaperone has become violently ill with sickness and diarrhoea.

Twenty minutes later, I knock timidly on the bathroom door. 'Are you okay? Can I help you in any way?'

'Not unless you are a trained doctor,' she manages between retches. 'Leave me alone.'

Charming.

The next day, I swim, sleep, read and spend the entire time nibbling fruit, unable to contact the outside world or to be contacted by anyone. I keep expecting Cam to turn up and rescue me but so far, there's been nothing and no one. I listen to the chaperone slamming doors and hurling chunks and go to bed starving hungry again.

Living the dream.

The following day, I wake up feeling dazed and confused. There's a knock at the front door. I race over and yank it open.

'Thank goodness,' I cry. I am greeted by a smiling face, unfazed that I am wearing a hospital gown and have not been able to wash and condition my matted hair. He is carrying a box of groceries. I step aside as he carries it inside and places it on the counter.

'I'm Jake. Your runner. Anything you need. Just ask me.'

'Thank you so much,' I say gratefully. 'I've been trapped here on my own for two days without food or water. Or shampoo. Or clothes.'

'I wondered why you hadn't put in an order, so I took a guess at what you might need. I'll add shampoo and conditioner to the list for next time. I'm the runner for six of the contestants in isolation, so I'm always around. Hortense, she should have told you about me?' he asks.

'Who?'

'Hortense, your chaperone?'

'Oh, her.' I must sound deflated because he tuts.

'Yep. She's not the best chaperone. We get a lot of complaints about that one. Half French, half Mexican. It's a fiery combination. She was born angry.'

Good Lord.

'She's not even introduced herself properly. She's... she's in the bathroom. She's been in there since I arrived. I'm not sure she's very well, judging by the sounds she's making.'

Right on cue, she makes a sound like a distressed cow giving birth to a calf that's half its own size.

His eyes grow wide with alarm. 'I'll ring it in. Thanks for letting me know. Okay, I'll be off if there's nothing else you need.'

He can't get away fast enough.

'Oh, there is one thing that I need,' I shout after him. 'Would it be possible to get these clothes cleaned, please?'

'Sure, no problem,' he says coming back to take the bag of stained clothes from me. 'I'll get them back to you in a couple of days.'

'And has there been any news from the airport about my luggage?'

He shakes his head. When he sees my distraught face, he says, 'Don't worry. It'll turn up eventually.'

Once I've put the food away, made myself a steaming hot mug of coffee and some fruit and yogurt for breakfast, I slip into my bikini and head out to the pool to read. This is more like it. I haven't been on holiday for years so even being here, essentially alone, like I'm on a Trappist Monk's extreme intermittent-fasting retreat, feels nice.

After the whole morning reading and not a peep from my chaperone, I find myself drifting off to sleep only to wake some moments later to the slamming of doors inside the villa and the sound of a car pulling up. I hurry inside, throwing the hospital gown over my tiny bikini to see what's going on. The chaperone is green-faced and standing with her suitcase by the door.

'I'm off to a hotel. I think it is food poisoning from your sandwich, but the powers-that-be aren't sure and don't want me to pass any bugs onto you. And for you then to pass the bugs on inside the Love on the Island villa.'

She sounds as though somehow it is my fault that her own sandwich has given her the shits.

'So, I'm about to go in the villa? But what about my luggage?' I try to hide my anxiety. 'Will I be an original?'

'What did I say?' she booms grumpily. 'No questions about when or even if you're going on the show!'

'But who is going to look for my luggage? Who will look after me? I have no way of contacting the runner because you haven't given me any information since the moment I arrived.'

'Again. We're not babysitters.' She rolls her eyes. 'We're Emotional Support and Well-being Officials. And FYI, there are more important things happening in the world than what outfits you are going to wear.'

God, she's right. I'm letting this get too out of hand. It's just a gameshow at the end of the day.

'Important things like my entire village burned down while I've been ill,' she says accusingly.

Oh, my God. I open my mouth to apologise.

'And all my dragons died.' She is spitting feathers. 'All of them.'

I count to three in my head before I say anything. 'So, who will my new Emotional Support and Well-being Official be?'

I hope they are saner than she is.

She screws her eyes at me. 'Cameron. He'll replace me until they figure something out.'

Cameron is coming over!

I glance over to the hallway mirror. My hair is a mess. Where are my expensive beach waves? My face is slightly sunburnt with streaks of two-day old make-up under my eyes. I am barefoot with matted hair and wearing a hospital gown. Just add a knife dripping blood and I could be an escapee from a horror movie.

'When will he get here?' I panic as she throws her bags into the waiting taxi. 'I need shampoo and conditioner. I need to make myself look more... less... more... waxed and polished,' I say, making myself sound like a rusty second-hand car.

She shakes her head and gives me a condescending look. 'That gown makes you look mental.'

Sadly, she's right. I should turn it round and tie it at the front. And I will, as soon as I think of a suitable retort. She is really getting on my nerves.

She slams the boot shut. 'You'll not last five minutes in the villa. People like you never do.'

People like me? Distinctly average, underwhelming, under-achievers with no sex appeal?

In just a few words, she has popped what little confidence I had like a balloon. She's voicing my worst fears. How can they hire someone this judgemental?

'Maybe you need to take a long look at yourself first and concentrate on your own issues. It's easy to stand there and judge others, but your opinion doesn't make it fact. It just makes you sound bitter and jealous.' I do namaste hands like Lois. 'And by the way, dragons aren't real.'

'Fuck you,' she yells back. 'Why don't you try working for a living? And FYI getting your ass out on TV is not real work.'

This is becoming very tit-for-tat now, but she has hit a nerve. A very raw nerve. I have come halfway across the bloody world to get my ass out on TV.

'I will be reporting you to the ombudsman and requesting that I never have to see you again.'

She yanks the car door open and turns to me, 'I hope you get the shits real bad. And I mean REAL bad.'

Mean fudging cow.

'I hope you choke on your own vomit,' I retaliate, instantly regretting it.

It's the jetlag and two days without food.

A movement distracts us.

'Hi there,' says Cameron, getting out of the taxi looking very startled. Our eyes meet and he holds my gaze. 'Nice to finally meet you, Libby.'

Chapter 6

The taxi whisks Hortense and her bags away, leaving Cameron and I facing each other. He gives me a cautious look before reaching out to shake my hand.

I have blown my chance to make a second good impression.

'Hi,' I say, embarrassed to the core that I've been caught being so rude and that I look such a mess. The opposite of a bombshell. I couldn't look less of a bombshell if I'd hurled myself through the hedge and rolled around in monkey poo.

'Hi,' he says again.

I'm not sure he knows what to make of me. I'm pretty certain that he'll be regretting his decision to pick me for the show. He has a tall, firm-shouldered, slim-waisted physique, long toned legs and the sort of easy vibe that commands attention. I glance at the smart-looking suitcase by his side. And he has good taste. I see he has casual but expensive footwear. I'm trying my hardest not to gawp, but he's making it extremely difficult. He could easily be an actor/model/singer/the ex-husband of Gwyneth Paltrow. He is a hundred times better-looking in real life than on the video call which, unfortunately, has automatically catapulted him way out of my league.

'Shall we?' He indicates for us to go into the villa.

I hear him clear his throat and realise, too late, that my gown will be flapping open at the back, revealing my backside like a randy baboon to a prospective mate. I grab the flaps and pull them closed, not daring to turn around.

'Good trip over?' he asks politely as we make our way through the villa to the lounge area.

'Sort of,' I say, one arm clamped behind me to keep the flaps tightly together. I wave the other hand around to make my point. 'Apart from the jetlag. The lost luggage, the unfriendly welcome and two days without food or water. Not to mention the serious lack of shut eye, because it has been like trying to sleep in a bovine birthing suite. But yes, it was all fine, thanks.'

Cameron bursts out laughing, revealing the cutest little gap between his two front teeth. 'Sorry,' he says, trying to hold it in. 'I don't mean to laugh. You Brits are so funny.

It doesn't sound like you got off to a great start. How can I help?'

I melt at the kindness in his voice and oh, that accent. That dreamy Canadian accent.

He leaves his case by the table and flops down on the sofa. He looks very tired.

'It would be great if you could help me to get my luggage back,' I say, indicating my gown.

He stifles a huge yawn. 'Yeah. No problem. I'll call them now.'

'No, please. Let me make you a coffee first. Take a seat in there while I go make it,' I say, pointing to the lounge area.

'Coffee would be awesome, thanks, Libby.' He has such an infectious easy smile. At the sound of him saying my name, goosebumps appear on my arm. 'I'm really sorry we've let you down like this. I'll do what I can to make sure you settle in comfortably, and I'll order some nice food and supplies. Let me know what you like.'

'That's so kind, thank you.' I am instantly lifted by his lovely thoughtfulness.

I disappear backwards into the kitchen and quickly switch my gown around so that the ties are at the front. He remains silent while I flit about making us both a coffee. I rummage around in the cupboard for the biscuits that I unpacked earlier. I imagine Cam could do with a pick-me-up, so while I wait for the coffee machine to finish whirring, I arrange them neatly on a plate ready to carry them through.

I'm so nervous around him. Partly because he is so much better looking in real life than I'd thought and secondly, because he obviously keeps himself trim with his part-time veganism and exercise. Only a blind woman would fail to notice how well his t-shirt and shorts contour the shape of his tanned, athletic legs and torso. The last time I used my legs for running purposes, I was ten years old. I also didn't expect him to be quite so cool. He's got a competent and professional air about him that is very charismatic.

In truth, he could just as easily go on the show himself, he's that good-looking. I'd put him around thirty so too mature for the show. In fact, I think, even with my dreadful track record in matters of the heart and hanging around with eight and nine-year-olds all day long, I'll still be too mature for the show.

'It must be exhausting to organise a TV show like this, is it? Who knew there was so much involved? Contestants in secret villas, runners, chaperones, producers,' I shout through from the kitchen, genuinely interested in what goes on behind the scenes. But more than that, I'd like to draw his attention away from the fact that I look horrific and greeted him with my pale bare bum cheeks in this piece-of-string bikini. 'I imagine there's so much to do.'

I slam cupboard doors looking for a tray, some sugar, spoons. 'I know you probably aren't allowed to tell me, but do you think that I'll be going in the villa soon?'

Slam, open, slam.

'As a bombshell? Or as an original?'

I'm like the prosecution leading the witness.

Silence. Plenty of it.

'It's just because I need to have my luggage back before I go in, otherwise I will look like a complete horror-show. A bit like I look today.' I let out a nervous laugh and wait for him to refute everything I have just said because, as I'm sure he will remember, he told me that I am gorgeous, stunning and naturally beautiful. All in the same sentence.

More silence.

I carry the tray of coffee and biscuits through to the lounge area to find Cameron flat out asleep on the sofa. His long legs are spread wide. His head is thrown back on the cushion and his arms are flopped on either side. He's still holding a bunch of keys in one hand and a pile of papers in the other. They have CONFIDENTIAL written across the top.

I glance at the papers. They look like the schedule papers for the show. It's nerve-wracking not knowing. I am tempted to take them from him but knowing my luck he'd wake up to find me manhandling him.

I look at the papers.

You do have to wonder if this level of secrecy is strictly necessary.

'They're hardly the Whitehouse nuclear codes,' I mutter quietly looking for a place to put the tray down. Cam shifts in his sleep, loosening his grip and the papers slip gently onto the floor.

I will not look.

No. I have strong moral fibre that prevents me.

I will not even tidy the papers back into a neat pile for him, in case he thinks I have been peeking.

I will put the tray down on the coffee table and go outside. I will enjoy my swim and read my book. I won't give these confidential papers a second thought. Nor will I obsess over how adorable he looks in his sleep. Or whether he is single and attracted to me.

I'm mid-swim when Cam appears at the patio door which leads out to the pool area from the lounge. He fills the frame, reaching casually up to stretch his arms out to yawn. He shakes himself awake and stands watching me.

'Sorry about nodding off like that,' he says sheepishly. 'I didn't realise I was so tired.'

'That's okay,' I shout back from the far end of the pool as I swim back towards him. Trust him to wake up now. I'll have to stay in the pool or else climb out and give him an eyeful of the world's skimpiest bikini. It's so skimpy I can barely feel it. I look down to double check that it is still tied to my body.

'Erm, I hate to ask this...' Cam rubs one side of his face sleepily. 'But did you by any chance...?'

Oh, my God, he thinks I've peeked at his stuff!

'Did I by any chance look at the confidential papers?' I say, pretending to be shocked. 'No, I did not. I would never. I'm the sort of woman who would NEVER betray a confidence. Those confidential papers fell from your hand, and I did not so much as glance at them. I swear to God. That's the truth of it.'

I couldn't sound more guilty if I tried.

Cam's face breaks into a huge smile. 'I was trying to ask if you by any chance brought some insect repellent?' he finishes. 'I forgot mine. And boy, do you need it over here, but it's impossible to get hold of in the village. Especially the spray bottles.'

'Oh. Insect repellent. Yes. It's in my room. I'll get it for you.'

Now I have the awkward dilemma of getting out of the pool without him seeing me. Ridiculous really, as soon I could be swanning around in a bikini for almost a billion people to watch on repeat for all of eternity.

I reach the steps and hesitate, plucking up the courage to just go for it, but Cam seems to immediately sense that I'm shy about him seeing my near-naked body.

He swivels around and goes back into the lounge. 'I'll just make some fresh coffee!' he yells.

I find his thoughtfulness very endearing as I quickly leap out of the pool, grab a towel and scuttle like a crab across the patio to my room. One glance in the mirror at my wet hair and face tells me that at least the streaks of make-up have washed off, leaving me fresh and natural-looking. And because, out of sheer fear, I have barely eaten anything since I decided to come on the show, my stomach looks flat and toned. I throw the hospital gown back on as though it was a dressing gown, grab one of the small canisters of insect repellent and walk through the villa to find Cam.

'You are a life saver,' he says. 'Thank you so much. Mosquitoes seem to love me.'

I'm not surprised.

As I hand it over, I glance down to see there is no wedding ring on his left hand. A small bolt of hope flashes through me.

'I'm going to do some work on this dining table if that's okay. And then I thought I'd cook us some dinner seeing as you haven't eaten for days. Does gluten-free salad sound good? I'd hate for any mishaps.'

Ah, so he's remembered my overshare. My cheeks flame instantly. 'Does the salad come with roast chicken and chips? I'm starving.'

'Chips? You would have potato chips with chicken?'

'Ah, no. It's the language barrier. Not crisps, I mean chips as in fries?' I forgot about this huge cultural difference.

Cam seems delighted to have a roomie who likes to eat complex carbs. 'Perfect. That's settled then. About seven for dinner?'

'Great. It's a date.'

Not a *date* date, obviously but I will simply make this worse if I try to clarify. A thought pings into my head as I make for the sun lounger. Do Canadians wear wedding bands on the left or right hand?

I'm halfway through my book when a splashing sound draws my attention. Cam has dived into the pool and is doing lengths. I peer over the top of my book to see him slice through the water, his arms are pumping, and his head is coming up for air every so often. It's very impressive.

He catches me watching him and stops swimming. 'I thought we could dine out here,' he calls over to me from the far end of the pool. 'What do you think?'

That would be very nice, is what I think. The sun is setting, the pool lights are beginning to twinkle, there are lights strung up around the garden and in the trees, and the table and chairs under the parasol will seem like the perfect romantic setting for dinner with the most attractive man I've ever laid eyes on. All we need is a string quartet and some wine for our non-date.

'I'll open a bottle of wine too, if you're up for it?' he says, as though reading my mind.

What. No quartet?

I nod enthusiastically before remembering I have only my hospital gown to wear; an outfit that will ensure nothing romantic happens. I will have to put any romantic aspirations firmly to one side until my cases turn up.

When I hear Cam getting out of the pool, I stare hard at my book so as not to look at him. It's only when he disappears into the villa that I realise I was holding my breath. I am making this whole scenario much tenser than it needs to be. It's not his fault I find him so attractive. And Lord knows he is not giving off any vibes that suggest he is feeling the same towards me. If anything, I have done my utmost to put him off.

I quietly slide into my room to get ready. After showering and drying my hair, I pile it up onto my head. Without the aid of straighteners, it would cascade wildly down my neck in one big frizzy lump, far from the sleek long choppy bob I arrived with. I have no make-up with me, so shiny cheeks will have to do. And after a few tries, the gown has become a casual wrap-over dress that goes nicely with the free slippers that were lying on my bed next to a stack of fresh fluffy towels when I arrived.

Cam calls through that dinner is ready. I step out onto the patio to find all the fairy lights are ablaze. It looks amazing.

'Dinner is served, madame.' Cam is wearing cargo-style shorts and a t-shirt. He has flip flops on and looks every bit like a dot com billionaire crossed with a model for surf boards. He waves his hand over the table which is set out like a five-star restaurant with gleaming cutlery, plates of sumptuous-looking food and candles that twinkle against half-full wineglasses. He pulls a chair out for me. A quick flick down reveals his right hand is ring-free too.

'Thank you so much.' I've had to look away in case my feelings are written all over my face. I've never been good at hiding my emotions and, at the present moment, they are fluttering out of control. He is such a gentleman. He is such a single gentleman.

'You're welcome,' Cam says, sitting down opposite me. 'By the way, the cleaner came and dropped off some towels and fresh bedding in case you need any. Mentioned something about a terrible stain on your clothes. She's giving it another go.'

How embarrassing.

'Great, and I could really do with my suitcases back, that's for sure,' I say, pointing to my gown. 'Otherwise, I'll be making togas out of the bed sheets.'

Cam chuckles. 'Sorry, I totally forgot. I'll get straight on it. You have at least a few days before anything happens. You may as well soak up the rays and relax before we start shooting.'

'Sounds great. Is that so the contestants can get a tan before they go on TV?'

'Yeah.'

I gulp. The contestants never have tan lines as far as I remember. Lois and I once discussed the angles one would have to contort the body, in order to get the sort of coverage required. We decided they must all do yoga in the nude for eight hours a day.

'Will I be expected to have an all-over tan?' I ask nervously.

Cam looks down at his plate. I see his cheeks colouring, even in this fading sunlight. 'Erm, that's erm, well, I mean, that's entirely up to you. Entirely. It's not mandatory by any means. But I suppose I can work in the bedroom during the day if you need some... privacy.'

He pokes around at his salad.

I have basically given him this mental picture of me lying stretched out naked on the sun loungers. Legs akimbo. Tits out, fanny out. Just as he is about to eat.

What is wrong with me?

Chapter 7

'So, Libby, what motivated you to come on the show? Apart from wanting to find love and win a hundred thousand dollars, of course.'

I am still picturing myself lying naked on the lounger while he brings me grapes and other erotic foods. I snap out of it. 'Good question. There's a lot I could do with a hundred thousand dollars.'

For a start, it would buy an awful lot of grapes.

Pull yourself together.

Cam tilts his head, waiting for me to answer. He'll be expecting me to say something obvious like a vanity project, designing my own range of edible thongs or an Instagramable trip to see the Dalai Lama. If I tell him the boring truth that it would go on two deposits for mortgage downpayments. One, so that my newly engaged sister can buy her first home, and two, so that I can start to rebuild my life after being unceremoniously dumped by Arrogant

Josh and let go from my job - he'll think I'm a sad loser. I'm so desperate to impress him that I default immediately to some meaningful, low-level lying.

'I was thinking I could take a year off teaching to help build an orphanage in Botswana.' I make sure to keep my eyes level with his, so as not to arouse suspicion. 'Or to help build a school in India for... you know... street urchins.'

Any sane person would stop there.

'Have you experience in construction?' He seems very interested.

'No. No, I haven't.'

'Oh.'

There's a silence hanging in the air that needs to be filled with more lies.

'Or I could go on one of those environmental boat trips clearing up plastics from the ocean. Rescue dolphins. Save some turtles.' In a panic I do namaste hands and bow my head. It is wildly inappropriate. 'Those sorts of things, really.'

He stares at me to see if I'm serious. He has no idea.

I will leave him wondering. Best he sees me as a kind soul, a touch benevolent and mystical, especially after the way he caught me yelling at my chaperone to choke on her own vomit.

'And you? What do you do when you're not working on this show? Do you go back to... the capital, LA? The city of angels.'

It's very apt because he has very angelic eyes. They are kind and expressive, with fine crinkles at the sides when he smiles, which is a lot. Despite the Year Three project, my geography of the USA is appalling. But everyone the world over, knows LA is where all the good-looking people go. I pour us both a hefty measure of wine, filling the glass right to the brim.

'I think you'll find Sacramento is the capital of California.' He raises his eyebrows playfully at me. 'I'm mostly in San Francisco.'

Capital cities are very cool and interesting, and more importantly a very safe topic of conversation. And yet...

I take another swig of wine. 'It must be hard to work away from home and leave family behind.'

He shrugs.

'Are you leaving a trail of broken hearts behind in San Francisco?' I joke.

I'm getting very personal, very quickly and making a lot of assumptions, but mining for personal information as to his single status is becoming something of a drug to me after two glasses of wine and nine days of barely eating.

'The shoot only takes around ten weeks in total. Eight of those just to set up. I thought you'd know that. As a super fan.'

'Super fan?'

'Yep. The show's number one super fan is what you told me in your interview,' he says smiling. 'Although, that's what they all say.'

Trust Lois. She is obsessed with the show. She would know all there is to know. 'Oh, yeah. I'm a total super fan. So, back to this trail of broken hearts...'

Cam laughs and gingerly picks up his wine to slurp carefully at it. 'I don't usually drink.'

'Me neither,' I say, knocking the rest back and topping myself up.

This causes Cam to half choke on his drink. 'I like you. You're different to the usual contestants. You seem very laid back about it all.'

'That's because...' I search for a plausible reason as I stare into his gorgeous eyes. 'That's because I'm really looking forward to the personal challenge rather than becoming world famous.'

He looks unconvinced.

'And I'm hoping to find my soulmate while I'm here.'

A vision pops into my mind of me in white, floaty chiffon. Him in rolled up white trousers and a loose linen shirt open to the stomach. The pair of us standing hand in hand on white powdered sand while locals shower us in bright pink flower petals. Now, because I've come this far, it's like I'm obsessed but thankfully, the film reel running in my mind is not playing out on my face.

Cam pretends to look serious. 'Oh yeah, for sure. For sure. Out of the 4 billion men on the planet, he'll definitely be one of the five we managed to pick out.'

He's funny.

'And the trail of broken hearts?'

Christ, I'm like a rottweiler but I can't seem to let it go.

Cam puts down his fork to look at me. 'There are no broken hearts. Only this one.' He points to himself.

It's my turn to act surprised. 'Somebody broke your heart?' I can't believe it. Who would do such a thing? 'Who was it? Taylor Swift?'

Cam chuckles. 'It was a long time ago.' Then I see something like pain flicker in his eyes as he reaches for another sip of his wine.

'I'm sorry. I didn't mean to get personal.'

I did. I would like to know everything, the deepest ins and outs and ups and downs of your entire love life, please.

'I'm a professional nosy parker. Please forgive me.'

This makes him grin. 'So that's all you need to know about me. What about you? Any broken hearts to report?'

I shake my head and give him a sad look. 'There was someone but he... ended it. I just wasn't... anyway, I'm over it now. Imagine, twenty-six and looking forward to life as a dusty old maid. Which is fine.'

His jaw falls open slightly.

'Because I'm married to my job,' I explain. 'Not because there's something wrong with me... you know.'

It very much feels as though I'm accidentally planting seeds that there is definitely something wrong with me.

'I really like my own company,' I say quickly. 'So, I don't go out much. University came and went, and before I knew it several years went by, and I'd forgotten how to flirt. All the men my age settled down with girls that were quicker off the mark than me and so now, there's hardly any decent men left in the town I live in. Just one rather arrogant male.'

Cam is looking at me in a thoughtful way.

'But what about all those men at university? Those wild nights working as a cocktail waitress? The exotic pole dancing?'

Oh. My. Fudging. Word. I am going to kill Lois.

'No! Absolutely not. I did no such thing!'

'So, you made that up just to get on the show?' Cam smiles. 'It's okay. We hear all kinds of horseshit from people desperate to get on the show.'

I love my sister and she did rather have fun for the both of us at college, but she's obviously thought nothing of telling a whole load of lies to get on the show.

'No. I must have... it must have come out wrong. I was actually co-vice-captain of the hummus society.'

'The hummus society? Sounds wild.'

I nod keenly. 'Yes. It was. There are over twenty-six different types. There were tastings to organise every single weekend. Did you know Mexico is the hummus capital of the world?'

He sips his wine again, this time taking a bigger slug. 'Surely, the Middle East is the hummus capital of the world.'

'I meant Western world.' I quickly top him up. 'It originated from Egypt if you're going to be pedantic about it.'

He's so culinarily literate.

'Anyway, I'm not desperate to get on the show. I just thought it might challenge me. I've been a bit stuck lately.'

'You're finding it difficult to move on?'

'Yes,' I admit. 'I guess this is my kick up the backside. Something to jolt me out of my boring routine.'

Cam nods. 'I totally get that.'

We share an intimate look. He really does have the loveliest kind eyes. They are glinting in the candlelight.

'You don't want to risk getting your heart broken again,' I say understandingly. 'Well, let me tell you, sometimes it's best to just let it go. Not all girls run around breaking hearts. Sometimes it is the men who do the breaking. They say the first cut is the deepest.' It's just one cliché after another tonight. 'I'm sure whoever it is regrets it big time.'

A half-smile tugs sadly at his mouth. 'I'm sure if she wasn't married to my best friend, she would.'

'Oh, I'm so sorry!' I gasp. 'I had no idea. That was terribly insensitive.'

'That's okay. It was a long time ago.' Cam picks up his drink, avoiding my gaze.

I gulp back the desire to sweep him up into a hug. 'That's awful. Such betrayal must have really hurt.'

He looks up to meet my gaze. It did hurt him. It's in the haunted look, and in the brave smile that doesn't quite reach his eyes.

'I hope you find peace with it,' I say, lifting my drink. 'Sometimes people just make no sense.'

He clinks glasses with me. 'No, they don't.'

We busy ourselves eating for a few moments before Cam breaks the silence. 'What do you think of the chicken? Is it spicy enough?'

'It's delicious,' I say. 'I love spicy chicken. Being gluten intolerant means I get most of my protein from chicken and fish.'

'Interesting,' he says, giving me a quizzical look.

'How so?' I stop eating.

'Because in your interview you told me you were a very strict vegan.'

I gulp. Of course, Lois would have said that. She has been trying to 'turn' me for over four years.

'I am. I mean I was. Until erm, yesterday.'

Lies upon lies upon lies.

Cam has not taken his gaze from mine. 'Yesterday?'

I nod slowly.

'You are full of surprises.'

I'm full of shit, he means.

'It's almost as though you're a completely different person to the one I interviewed last summer.'

I'm like a rabbit in the headlights.

'I am?'

'Tell me about this sister of yours. Do you have any photos of the two of you together?' *Crap.*

Chapter 8

'I do not have any photos... of me and my sister together... about my person,' I say in a flat robotic tone, annunciating each word carefully as though it might be taken down and used as evidence against me in a court of law.

'Tell me about her. Are you alike?'

Oh, Goodness. He is not going to drop it. I can't read his face either.

'Well, she's a little older than me.' Not technically a lie as she is three and a half minutes older. 'And she's a nurse. Which means she's very outspoken and quite bossy with it.'

Cam is stroking his chin stubble, taking in every word. 'How much older exactly.'

'Three, she's older by three, erm...' I take a deep breath in.

'Years?'

I shake my head.

'Months?' He is looking confused.

I can't lie any more. I can't. I will come clean. 'Three minutes.'

I've cracked under virtually no pressure.

Cam blinks slowly, letting out a calm sigh. He gets up from his seat and disappears into the villa in one long fluid movement. He's so incredibly easy on the eye, and as attractive from the front as he is at the back. Almost as though he was dreamt into the world to make it prettier. I hear the faint bleeps of the safe being opened.

What will I say? What excuse do I have?

Cam returns moments later and plonks my phone down on the table. 'Show me the photos. Please.'

I pick up the phone and scroll to me and Lois having the world's longest goodbye at the airport a couple of days ago. Tyrone took lots of pictures and a lovely video of us, so she'd be able to look at them while I'm in isolation without my phone.

I press play and turn it around for Cam to see. He watches our teary goodbye. He listens to me telling Lois how much I love her and how much I'm going to miss her. He listens to Lois mothering me and making sure I have everything. He listens to her ask once again if I'm positive I'm flying to Mexico for the right reasons. Cam briefly flicks his eyes to mine and back to the screen. He listens to Lois tell me how proud of me she is. How she knows these past few years have been really hard for me. Losing our mother. Losing my home. Losing my sense of purpose.

Cam pauses the video.

My eyes fill with tears as suppressed memories flood back. 'I gave up work to care for her while she was sick. There's only ever been the three of us. It kind of killed my career, but I'd do it again in a heartbeat.'

Cam's face slackens and we share a real look of understanding. The kind of empathy that comes when you've lived through the horror of losing a loved one. He slides the phone back towards me.

'I'm sorry,' he says. 'Sounds like you've had it tough. She did well raising twins on her own.'

I nod.

'So, you're identical, huh?' he says, trying to lighten the mood.

'I'm sorry,' is all I can manage. 'I should have been honest with you last week on the phone. Lois is engaged to a great guy, Tyrone, so she couldn't come on the show. I'd just got out of that... erm, situationship, and I thought maybe it would be a good idea to come here.'

I wonder if he is going to be angry at the deception, but he surprises me by not seeming that blown away.

'So now you've come clean about your sister, do you want to tell me about this relationship you just got out of?' Cam asks.

'Honestly, not much to tell. I thought I was in love with him but really, we never did anything together to create any sparks. I was boring. I worked all the time. I suppose in a way I'm not surprised he dumped me. I'm just upset that he did it by text.'

'Ouch. That's harsh. What a dick.'

'Yeah, right?' And before I know what I'm saying I admit the truth as to why I'm here. 'I wanted to take Lois's place on the show to get back at him. To make him see I'm not just a frumpy old maid. To make him regret dumping me.'

It sounds very childish.

'That's a lot of effort and a long way to come just to make him jealous. You must really want him back.'

I shake my head. 'No. I thought I did, but I guess I just felt rejected and insecure.'

'I get it. But listen, Libby, you've put me in an awkward spot here. I'm going to have to tell the executive director that you're not the original hire. You and your sister have two completely different personalities. She will have passed the psychometric tests and you... probably wouldn't have.

What if we put you on the show and you crack under the pressure? It wouldn't be fair to you.'

'I won't crack, I promise. I'm sorry to put you in this situation. I was desperate at the time, and then you rang, and we spoke and...'

... and I fancied you from the moment I saw you and decided to throw caution to the wind and kill two birds with one stone.

Cam looks at me thoughtfully. 'We all do stupid things for love.'

I'm taken by surprise. 'Now look at who's rolling out the clichés.'

He smiles and leans back in his chair.

'Do you want to tell me how your ex ended up with your best friend? I'm quite the expert on trust issues.'

Cam hesitates. 'You know what? Women never ask me about it. They just want to know if I'm single.'

Who can blame them?

'Well then, I'd like to apologise for all women. We can be occasionally thoughtless and self-centred and very determined when faced with men as handsome as you.'

Cam grins. 'Really? So, it's almost my fault women behave that way around me?'

'Oh, yes. Definitely. Now, this crazy cheating ex, tell me what's wrong with her.'

I almost instantly regret asking when I find out Megan is a former model turned fashion editor and runs her own very successful ethical clothing website and charity for abandoned horses. A real triple threat; brains, beauty, kind-hearted. She sounds too good to be true. I listen as he talks very briefly about his past relationship and his regrets at how he handled it. I get a warm glow of satisfaction over how comfortable we are with each other.

'God, I must be drunk to be telling you any of this,' he says, before calling it a night.

'I'm relieved to hear she has fidelity issues. She sounds too perfect otherwise.'

Cam chuckles. 'She definitely wasn't perfect. She couldn't be spontaneous. She needed at least six hours' notice to get ready. She'd never be seen without her face on, and hair done. It meant we missed out on things that would have been fun.'

I look down at my raggedy outfit. My hair is in a wild bun, and I have no make-up on. My career is down the toilet and the last time I raised money for charity was nine years ago. I am the exact opposite of his former girlfriend. In other words, the opposite of his type.

'I'll clear away,' I offer, getting unsteadily to my feet after the best part of a bottle of wine.

Cam puts his hand out to steady me, and it feels like a jolt, a spark of electricity. It causes me to look wide-eyed at him.

'I'll do it. You head to bed, and in the morning, we can decide whether I'm sending you back home to England...' He fixes me a stern look so that I know he hasn't forgotten that I am here by pretence. '... or whether you are staying in Mexico for a shot at finding true love.'

'Yes. True love,' I repeat, for no reason other than I'm very, very tipsy and I want to keep talking to him for the rest of my life. I carefully enunciate every word to hide this fact. 'Actual. Heart-stopping. Soul-melting. Sparkles-in-your-eyes. True love. That's what I want.'

'That's a tall order, Mrs Cliché, but I'll see what I can do,' he says, giving me a sleepy half-smile. 'Although you forgot the butterflies in the stomach and the tingles down the spine whenever they walk in the room.'

He gets it. He totally gets it.

'I'm not a TV producer on the world's most over-rated show for nothing. I have to warn you though, we have a very poor track record. There's a zero point one chance of you staying with anyone you meet on the show. They all split up eventually.'

He is horribly drunk. Otherwise, he'd know that I am talking about him.

The following morning, I awake from a series of torrid dreams in a bit of a sweat. I tossed and turned. Vivid images of me making out with Cam, his delicious hot mouth on mine, his hands in places they shouldn't be, had morphed into awful images of me drowning in the pool. In one of the dreams, I was parading down a catwalk in a crowded city centre. Me in a skimpy bikini and struggling in skyscraper heels, while everyone else is in boots, coats, hats and gloves because it is snowing and I am ridiculous, and they were laughing at me. I may as well have been a fish out of water in that dream, the meaning was so obvious.

Maybe it is a good thing that Cameron sends me back home. He is clearly not ready to move on. And even if he was, it wouldn't be with someone like me. And there's no point in me going on the show because I'll get thrown off for being too dull and boring, and Josh probably won't even know or care that I've been on it.

I wander through the villa to find Cam bashing away at his laptop, a slew of papers covering the table and multiple phones on the go all pinging and bleeping at once.

'Planning a major heist? Shouldn't we be in an abandoned warehouse?'

Cam looks up grinning. 'Good morning. Please don't peek at these confidential papers. I know that will be very hard for you.'

'Cheek! I did not peek at them yesterday while you were asleep, so I'm hardly going to bother now, am I?'

He screws his eyes at me in a friendly manner.

'Honestly, I don't want to know. I mean why would a woman, isolated in the middle of the jungle, be curious that the man she is stuck with has over ten burner phones on the go?'

'They are for the contestants. Each of them will get their own phone, but only to take selfies and to receive instructions to gather round the firepit from Destiny, this year's host. On that note,' he says. 'I've reached a decision about you.'

Suddenly, my time here seems too short. It's such a long way to come to stay stuck in a villa that could be anywhere in the world.

'Wait. Before you tell me. Can I just say that I'm so sorry I lied to get on the show, and I'm sorry it was for the wrong reasons. I completely understand if you want to send me home.'

Cam looks at me as though weighing up whether I'm worth the hassle.

'But can you please wait one more day to decide?' I beg. 'After last night... you helped me see that getting back at Josh isn't what will make me happy. It's petty and desperate. Moving on and never looking back will make me happy. And that's what I intend to do.'

He raises his eyebrows. He's curious. He leans back in his chair and folds his arms. 'You don't need to go on the show for that.'

'True and that's fine.' I watch him get up. 'But my sister and her fiancé won't have had nearly enough alone time. Please let me stay here for a bit longer.'

'You want a free holiday basically?'

I feel my cheeks glow. 'I won't get in your way. You won't even notice I'm here. I won't bother you at all while you are busy checking phones and... writing secret papers,' I say, following him into the kitchen. I stand next to him as he washes his cup in the sink. 'I'll help with the chores.'

He has nice hands and clean manicured nails but more importantly he is thorough with the rinsing and double checks the cup, holding it up, to make sure it is super clean.

'Look, we even do the dishes the exact same way.'

'Fascinating,' he says, picking up a plate to do the same.

'I'm a primary school teacher so I'd be good company for you.'

He nods. 'I do have a lot on. I'm not sure how much company you think I'll need.'

'I'll do all the cooking. I'll do vegan meals if I have to. Please, just a few more days.'

I sound desperate.

'One more day,' he says firmly. 'I'll need to check in with the boss to see where we are at with the other contestants. It's around about now that we start pulling the cast together, so I guess another day won't hurt.'

'Thank you. Thank you so much. You won't regret it.' I could give him a massive hug but settle for flashing him the biggest smile my face can make.

Cam wipes his hands dry on a cloth, neatly folding it before placing it on the bench.

'It's fascinating to hear behind-the-scenes stuff. I've always wanted to know what a TV producer does. How is it different to a director? And why are there so many executive producers and directors? And there's always thousands of Key Grips, what the heck are they?'

He shakes his head playfully. I am already bothering him, less than a second after saying I wouldn't.

I follow him back through to the dining table as he talks.

'I manage both the crew on set and oversee the two-hundred or so crew who live and work in the make-shift production village just outside the *Love on the Island* villa. I'm responsible for the music, the daily rushes, the monitoring of the camera hides and microphones, as well as the general welfare of the contestants, those who make it onto the show and those who don't.'

'Wow. That's a lot of stuff to manage.'

Cam nods. 'Last year one of the Islanders failed to disclose that he'd starred in some pretty graphic adult movies. It threw the opening episode into chaos.'

'All the more reason to play it safe with me. The most interesting it ever got at my school involved a dead pigeon.' The words are tumbling from my lips, and I am powerless to stop them. 'And little Patrick's stepdad has been having an affair with Geoff next door for over two years. His wife is livid about it.'

For the love of God, please refrain.

After giving me a long look, Cam picks up his phone, and after a series of clicks and pressing numbers on the keypad, he gets through to a person. I listen to him speaking fluent Spanish, an instant aphrodisiac, before he turns to me.

'If you're going to stay then you'll need your things.' He points to his phone. 'Lost property. They think they have your luggage.'

I suppress a squeal of excitement while he finishes the call.

'You can tell me more about this dead pigeon on the way to the airport. Let's go.'

Chapter 9

Even though I've only been without my things for a few days, it seems like forever, and I am desperate for fresh clothes and my familiar toiletries. I am smiling at Cameron as though I have Stockholm Syndrome. He keeps shaking his head at me and grinning to himself as we drive down the secluded road, hemmed in by thick tropical rainforest on either side.

'It seems magical, doesn't it? As though an elephant is going to pop its head out any second,' I gush as we speed along.

Cam slides his eyes to mine. 'Wrong jungle. Wrong continent. Are you sure you're an educator?'

'I was speaking hypothetically.' The only jungle I've ever seen is Jungle Book. 'I meant tiger.'

'Try a monkey or a jaguar.'

'Good job I don't teach Zoology then,' I laugh.

'I think you'll find the study of animals comes under Science. And I'm pretty certain you teach that in schools.'

He's right! It does.

I will try to style it out. He couldn't possibly know the National Curriculum. We can barely keep up with the changes ourselves. 'Which one of us is the teacher here?' I ask in a light tone.

'Judging by this conversation, you could hardly tell,' he says wryly, keeping his eyes fixed on the road.

He's cheeky but I will let it go because one, he's in the right and two, he's woken up this morning looking perfect. Whereas I am a sweaty, hot mess.

After forty minutes of revealing how little research I have done on this fascinating country, we pull up at the airport and make our way inside the terminal. Stepping into the cool air-conditioned hustle and bustle is bliss. Even the walk from the car park has rivers of sweat pouring down my face.

A mere thirty minutes of queueing, two minutes of Cam sounding very annoyed in Spanish and some shaking of heads and slapping of papers, we are leaving the airport terminal empty-handed and making our way back to the car.

Cam is muttering expletives under his breath. 'Why tell me they have it when they clearly haven't?'

'What do you mean? Why can't they find my luggage?'

Cam stops marching to face me. 'Oh, they've found it. They know exactly where it is.'

'Great! Where is it?'

'Dubai. It's being treated as a terrorist threat. Apparently, they found suspicious items. A digital thermometer, a tourniquet, bottles of antibacterial liquids and a penlight?' He doesn't seem impressed. 'It's hardly going to be your case, is it?'

Ah. I should explain.

'Lois. My sister the nurse? What you're describing is essentially a complete medi-pack. It could save lives.'

The frustration falls from his face as he laughingly rolls his eyes. 'Hah. I should've known. Well, I doubt you'll get any of that back, but the good news is they have promised to forward the rest of the luggage, you know, the really important stuff, your high heels and your hair pieces. It should be on a flight today or tomorrow.'

'I love how you are taking my wardrobe so seriously.' My voice dripping with playful sarcasm. 'Thank you so much for helping me get it back. I really can't live without my stick-on eyelashes.'

'Who could?'

'Does that mean you might even let me go on the show?' I say, treating him to my best adorable smile.

'I could get into a lot of trouble if I do.'

Now that I'm here, I feel it would be rude to at least not to try and win the hundred grand.

'Would it help if I said mine and Lois's signatures are virtually identical and that her fiancé says only a thorough forensic investigation would tell them apart, and that unless either of us confessed, LoveIt TV would never know? And he's an up-and-coming lawyer so...'

'Except, as the show's producer, you have confessed to LoveIt TV. Twice.'

I am never drinking free wine ever again.

'You're right. I'm sorry for putting you in this situation and I'm sorry we've had a wasted trip to the airport, but I did enjoy the ride through the jungle. It was worth coming all this way just for that. Maybe we'll see some giraffes or zebras on the way back.'

Cam studies me as I fiddle with my hospital gown, exposing my bikini in the process. 'We can do better than that. Come on. I need to show you something. But first, we'll pick up some clothes for you in town. Get whatever you need. You can also send a list to Jake, your runner when we get back. We can always say you didn't confess until tomorrow.'

'Cool. Thanks. One more day in paradise. I'll take it.'

I am beyond grateful.

Apparently, the only clothes in this small one-horse town on the way back to the villa, are to be found in a charming artisanal street market. It is bustling with locals. There is one stand, amid two kebab meat vendors, selling clothes. Traditional embroidered loose tops and lots of colourful ponchos leap out at me. I've never worn any bright colours in my life. The gap-toothed lady looks me up and down, indicates for me to twirl around and disappears behind a huge mountain of clothes. She emerges to thrust a small pile into my arms.

'Thirty dollar,' she says, all gums.

'Gracias,' I say, too polite to argue. 'Is there anywhere to try them on? Pongo las ropas?'

She shakes her head at my pidgin Spanish. 'No need. They perfecto. She very lovely.' She holds out her hand to a laughing Cam who is nodding in agreement. He hands over the money while I feel a small tickle of pride ballooning inside. He thinks I'm lovely.

'Thank you,' I say as we leave. 'I'll pay you back.'

'No worries,' he says as I bundle the kebab meat-scented clothes onto the back seat. 'Even if they don't fit, at least you'll smell delicious in them. Nice try at the Spanish by the way.'

He thinks I smell nice and that I'm culturally sensitive.

We pull off the main road leading away from the airport and follow the signs to Cenote Maya. I can see all manner of tropical birds flying around, flashes of yellow, purples and blue as we whiz by.

'How spontaneous would you say you are?' he asks.

Compared to your glamorous over-achieving not spontaneous enough ex-girlfriend? 'Erm, very. I mean extremely.'

'Extremely?' Cam asks, trying not to laugh at me.

'Yes.'

As in not in the slightest.

'You're wearing a bikini underneath the gown, correct?'

I nod slowly. 'Sort of. It's one strap short of being a single shoelace.'

I just have time to notice Cam's eyes widen. 'How about a swim? You said you wanted to do something amazing before you leave, didn't you?'

He swings the car into a car park area packed with buses and people coming and going. I slip on my new clothes over the bikini while Cam turns his back to give me some privacy. It's a chance for me to appreciate his clean, smooth lines. He is literally the perfect shape. Not big and bulky, just lean, and athletic, the sort who could sweep you over his shoulder in the event of an emergency and still be able to save the dog.

A waft of roast pork follows me around. 'I hope I don't attract every wild carnivore in a ten-mile radius,' I joke, discreetly pulling my new denim shorts into place to avoid a camel toe situation – that crafty, gummy old doll has given me a size too small. I smooth down the top, also close-fitting, before asking Cam where we are.

'Probably the most magical place on Earth,' he says, causing ripples of excitement to flood my brain.

We approach the entrance and Cam pulls out some American dollars before we trek through the forest to an opening. We reach a busy scene. People are stripping down to their swimwear, kicking off their shoes, throwing bags onto wooden benches and racing over to a large wooden platform to queue up. There's an excited buzz and much animated chatter. We go over to do the same. I get the feeling that Cam is purposefully trying not to look at me in my skimpy bikini.

Once we have joined the queue, it is very fast moving. As we get to the front Cam's face lights up. 'Hold onto your bikini straps!' he says. 'This will blow your mind.' He points to a large wooden structure with all manner of pulleys, ropes and harnesses.

'What is it?' I ask him but before he has a chance to answer, we are being strapped to a harness each and two men are lowering us gently into a huge sinkhole in the ground. It is surrounded by lush green plants and leaves and there's a bright turquoise pool down at the bottom.

'Oh, my word!' I squeal as soon as we clear the fauna and are lowered further down on the rope. We pass through the gap into an underground cave full of sparkling stalactites and glistening rock formations. It is terrifying and breathtaking at the same time.

Cam and I look at each other. He seems very excited while I am petrified and cling tightly to the rope. Within seconds, we reach another wooden platform like the one above and again two staff members unclip our harnesses.

'Wow,' Cam says, as he looks around. 'You okay?'

'No,' I say nodding my head. 'I mean yes. No.'

'You wanted to challenge yourself, right?'

Trust him to have such a good memory.

The staff instruct us on how to hold the zipwire before we plunge into the pool. 'Wait until you are closest to the water and let go,' one of the guides says, as though hurtling through a massive cave and dropping twenty feet into an underground pool is something I do every day of the week.

He must sense fear in me. 'Questions?'

'Yes,' I say, trembling. 'Are there any alligators in there? Should I be worried?'

He starts laughing. 'No. Hahaha. Alligators! Hahahaha. No!' He looks at me as though I'm insane. 'No alligators in whole of Mexico. Alligators in Florida. Long way away.'

What a relief! I am seriously going to watch all the Blue Planets when I get back home.

'Florida is a state in America,' Cam leans across, his lips twitching.

'Is it really? Thank you. Good to know.' I turn my attention back to the helper as he guides my hands to the zipwire and puts them firmly on the crossbar.

'Seriously, lady. Don't worry. No alligators here. Only crocodiles! Big, big crocodiles!' the instructor says, giving me a push off the ledge. 'Biggest in world, hahaha,' he yells unnecessarily.

After an eternity of screaming, I land with an almighty splash in the pool. I splutter to the surface to see Cam and the two staff are howling with laughter at my expense. Cam leaps off the ledge and hurtles down the zipwire to splash into the water beside me.

He emerges to shake water from his hair and flashes me an excited grin. 'What do you think?'

'Loved it!' I say.

'Want to go again?'

I'm never doing that again as long as I live.

'I might swim a little first.' Adrenaline is pumping through my veins. I take a few deep breaths as the shock turns to curiosity. Every rock surface is reflecting the sun, and the water is causing a rainbow of colours to ripple around the cave. People are splashing about around us on various rope swings and bridges.

'It's like a movie set for Indiana Jones,' I marvel. 'The water is so clear.'

'It's thousands of years old,' Cam says, treading water. 'The waters have healing powers. Local myth says they can fix you. Fix the soul, so you can be reborn. Start again.'

'I'd like that.'

'Me too,' he says.

'I'll start again as Beyoncé or Taylor Swift.'

Cam laughs at me. 'You're better just being yourself. You are enough. Repeat after me. You, Libby Jackson, are enough.'

It's almost like he wants me to fall in love with him.

'You're right. I am enough. It's time for me to try new things. Move on,' I say, bobbing around, trying to converse while keeping an eye out for creatures lurking.

'Moving on sounds like a plan. I have an idea,' Cam says as the instructors start shouting from the rigging for people to clear a space. 'We could... if you... I'd be... the village... on a date... No one from... would see us.'

He's giving me the strangest look.

'We should give it a try,' he yells over the nearby splashing. A group of tourists are ruining our private moment.

'Give what a try?' I yell back.

'Me and you,' he says pointing a finger back and forth before flipping out of the water like a dolphin to dive back underneath.

Splash, splash.

Oh, my God. Can this be happening? Is he suggesting a secret romantic liaison?

'What do you think?' he says, emerging to catch his breath not far from me. It's like looking into the eyes of my soulmate. As though he can see through me. He can sense the turmoil I'm in, the toll of the past few years bumping against the fear of being in my late twenties without a clue of what my future holds and no mother to guide me.

Splash, splash.

Yes, please. A thousand times yes.

'Might be harder but it'll be worth it.' His face is lit up like a Christmas tree, reminding me of Lois.

'Harder?' I say. I suppose he's got the busy job to do, never mind keeping a new relationship under the radar from his boss. Our heart-to-heart last night must have made him rethink taking a chance on love. 'Harder but worth it!' I repeat back to him. My heart is beating so fast, I'm having palpitations.

Splish, splash.

My arms and legs are going like the clappers under the water to try and keep me afloat. I'll drown if he says anything else. I can't believe he's being so calm about asking me out.

'No, not harder.' Cam swims towards me. 'I said wait until you taste the michelada'.

'Michelada?'

'You'll love it. It's authentic spicy beer.'

'Spicy beer?' I splutter. *Who the fudge wants spicy feckin beer?*

He's nodding enthusiastically. 'Brewed with ancient cenote waters. Totally worth the one-hour trek, you think?'

And our potential union? What about that? I am so aghast at my obvious mistake I need to take five. I point to the jetty. I need some time out to have a word with myself. Of course, I can't compete with a model turned fashion editor. Why would he be interested in me?

'Good idea,' he says. 'Let's do the zipwire again.'

Fudge.

'I can't wait to try this,' Cam says as soon as we have dried off and made our way back to the car. 'I googled it and the best place to get michelada here on the Yucatan Peninsula is this local street food vendor back at that village. It looks incredible.' Cam is giving off major excited tourist vibes.

I am still reeling from my near miss at being caught out thinking he meant we get together physically and emotionally, instead of just for food. Still, thank goodness for small mercies. It's not Cam's fault I'm finding him increasingly magnificent with every passing second. Although sadly, it would seem I've barely made an impression on him other than my leanings towards being fraudulent and deceptive.

Apart from that though, I am buzzing. Tingling from top to toe at the cenote experience. What a thrill. Me on a zipline hurtling through a sinkhole in the jungle. The cenote has more than made up for my awful first few days here.

'This has been one of the best mornings of my life,' I say. 'I'll go anywhere and do anything. What did you say the spicy beer is called? Bring it on!'

WHO. EVEN. AM. I?

This makes Cam beam even more widely. He turns the radio up and Mexican salsa music floods the car as we race through the leafy road towards our next destination.

Two hours later and I AM STUFFED. We have eaten the best tacos and the creamiest guacamole and drunk the spiciest beer I have ever encountered in my life.

'It's like an explosion in my mouth,' I say in awe. 'I have nuclear warheads detonating in my brain.'

'I know,' says Cam, agog. 'My tastebuds are screaming for more. Who knew food and beer could taste so good?'

He's not wrong. We have eaten our way through the menu. It is delicious, even though they put chillies in the beer! Chillies in beer!

PING.

'Excuse me. I'll have to get this,' says Cam, sliding off his stool, phone clamped to his ear. He struggles to get reception and disappears outside while I look around at the authenticity of this place. The hotplates sizzling away behind a cloud of steam, as the chef cooks everything in the centre of the bar. Fresh colourful ingredients are being tossed high in the air releasing an aromatic hiss as they land. People are chatting away and clinking glasses. I look down to admire my new outfit. I blend in perfectly. The gummy lady was right. The denim shorts and beautiful embroidered peacock blue top are very flattering. She has given me an orange and pink swirly patterned poncho to go over it and a floppy purple hat. I look like a bird of paradise. Even though I have piled my drying hair on my head out of the way, I get a sudden urge to shake it free to try on the big floppy hat while Cameron is taking his call.

I undo the elastic and my hair cascades down my back, soft and shiny thanks to the magics of the ancient cenote water. I run my hands through it and swish it this way and that, as though I'm in a hair commercial. When I open my eyes, Cam is standing right in front of me, staring. My heart skips a beat in response.

Why does he have to be so incredibly gorgeous?

He blinks a few times before he speaks.

'Drink up. There's been an emergency. We have to go.'

Chapter 10

'What's happened? Where are we going?' I ask as we jump back in the car. Cam seems very stressed even with his adorable and calming Canadian lilt.

'It's the head of cabling. He says the team of electricians we contracted with have wired the conductors and connectors for the camera hides all wrong. It could set us back days if not weeks. I need to get to the production village to find out what's going on.'

'Where's the production village?'

Cam sighs patiently as though he could really do without me tagging along. 'About fifteen minutes up the road from the *Love on the Island* villa.'

'And what happens at the production village?'

Professionally nosy, remember? It's a condition. I can't help it.

'I'm afraid it's classified.'

OMG, it's the nuclear codes all over again.

'I promise you can trust me.'

He looks uncertain, almost as though thus far, our relationship has been based on a bed of lies.

'It's where all the crew stay so that we can make sure all the dailies come in and are monitored correctly twenty-four seven,' he says eventually as we hurtle away from the village. 'The kitchen staff make food for the crew and contestants from trailers, the camera operators work remotely from a makeshift office, we have technicians working on cabling and lighting, we have runners checking on the contestants in over twenty nearby villas.' He gives me a pleading look. 'Keep it to yourself. Do you promise?'

I nod. 'Of course. Not one word.'

'I'll need to drop you off at the villa first before I head to the production village,' he says, pinching the bridge of his nose like I do when figuring things out. 'Then I'll need to get to the Love on the Island villa before dark otherwise without electrics we can't see what we're doing.' I can see his mind trying to work out how he'll squash it all in. 'But it's about a two-hour round trip. There's just not enough time to do it all.'

'You're forgetting I'm a teacher. Doing a hundred jobs at once is my superpower. There is time.'

Cam takes his eyes off the road to give me a quizzical look.

'You'll have time if you take me with you, and I hide in the car.'

His face lights up. 'Man, that would be so great. Are you sure? Absolutely no one can see you or it's game over. They'll send you back home for sure and I'll get sacked on the spot. It's like one of those sacred rules.'

'Roger that,' I say, giving him a salute. 'I will stay hidden.'

I think I'm a bit tipsy from the spicy beer, but he is so relieved that I don't think he's noticed.

We arrive twenty minutes later to a park full of trailers, prefabricated square offices, what seems like millions of people scurrying around, cables everywhere, portacabins and lots of gazebos with tables and chairs dotted about with people sitting staring at laptops. I look at a huge wooden pole acting as an electricity pylon. It has signs nailed onto it for toilets, washrooms, a kitchen area and a medical tent.

'It's too crowded,' Cam says, as I slide down the seat covering my face with my huge floppy hat. 'I'll drive to my trailer. You can hide in there until I'm done.'

His trailer! An actual American-style TV trailer. 'Wow. I can't wait to see what's inside your trailer,' I say without thinking. He frowns at me. 'I mean to get out of the heat. It'll be more comfortable.'

He swings the car round the back of a huge trailer and jumps out. 'Wait here until I unlock the door.' He fiddles with some keys, looks quickly to his left then right and beckons me to follow him in. I scurry up the two stairs, and he shuts the door behind us before rolling down the blinds over the windows. Only two narrow window slits along the top allow the light to pour in.

He looks a bit flustered that I'm in his personal space. 'Make yourself at home. I'll be back as soon as I can. Help yourself to whatever there is. Try not to read any confidential papers if you can help it.'

He closes the door quietly behind him while I cast my gaze around. I've never been inside a television trailer. It's very nice and compact. There's a slim desk with a laptop, what look like scripts and charts scattered on top and a huge mirror. Opposite is a tall thin wardrobe in shiny walnut wood. I pull the long golden handle and it slides easily open. A waft of clean freshly laundered shirts fills my nostrils. It's a lavender smell. He obviously likes his tops and shorts ironed because everything hanging up looks pristine. I close the wardrobe and notice that next to it there is a door leading to a tiny bathroom with a shower. I breathe in a musky woody scent blooming from the cabinets. He has good taste in toiletries. Next to that a kitchen bench runs the length of the trailer with a microwave fixed to the wall and a built-in fridge stocked with cold drinks and snacks. There's a sweet little dining area opposite with a table for two. It looks unused. Then the trailer opens out into a spacious living area with an L-shaped sofa and a giant TV on the wall. The last door is obviously the bedroom. It's closed so I shouldn't go in.

It would be the very essence of borderline stalking and personal disrespect. Besides, a bedroom says a lot about a person. If nice and tidy, it could make a lasting impression and have you signing up to a lifetime of wedded bliss. If utterly disgusting, it could have you running screaming for the hills. I sit down on the sofa and stare at the wall. I can't put on the TV because it will make a noise.

A few minutes of me drumming my Shellac nails on the table go by. I get back up again and pace the length of the trailer. There's not an inch unused. Every surface is multi-purpose. Shelves flip up, hidden drawers pull out, the sofa is also a bed, the bench is also storage. It's so clever. I wonder how big the bedroom is in terms of square footage. Just from a professional point of view. Not that I'm thinking of leaving teaching and retraining as an interior designer any time soon. But what's the harm in peeking? Just a little look. I reach out to push the door open when the trailer door rattles suddenly, and two loud voices begin talking outside.

'Is Cameron in?' someone shouts before banging on the trailer door. 'Cameron? CAMERON?'

'I'll look through the window,' I hear a man reply.

I barely have time to dive onto the bedroom floor as I swiftly pull the duvet down over my head.

'No one in there. I can't really see for the blinds. I'll go round the back and you knock again.' He thumps so loudly it shakes the whole trailer causing me to jump with fright. I only just manage not to shriek and pull the duvet further down to cover me thoroughly.

'He's not in. We need to make a judgement call. Come over here.'

I hear the sound of footsteps right outside the bedroom and the two voices lower substantially. 'We don't have to tell him.'

'No. I disagree, Gram. I think we do have tell him, otherwise what if they find out?'

'How will they find out? Only you and me know, and the idiot who put the camera up in the wrong spot. He'll be off-site and away by now anyway.'

'True, but if the producers find out there's a blind spot and the contestants realise it's there, then we are fucked. You know what Porscha is like. She's got microphones in every toilet, shower, nook and cranny. She's even got them hidden in the bushes in case any of them try to have a quick snog without her seeing.'

Toilets? Bushes?

'Either we come clean and put production back three or four days, or we keep quiet and pray no one notices. There's only a square metre of blind spot where neither camera nor microphone will pick up. I could even put a recycle bin there. Who would sneak round the back of the beach hut to have bin-sex anyway? It's not like it's an actual alleyway.'

Who has bin-sex down alleyways? Is this a thing? Is this what contestants do?

'Doubt they'll recycle either. Good plan. That's what we'll do.'

'What about the secret door at the back of the pantry? Did you get that fixed?'

'Yes. Just don't tell her the camera is there instead of outside. Anyway, it's the camera connectors in the hides that have got Porscha's knickers in a twist. She wants connectivity and she wants it now. We're shooting the originals entrances tomorrow and none of them are working. She is on the war path. If we tell her we are going to delay the shoot for a few days, she will sack us all.'

The show starts tomorrow? And I'm obviously not one of them!

'Shit. Here they are. Quick! Hide down here so they don't see us.'

I hear a rustling noise, and a scraping sound, as though they are crouching down under the bedroom window. At the opposite end of the trailer, I can hear Cam raising his voice outside.

'It's under control, Porscha. I'll let you know as soon as it is sorted.'

She says something back that I can't quite hear, then Cameron responds.

'You want to come into my trailer?' he is saying in an exaggerated voice that is getting nearer. He sounds like a pantomime villain with something to hide. The irony that he is hiding me, and I'm hiding from the two men outside who are hiding from him, is making me want to giggle. It's ridiculous. This is a multi-million dollar show that is broadcast all over the world, and yet here we all are, hiding from each other like some kind of cheesy romcom.

'Sorry, but I'm on my way to fix the problem with the connectors. I just need to pick up my laptop and then I'll be off to the villa to meet the electrical team. Can we video call later?'

I am dying to see this Porscha she-devil that they all seem to fear. I sneak out of the bedroom and tiptoe along past the sofa, the kitchen bench and slide into the desk seat to peek through one of the windows. I slide the blind out just enough to see the back of Cam talking to a tall woman. She has flame-red hair falling like curtains to her shoulders. She is wearing beige platform wedges and standing with her legs crossed, her hands on her hips and her head tilted attractively to one side. She is beautifully made up with full make-up, tight-fitting t-shirt, denim shorts like mine and legs up to her armpits. And she clearly likes him because she is doing the hair twirl thing. I watch as she reaches out to rest her hand on his shoulder. Now she's gently rubbing her hand up and down his arm. Her body language is screaming, 'Quick, take me, take me now Cameron! Up against the bins!' and now she is pouting sulkily because he won't let her inside his trailer.

I feel a tiny stab of jealousy. What would he do if he wasn't hiding me in here? Would he have let her in? Is the attraction reciprocated?

She is biting her lip and batting her lashes at him. *Pur-leese.* It's too obvious. She hands him something and laughs. He's almost dropping them. I wish I could see his face. I can't make out what they are saying to each other, but she is nodding her head and waving her phone at him. Finally, she heads off and Cam spins round. He looks relieved.

I still jump a mile when he barges through the door and slams it shut with his foot. I am sitting innocently at his desk when he comes over and dumps loads of small packets onto it. There's an awkward moment where I look at the packets and realise that they are all condoms. Gold glittery condoms in the shape of hearts. Then Cam looks at where I am sitting. Right next to a pile of confidential papers.

'I haven't read them!' I whisper loudly, sounding guilty even though I'm not.

'What have you been doing for the half hour I've been away?' he whispers back just as the door to his bedroom flaps open. The quilt is crumpled on the floor. It looks like I've been in and ransacked the place.

How do I explain that I was hiding from people who were hiding from him? He wouldn't believe me if I tried.

'I've been eavesdropping,' I mouth, pointing outside. 'There are two people hiding outside your bedroom.'

Cam immediately throws open the front door and marches round the trailer. He comes back in with a confused look. 'There's no one there.'

'I promise they were there. I heard everything.'

He looks unconvinced.

'One of them had a funny name!' I suddenly remember. 'He's called Gram. I mean what sort of name is that? Where I come from, it's a basic unit of scientific measurement.'

'Where I come from it's what we call our senior technician.' He points a thumb to his bedroom, giving me a stern look. 'But first, could you please explain what you were doing in my bed?'

Chapter 11

Cam flops down on the trailer's hard-looking corner sofa. He looks shattered. The youthful exuberance of our morning adventures together has disappeared.

I hope he doesn't think I'm some weirdo who climbs into every man's bed she comes across. 'I swear I wasn't in your bed. Just hiding beside it. I panicked that's all. I'd never get into a strange man's bed.'

He screws his eyes at me.

'Not that you're strange.'

Someone, pass me a spade.

'Obviously, I meant I don't bed hop. I wouldn't ordinarily be found in a male companion's bed chamber –'

'You really heard voices?' Cam interrupts before my nonsense gets too out of hand.

'Yes. They said something about a blind spot.'

Cam's jaw drops. 'Blind spot? Graeme is a senior technician. He's solid. If there's a serious problem, then there's a serious problem.' He looks at the pile of papers waiting his attention. 'Those schedules will have to wait until I track down Graeme and find out what's going on.'

'Let me help,' I say. 'I'm a teacher. I can basically solve every problem known to humankind.'

'What about top-secret work schedules?'

'My speciality.'

At least this raises a smile from him. I reach out to touch his arm. 'It's been a really fun day. I owe you one,' I say, pleased that he looks more relaxed. 'Now, what can I do?'

Cam considers me for a moment. 'I know Geography isn't your strong point but are you any good at organising people?'

'Are you kidding me? I'm a professional people organiser. It's my superpower.'

'I thought you said doing a hundred jobs at once was your superpower?'

'That is the very definition of being organised, Cameron.'

Me using his full name is causing some amusement. 'And can I trust you here on your own while I go look for Graeme?'

'Yes, but only if you stop calling him Gram and start pronouncing his name correctly. It's GRAY – UM.'

Cam doesn't rise to the bait. 'And you haven't just violated my trust by snooping at confidential papers or prying around in my bedroom?'

'No, absolutely not. What a ridiculous thing to assume.'

We look again at the CONFIDENTIAL papers scattered beside me, the upended bedroom that looks like the aftermath of an orgy and the pile of condoms in the shape of glittery gold hearts spilling over the desk, and start smirking.

'You had better tell me everything you overheard then,' he says, shaking his head in disbelief. I'm just about to tell him when there's more banging on the door. Cam throws his hands in the air, frustrated. Without saying a word, I dash into his bedroom, quietly close the door, and press my ear to it.

'Hi Porscha. What's up?'

'Sorry to bother you, Cameron,' says Porscha, her voice like honey. 'But I forgot to mention something earlier.'

Sure you did.

'Okay. What is it?'

'Did I just hear voices?'

Oh dear.

'I was on the phone sorting an issue,' Cam lies smoothly.

'I'll need to come in. It's, it's rather… delicate.'

My hairy backside it is.

Cam sighs loudly. 'Can't it wait? Like I just said, I'm really busy.'

'No, it can't.' She sounds a bit frosty now.

The trailer shakes slightly as she, presumably, forces her way in.

'I'd kill for a coffee,' she says.

'If we could get right to the point. I'm just on my way out to find Graeme.'

'I've just seen him heading to the catering tent. He'll be there for hours. I'll do two coffees. Want one?'

'Uh, no thanks. Here, let me do it.'

I hear a whirring and fizzing followed by Porscha oohing and ahhing. 'Thank you so much. Is there nothing you're not good at?' She laughs as though she's told a funny joke, while I bristle at the horrendous use of a double negative.

'Seriously, though Porscha. I really need to speak to Graeme urgently.'

'It can wait. Sit,' she instructs as though he is her pet dog. 'I need your advice.'

'Sure. What is it?'

'It's about...'

I can almost hear her mind whirring while she makes up a fib. She's totally stalling. She's making it all up so that she can flirt with him. I know because I have done it myself so many times since my arrival. It's not his fault he emits a sort of sexy hunk pheromone. Like a drop of blood in the ocean, he attracts women from miles around.

'It's about these trailers.'

Pathetic.

'What about these trailers?' Cam sounds frustrated.

'I'm thinking of changing mine. It's too small. I wondered if I could have a look around yours. Do you mind?'

Genius.

'Go ahead.' He lets out a huge, bored sigh until he yells, 'No! Not in there!'

There's barely time to react so I do the only thing I can and dive onto the bed covering myself with the quilt.

Porscha laughs. 'Why? Are you hiding a woman in there?'

'No. Well, yes, actually.'

Does he struggle with low-level lying too? We really do have a lot in common.

Porscha stops walking. 'Excuse me? You've brought a woman back to your trailer? You've brought a woman to this secret location? Well, I hope she's worth it because it'll cost you your job if the boss finds out.'

'I can explain.'

'No. Hang on. I am the boss!' Porscha spits, not letting him explain.

'It's not what you think.'

There's a thumping sound vibrating through the trailer. I imagine Porscha tapping her foot, waiting for an explanation. Then more thumps and a hand on the bedroom doorhandle. Lord knows what he'll come up with.

'CHAP 3 was in there. She's been sick. The hotel couldn't check her in before two o'clock, so I offered for her to use the trailer. I haven't yet disinfected the place. So don't go in. You might catch what she's got. Even I haven't been in.'

Very impressive. But only if he's lying. I do not want to be in this bed if that awful woman has been in here.

'Thank God, you stopped me in time.' Porscha sounds as though he's just saved her from accidentally walking off a clifftop. 'How disgusting. I'll get cleaning over here immediately.'

The whole experience has clearly put her off evaluating its suitability as potential accommodation. I hear the trailer door open and feel Porscha's weight on the steps.

'Maybe I'll come back another time. When you have fresh sheets,' she laughs. 'Ciao.'

The trailer door clicks shut and, a few moments later, there's a gentle knock on the bedroom door. 'The coast is clear.' Cam opens the door and spots me still hidden under his quilt. It smells of lemon-scented woody after-shave. Just like his shirts. Fresh and clean. The CHAP 3 story was a complete lie. I'm impressed.

'That woman is stress on legs, isn't she?' I say, sitting up in his bed. 'I'm surprised you're not on permanent ten-terhooks. It's almost sexual harassment in the workplace the way she's throwing herself at you.'

Says the woman making herself comfy in his actual bed.

Cam's cheeks flame.

'Sorry. I didn't mean to embarrass you. I just as-sumed...'

I just assumed you aren't attracted to forceful man-eaters with extra-long legs.

'No. It's not that. It's just the whole unrequited situa-tion. I'm not ready for... anything just yet. And definitely not while I'm working.'

Oof. A double blow.

'That's completely understandable,' I say, vowing to back off completely. 'It must be hard to have beautiful women constantly throwing themselves at you every minute of every single day. If only you'd gone into nature documentaries. Although, knowing your luck you'd be carried off into a South-African rainforest by a randy Silverback.'

Cam shakes his head, trying not to laugh. 'Wrong terrain. Wrong continent.'

'I'm going to have a word with the British Government as soon as I return to England. Our education system is clearly lacking.'

Cam throws his head back and laughs causing an unexpected feeling of joy to spread through me. I throw off the quilt and follow him back to the lounge area.

'What's that?' I say pointing to the L-shaped sofa.

Cam groans. 'Oh, man. She left her walkie talkie behind.'

'Meaning she'll be back as soon as she thinks you have clean sheets,' I giggle. 'She's admirably persistent, I'll give her that.'

Cam smiles.

'What?'

'Thanks,' he says simply. 'I appreciate it.'

'Appreciate what?'

'What you're doing. It's very kind. Making me laugh to take my mind off the stress.'

I gulp, heat rising from my neck. I'd hate to embarrass him with another unrequited crush situation. 'I have no idea what you're talking about.'

'Well, let's just say I'm not like this around everyone.'

My cheeks are on fire. 'You best return this to Porscha before she has time to come back in her stripper basque and peephole bra.'

If he thinks Porscha leaving objects in his trailer might be obvious and tacky, it's nothing compared to me flying thirteen thousand miles across the planet just to see if there's a spark of interest in those glorious eyes of his. The shame.

'I'll drop it with her assistant. Then I need to swing by the main villa to drop some kit off and check in with the technicians. You'll be stuck with me for another few hours. Is that okay?'

I'd like nothing more.

While Cam has gone into the *Love on the Island* villa, I have remained hidden in the car behind a section of trees. I've tried peeking, but the villa itself is hidden behind a massive purpose-built wall and ironclad gate. They are obviously leaving nothing to chance, and security is disappointingly rock solid. He has left me with a plethora of things to schedule. I need to work out the driving times from each of the ten villas housing the contestants, so that I can co-ordinate the drivers and entry times and match those with camera operators and runners. And according to the notes, I need to cross-reference those with the timings of kitchen and housekeeping crew who need to be in, set up, cooking the food, doing the final sweep to check all the cameras and microphones are working and then need to disappear before the *Love on the Island*-ers gather by the firepit for the first big welcome to the show. It's very exciting. I have goosebumps. I'm much better suited to behind-the-scenes. Before I know it, Cam is climbing back into the car.

'How did you get on?' he asks, looking at my clipboard.

'All done,' I say, turning it round to show him. He makes a big 'O' with his mouth. 'You're welcome, Cam. Least I could do after such an awesome morning.'

'I really appreciate it, thank you. And you were right. There's a blind spot exactly where you said it would be.'

'What are you going to do?'

Cam shrugs. 'Not sure yet. Every day we are set back costs roughly four hundred thousand dollars at this point, plus penalties from sponsors if we don't air on time. It's a shitshow, all right. I'm tempted to let Gram get away with it. If you were on the show, would you go looking for blind spots, or would you just assume there are cameras everywhere and there would be no point?'

I want to reassure him. 'I'd assume the worst, cameras everywhere. Did you know that they have microphones in the toilet and cameras in the shower?'

Cam looks uncomfortable. 'Just for the record, I never agreed with that. It's disgusting, but what Porscha wants, Porscha gets.'

'Hmmm. I got that impression. She looks the forceful type, that's for sure.'

'How do you know what Porscha looks like?'

'Erm, well, I kind of saw you two together outside your trailer before she came barging inside. And those two workmen had plenty of things to say about her that weren't entirely complimentary.'

'She is kind of a ballbreaker, I'll give her that. But then you have to be, on a show like this.'

'How long have you worked on this show?'

'Just since the last series. It's a stepping stone to what I'd ideally like to do.' Cam leans an arm across my seat while he twists around to reverse expertly out of the tight spot we are in.

'Which is?'

'You ask a lot of questions, don't you?' he says, turning back around and jamming the gear into first. He pulls on the steering wheel to navigate the rough terrain.

‘Like I said. I’m a teacher. Being nosy is a huge part of who I am professionally.’

Cam starts chuckling as he swings onto the road. ‘Okay. Why don’t I show you instead? Do you have one more spontaneous surprise left in you?’

'Do we have time?'

'I'll make time.'

Oh, gosh.

‘Then, I love surprises,’ I lie casually as we speed along the isolated road back to our villa.

Who am I? Who is this woman?

Chapter 12

Cam drives a little further on and then turns off the road at a sign for a nature park. We bump along for a few miles until the track opens up onto a dusty carpark and a hut with a small window and a tired-looking fella sitting up, but quite asleep, behind it.

We jump out and Cam opens the boot. He drags out a big camera and a tripod. 'Hold this please,' he says. 'And this.'

Soon we are paying ten dollars entry and are essentially walking into a jungle. My stress levels are climbing. The light is fading. It will get dark soon.

'Do you know where we are going? What if we get lost? Do you have a phone signal? A first aid kit? Who else knows we are here? Do you have your mobile tracker on? These clothes still smell like fresh kebab meat. Am I going to get my tits ripped off by a pack of rabid hyenas?'

'For a start, hyenas live in Africa.' Cam stops to look at me.

I instantly stop panicking at his calm, soothing tone.

'Huh. Not much of a risk-taker, are you?'

I shake my head. 'I struggle a little bit with change... and with anything that's not organised with military precision.' This is a gross understatement. 'And... surprises.'

He jokily rolls his eyes. 'Well, don't worry. I have you covered. Trust me. Look, it's just up ahead.'

He has such a reassuring manner that it puts me at ease straightaway. Two minutes later we come to a clearing.

The scene takes my breath away as I sweep my gaze upwards. 'We've stepped into paradise,' I whisper. Exotic birds are swooping through the air, monkeys are swinging through trees, all manner of creatures are scampering around. 'Have we just walked into a Disney film?'

Cam laughs quietly and sets up the tripod, fixing the camera deftly on top. 'I produce nature documentaries by trade. You kinda hit the nail on the head back there with your Silverback assumptions.'

I nod in understanding.

'I don't usually bring anyone here. It's my special place.'

My heart flutters at his confession, but I try not to read anything into it.

'Documenting wildlife, especially those close to extinction, is my absolute passion. Filming anything else seems meaningless,' he says, twisting the giant lens and swinging the camera round. 'I'd love to film in the UK someday. Man, you have some spectacular scenery and wildlife. But you just gotta take what work's offered, you know? Even if you don't enjoy it.'

'I totally get that,' I say. When my mother died, so did my zest for life, my ambition, my passion. Everything seemed meaningless afterwards, so I allowed myself to drift, doing crappy supply jobs for hardly any money, and even less respect, while I took time to figure out how to cope.

While Cam has his head down, peering through the camera and twiddling with buttons, he starts speaking to me in hushed tones.

'I filmed here once. In this exact spot. In fact, it was while I was here on location that Megan and Pete first hooked up behind my back.'

Oh. This must be hard for him. He keeps his face hidden behind the camera. Just because he's comfortable and trusting enough to confide in me and because I'm incredibly easy to talk to, doesn't mean he has romantic feelings for me. I try not to let my hopes soar.

'Must have been so tough to lose both your best friend and your girlfriend at the same time,' I say quietly. 'That's why you don't mind being away from home so long.'

A comfortable silence settles between us and for the next hour we simply watch the jungle come alive in all its glorious technicolour. When we pack up and trek back to the car, Cam says, 'Thank you, Libby. That meant a lot.'

One look into his kind, sad eyes and my heart melts for him. I reach out to take his hand lightly. 'It's okay to still be sad.'

He clears his throat, dropping my hand. 'We'd best hurry. Porscha will be calling soon. I'll need to be at my desk, or she'll get suspicious.'

'You could tell her to back off.'

He gives me a tiny half-smile as we set off, navigating the difficult compacted terrain in partial light.

'Yeah. She's been after me for a while. It's kinda difficult because, well, for one she's my boss and two...'

'You're not interested? She's not your type? Too bossy? Too scary? Too in-your-face?'

'I was going to say I never mix business with pleasure.'

My chances with this glorious man are plummeting by the second.

'I could tell by your body language,' I say, ignoring this devastating blow. 'Usually, if a woman muscles her way into your trailer under false pretences, twirls her hair and gives you a year's supply of condoms, you'd do more than hurry away at the speed of light.'

Cam chortles. 'Was it that obvious?'

'For your sake, I hope she's not one of those women who loves the chase. From what I hear, she always gets what she wants.'

'Are you sure you're a schoolteacher and not some spy from a rival TV channel? You seem to know an awful lot about things.'

'I am a teacher therefore I gossip.'

'Did you just coin a new phrase?' Cam looks at me and waggles his eyebrows.

It's almost like he is flirting with me.

'How do you fancy continuing this over dinner?' he says.

He is. He's flirting with me.

A bubble of joy rises from my chest. I must try to play it cool whilst also letting him know that I am very, very available. 'Sure. I'd love to.'

'As a teacher, I'd appreciate your take on using documentaries to drive home the need to save the planet in schools. Is it a mandatory part of the National Curriculum over there? How about the rest of Europe?'

I have never been so disappointed.

He is clearly only after one thing. My brain. Just then Cam's phone bursts to life. He presses the button on the dashboard to Bluetooth the call. It's Porscha. Cam slides his gaze to me and raises a finger to his lips.

'Cam, honey. Thanks for dropping my walkie talkie off. If I'd known, I would've made sure I was in the office to receive it personally. How did it go at the main villa? All sorted?'

Honey?

'Yes. All sorted. Just on my way back to the holding villa now.'

'Shame. I thought we could get together tonight. To go over the... schedules. Give them a thorough going over to make sure we haven't missed anything.'

She is making it sound filthy.

'That's okay,' Cam says quickly. He has obviously detected an ulterior motive. 'They're all done and checked.' He gives me a grateful look.

'Are they?' She sounds dissatisfied. 'Okay. Well, how about you head back to base for a debriefing? It's a while since anyone debriefed me.'

This too sounds like pure filth. I wonder again about that mountain of condoms she gave him. Is she hoping to test them all individually? That's quite the quality check.

'I would but I'm chaperoning our British contestant. Chap 3 went down with a stomach bug, remember? So, I'm standing in until we find a replacement.'

'Not a problem. I'll send Jake over to keep her company. He's losing three of his contestants tomorrow anyway when they go in the villa. I'll text him now. Which villa are you staying in? Is it Yucatan twelve?'

I gulp, suddenly feeling distraught at losing Cam so soon. Just as we are starting to get to know each other.

He shoots me a look. 'Er no, Porscha. Thanks, but it's fine. I have all my equipment set up ready to do the music soundbites. I'm gonna be working all night. So, no need to send Jake. We'll work something out tomorrow.'

There's a silence before she tuts loudly down the phone. Porscha does not sound happy.

'Fine,' she says tightly. 'I'll see you tomorrow then.'

Cam clicks off the call and exhales. 'Looks like I've escaped for another night at least.'

My heart does a little flip. I'm sure he only wants to stay with me to escape Porscha, but a tiny part of me hopes otherwise...

Three hours later we have feasted on goats' cheese and crispy bacon salad and have sung our way through most of tomorrow's playlist.

'Top up?' I ask, wandering over to the table to pour more wine into Cam's glass. I'm a terrible influence on him. I lean over him, making sure not to knock any of the screens, cables and mini mixing desk laid out. He has been working away diligently while I've been singing along from the sofa.

'I love that you have all these famous songs slowed down or speeded up just to fit each scenario. The being dumped clip is a howler!' I giggle.

'What do you mean?' Cam says looking up.

'Oh, come on,' I put my drink down so that it doesn't slosh over the sides. 'Go on now go! Walk out the door,' I sing at the top of my lungs. 'While the poor sod does the walk of shame out of the actual villa door.' I'm laughing hard at the very thought of it. 'Imagine? If it's not humiliating enough, you've got throwing out music to see you on your way.'

'I know. We're awful people.'

We lock eyes.

'Would you feel emotionally able to handle the show? Given your motivations for flying all the way over here just to make some guy jealous?'

'And to give my sister and her fiancée some space,' I reason. 'I'm not completely insane. Today has been the best day of my entire life but I'd hate to get you into any trouble.'

'Wow. You'd give up the chance to win one hundred thousand dollars just so I don't get into trouble?'

I nod slowly. 'Well, when you put it like that... I do sound insane.'

Suddenly I'm aware of the music changing to a slow romantic tune. I sip my wine to keep me from staring into those soulful eyes of his. Each sip feels laced with a frisson of something illicit. The atmosphere crackles between us. He picks his wineglass up and necks it.

'You are a terrible corrupting influence,' he says.

'Wait until you see me dance,' I say, beginning to sway sexily for him. I'm three glasses deep and quite sure beyond a shadow of doubt that it is anything but sexy. But who cares? Fortune favours the brave. I may never see him again after tonight. He might go back to the production village, and I might get sent home. The new me won't even have had her moment to shine.

'Dance with me.' I hold my breath while he visibly decides whether this is a good idea. He is staring at me. Now he is looking at my lips. He is putting down his drink and leaning towards me. It's happening in slow motion, but I think I'm moving closer to him. He takes my drink from me and finishes it in one go. I really shouldn't but I find his new tolerance for alcohol immensely sexy.

He reaches out to take my waist and I step closer. We start to move in time to the music. At first tentatively but then, my God, can he move. We are pressed up against each other, my arms round his neck and we are swaying in perfect time with one another. His scent is intoxicating, fresh and lemony. His eyes have not left my face. My heart is thumping through my chest as his hands move lightly over my back. I think he might kiss me. I bite my lip slowly and hear a low groan escape from him.

'You shouldn't look at me like that,' he whispers.

Yes, I bloody should.

I ease my head back to peer up at him from below my eyelashes, willing him with every fibre in my being to kiss me. I run my hand lightly through his hair. It's soft and silky just as I imagined. I trail my hand down his neck and trace the outline of his firm shoulders. I feel his bicep tense under my touch. When I see him gulp, I'm pretty sure I have him under my spell.

The sensual beat of the music is enhancing the mood, causing us to keep time. Cam's hands press firmly on my back, bringing me in even closer as we sway in time. He leans down towards me, our foreheads almost touching, his ragged breath light on my face. The energy between us is electrifying. My heartbeat is terrifyingly fast, my mind is spinning out of control with lustful thoughts for this man.

'Kiss me,' I whisper. Our lips are millimetres apart.

Before he can act on my instruction the beat of the music changes suddenly. It's almost as though it snaps him out of the trance.

The tempo thumps through our bodies demanding we keep pace. In one swift move he keeps one arm wrapped around me, takes my hand from his neck and twirls me slowly away from him Latino-style. He then pulls me back in and up close before we engage in what can only be described as having sex while dancing fully clothed.

IT. IS. THE. MOST. EROTIC. EXPERIENCE. OF. MY. LIFE.

The music ends and we stare panting and breathless at one another. The sexual energy in the room is off the charts.

I shouldn't have to ask twice for him to kiss me... but I will if he doesn't make a move soon.

It feels like ten of the world's slowest seconds crawl by and still no lip action.

'Goodnight then,' he says.

It takes a long moment for his words to sink in.

'Goodnight?'

He nods slowly with an almost pained expression.

'Goodnight as in you're off to bed?' I really need some clarification.

'Yeah, erm, big day tomorrow and you know, erm...' he says, running a hand through his hair and blinking his eyes as though to shake himself out of a daze.

No, I certainly do not know.

I must look distraught.

'I'm sorry, Libby. Even though I find you incredibly attractive. Unbelievably attractive,' he says. 'I can't get involved.'

'Oh,' I say, trying not to look or sound tearful as he hurries back to his laptops to put some distance between us.

He turns the music off with a noisy clang. The romantic atmosphere has been well and truly burst like a balloon.

Almost as if he has suddenly remembered that he does not mix business with pleasure after all.

Chapter 13

I can't even begin to describe how rough I feel when I wake up. The whole drinking too much wine and crushing rejection had me tossing and turning all night. My cheeks are burning with the humiliation of it. How am I going to face Cam today? I threw myself at him in the most shameful way. I did the whole lips pouting, bosom-heaving, lashes batting routine, and more or less demanded that he kiss me, and he still did not have the courtesy to act on it. After all, the attraction was mutual. He said so himself.

Or did he?

Was I so under the influence that I imagined he was more into me than he actually was? When he said 'I shouldn't look at him like that' did he really mean I shouldn't look at him like that? Was I, in fact, coming on too strong and it spooked him? He certainly seemed like he couldn't get away fast enough. But the crackling energy between us... he must have felt it. He must have.

Unless he didn't.

How mortifying. I'm never drinking that much again.

Without any way of telling the time, it takes me ages to summon the courage to get out of bed. Ages. So long in fact, that the sun is high in the sky, the heat is almost impenetrable when I step out through the patio doors, and the villa is completely empty. I wander through to the kitchen to find Cam has left a note on the bench to say that he has had to go back to the production village to sort out some things. Nothing about last night. Not one word.

I feel so deeply depressed about it. And what makes it worse is that it's all my own doing. He told me very clearly that he is not ready for a relationship and even if he was, he does not mix business with pleasure. He couldn't have been any clearer. And yet... here I am. Thinking about him all the time. Dreaming about him at night. And trying my best to make him laugh just to see his face light up and the sadness fade from his eyes. His kind, honest, worldly blue-green eyes.

He has already risked quite a lot for me. It's not his fault that I'm over-reacting, my emotions are running wild, and I've built up this elaborate fantasy where we fall madly in love with each other just because he's my newly discovered type.

The last thing he needs is for my massive unrequited crush to cost him his job and livelihood. I will pull myself together and behave like a grown-up woman. I will rein in my runaway libido and excessive flirting, out of professional respect for him. It's the least I can do.

Pep talk over, I decide to go for a dip in the pool to cool my passions. I came all this way to see if Cameron was my type. This has been undeniably confirmed. He is the perfect man. I find him attractive to the point of never needing to look at another man again in my whole life. Unfortunately, it would seem that every other woman on the planet feels the same way. But still, at least I can return home with that box well and truly ticked. I wanted to do a long-haul flight to somewhere exotic and I have, so that box is ticked, and so is the stepping outside my comfort zone to take a few risks box. I'd say hurling myself into an underground cave full of ancient healing waters, trekking into the middle of a jungle and falling head over heels for the only man that's not emotionally available in the whole of Mexico would definitely constitute self-challenge and personal growth. And as for Arrogant Josh... Josh who? Now that I've had a taste of what real men are like there's no going back for me.

By the time I have swum over thirty lengths, I reach the conclusion that my time here is done. I have no need to go on *Love on the Island* in search of love. I will save everyone a load of trouble and ask to withdraw. I would hate to get Cam into trouble if the TV company finds out I've swapped places with Lois, and he knew about it. And I could always ask them to keep my flight home open until I've had a chance to explore this wonderful country. I could even go island hopping in the Caribbean for the entire summer to give Lois and Tyrone some space to achieve their couples goals.

I float around face up in the pool making angels wings with my arms and legs. How lucky am I to be given this opportunity? I shouldn't be going home feeling anything but grateful that I met him and had this brief but wonderful and intoxicating experience.

'Mind if I join you?'

My eyes snap open as I stare up into a silhouette. Cam slips into the water with barely a splash. I swim to the end of the pool to meet him. Might as well get this sorry embarrassment over with.

I instantly regret it. Cam's handsome features emerge from the water to take in air. He swipes the hair from his forehead, water trickling seductively down his face, round his lips and down towards the firm chest not quite hidden below the water. He takes my breath away. He literally takes my breath a.w.a.y.

For a horrible second, I think I might burst into tears, my emotions are swirling around so uncontrollably. I wonder if it is the heat. Do extreme temperatures affect your ability to act normal?

Cam opens his eyes and I'm surprised to see my own sadness reflecting back at me. He holds my gaze for too long so that my cheeks feel like they are on fire. I find myself biting my lip and turning away from him.

'I'm sorry,' he says, causing me to look back at him. 'For last night.' It's almost as though he is dragging the words from the depths of his soul and that's all he can manage.

I try my best to smile bravely back. 'It's okay. I completely understand.'

I can't tear my eyes from his. If he has an ounce of understanding of how a woman works, then he will read between the lines and know that I am completely and utterly crushed. It most definitely is not okay, and I do not in any way, shape or form understand why in the heat of the moment he had to reject me so thoroughly.

His jaw falls open as though he is about to say something, but he closes it before the words reach his lips.

'I'll go back home,' I blurt out. 'It's for the best.'

Cam says nothing as we let the words hang between us.

'Besides, we both know I shouldn't have come.'

Again, Cam says nothing. He simply takes in what I'm saying.

'And anyway, I'm not really cut out for this sort of show. Or any show really.'

Still nothing.

'So, if... if you don't mind, I'll just... I'll just pack my things up and... you can keep the emergency first aid kit and insect repellent if you want. You might need it. And the Imodium might come in handy too if you're going to be drinking spicy beer. And the wipes might help you avoid catching any bugs. In fact, I'll leave you the surgical gown too, just in case.'

I can't read his face. I can't tell what he is thinking at all. He is simply standing staring at me until he finally nods.

'Sure. If that's what you want.'

I sniff back the threat of tears and chew my lip to stop it wobbling. 'It is.'

It sooooo isn't, I am practically silent screaming at him.

Why isn't he asking me to stay?

A heavy silence hangs in the air.

'I'll check out flight options back to the UK,' he says stiffly. He swiftly glides to the pool edge, clamps his hands on the side and, as though the universe is kicking me while I'm down, and hauls himself up and out in one languid movement.

My God, the man is magnificent. Taut muscles ripple across his back, as he picks up his towel to dab his athletic torso in slow motion, before he strolls into the villa without so much as a backward glance.

What just happened? One minute I'm here, there's sunshine, this amazing pool, the world's best human wearing only swimming trunks and a hunky smile and the next, I'm sulking for England in my room as I pack my one wet belonging into my case. I towel-dry my hair, pin it into a top knot, slip into my short shorts and yesterday's poncho top.

I wheel the empty case to the door and try to be grateful for the time I've spent here. I slap on a smile for Cam as he picks up his car keys. He's blissfully unaware that he's adding insult to injury by looking and smelling fabulous.

I open the door and feel the warm breeze blow through. My heart sinks a mile at the thought of leaving.

'Libby, wait. You came a long way to be on the show. I'm sorry if, in some way, I have ruined that for you.'

He looks so genuine. I ache to throw my arms around him. 'No. No, you haven't. It's not your fault I'm leaving.

I'm the one who shouldn't have come in the first place. I've absolutely loved the few days I've had here.' Now is a good time to inspect my footwear. I keep my eyes trained on my sneakers. 'With you.'

Silence and plenty of it while we think of what to say next. Me, trying not to let him see the effect he has on me, sparkles shooting from my eyes that type of thing, and him, wondering how to politely remind me that he isn't interested in me like that.

'Leave the case. You won't need it.'

I frown. 'Why? What's going on?'

Cam throws me a bittersweet smile. 'There isn't a flight available today. And...' He gives me a meaningful look. 'I'm not sure I made myself clear last night.'

'You seemed pretty clear to me.'

He tilts his head. 'I didn't want to confuse you.'

'Confuse me?' I say. 'I think we both know what I wanted. The confusion is with you. I mean I get it,' I tell him. 'Last night. You'd get sacked if we were caught... you know, wouldn't you?'

'It's not that. What if you'd got the call and decided to go into the villa. I didn't want you to feel awkward about having to go with other...'

'But I don't want to go with other...' I can't bring myself to finish the sentence. There's no chance any woman with a pulse would choose any other man over him.

He clears his throat nervously. 'Are you saying that you...?'

I blink slowly. 'Are *you* saying that you...?' I say, taking a step towards him.

You could cut the sexual tension with a knife.

He instinctively reaches for me. Our faces inches apart, his strong arms holding me tight. I wrap my arms around his neck pulling him closer. I feel the heat of his skin on mine. The energy between us suddenly changes. This is it.

The moment.

The build-up to the kiss has commenced yet again and fireworks are going off in my brain.

The kiss is forthcoming. Cam's gaze has shifted to my lips.

If he doesn't make a move, then I definitely will because he fancies me. I'm one hundred percent certain of it. I reach slowly behind me to close the door when a shadow falls over us.

'Well, this looks cosy!'

We spring apart. Porscha is standing looking furious, hands firmly on hips, legs wide apart as though she's a politician on stage at a public rally, head tilted to one side.

She looks from Cam to me, and back again. 'Someone want to tell me what the hell is going on?'

Chapter 14

Cam and I exchange a panicked look. We were so, so close to sealing the deal. I'm gutted. I can feel the dopamine ebbing from my brain.

'We were saying goodbye,' I say, stepping away from Cam. 'Cam was just helping... me... with my bags. I get very emotional at goodbyes. I'm not good with that sort of thing. I have overactive hormones.' I am speaking so quickly that it all sounds very, very untrue by the time it peters out.

Porscha looks down at my one tiny case and shakes her head at me. 'I can see why you need help with it.'

Sarcasm. The lowest form of wit.

There's an awkward air of silence where none of us say anything.

'God, I can't stand you British and your need for over-thinking things. You make terrible liars. I know that for sure. And where is it you think you're going?'

'Home.' It's out of my mouth before I barely know what's happening.

She glares at Cameron. 'And you didn't think to tell me this minor detail? You do know how this show works, right?' Her voice jumps up at least four octaves. She looks livid with him.

'Not my home,' I blurt. 'Another home. Another villa.'

'That's right,' says Cam. 'I thought I'd switch her to a villa that's nearer to the production village. So I don't have too far to travel.'

'You told her about the production village?' She looks incredulous.

It's time for the more experienced liar to step up.

'It's not his fault,' I say in a rush. 'I overheard him talking on his phone. I appreciate there's a lot that still needs to be pulled together.'

'Is she telling me what happens on my own show?' she says to Cam.

He shakes his head. He's probably wondering why I'm digging myself into a hole.

Porscha remains unconvinced and is eyeballing Cam. He has lost his words. I blame myself. I practically made him an alcoholic over the two days I have been in his care. And now

I have put him in an untenable situation with my desire to kiss him. Shame on me.

'Don't worry, Porscha, I have strong moral values that I guard with the utmost integrity. Your secret is safe with me. *Bono moralia, custodio integretate.*'

Christ. Trust our school motto to be the only thing to spring to mind.

'Excuse me?' she says, looking me up and down. I immediately take a step back.

'It's Latin. For the thing I just said.' I swallow a lump in my throat. Porscha should be a headteacher. She'd be perfect.

'Cameron. Can we have a word, please?' She looks sharply at me. 'We have strict rules about non-disclosure...'

'That's not his fault either,' I blurt. 'I'm a professional nosy parker. I'm the problem, it's me.'

Taylor Swift really knows her stuff.

'... and even stricter rules about getting involved with the collateral,' she carries on as though I'm not there.

'It was a hug goodbye. Nothing happened,' says Cam, holding his hands in the air as though he's been caught at a crime scene.

'He's right,' I say, the disappointment flooding out of me. 'Absolutely nothing happened. Nothing. It's border-line shocking.'

This causes Cam to start smirking.

'I think you'd better leave the adults to do the talking,' Porscha says condescendingly.

See? Perfect headteacher material.

'It's obvious I need to split you two up before one of you makes a fool of herself.'

'Now, Porscha. You're reading way too much into –' Cam says.

She cuts him off. 'I think we should send her into the villa if she's that uncontrollably horny.'

Oh shit.

'No!' I am in flight or fight mode. 'My luggage isn't even here yet. It's in Dubai. I have no clothes or make-up. I'm a mess. I haven't even got an all-over tan.' It's true. 'I'll look dreadful on camera. I'll get voted off straight away. Surely that wouldn't make any commercial sense?'

Porscha ignores me. 'Is she telling me how to run my own show, Cameron?'

It's like I'm invisible.

'No. No, of course she isn't,' Cam says defending me. Porscha stands blinking at him. He flashes her a bright smile. It has an instant calming effect on her. She tears her eyes away from him to look at me.

'So, you do want to go on the show?'

I nod. 'But it would be great if I could wait until my clothes get here.'

She takes a moment to stare at me. She can't believe the audacity.

'Oh, right. Of course. Of course, we'll hold the entire show up while we wait for your knickers to arrive from... where did you say you left them?' She screws her eyes at me. 'I'll send a car for you.' She looks down at her phone, rapidly clicks a few things with her two robotic thumbs and looks back up. 'Done.' She waves me off as though dismissing the hired help.

'By the way, Libby, you should know that any liaisons between a contestant and a member of the crew will result in a breach of contract.' She goes on to quote verbatim at me. It's so unnecessary. 'You'll be sent home, and the crew member will be sacked immediately.' She turns to Cam. 'Without severance pay. I'm surprised you haven't mentioned it to her. It's all in the small print.'

'I will try to keep my wandering libido to myself,' I say, furious at not being able to tell her where to get off.

'Please do. Save it for the islanders.' She gives me an evil stare. 'I'll have a word with wardrobe. I'm sure we can find something suitable.'

It sounds more like a threat than an offer of help.

Nor am I loving her perfect impression of my headteacher. Dismissive. Uncaring. Pompous. It's as though the whole world revolves around them and their careers.

'Cameron, you better come with me. You can pick your stuff up later.'

I see Cam's cheeks go red. He's struggling to keep his temper. I can tell because he has this tick that goes off in his cheek. It was the same when he was talking to her on the phone. She must really get his goat. 'You're making out that something has happened here when it absolutely hasn't.'

She is taken back by Cam's forcefulness.

'Porscha. You've walked in and thrown accusations around. Threatened to sack me. Assumed that I'm incapable of acting responsibly and now you don't trust me to keep my hands to myself?'

She is backfooted by him. Her mouth opens and closes. 'Very well. Have it your way.'

She swivels on her high wedged sandals and marches back to her car. With a loud crunch of gravel and an angry roar of the engine she drives off.

I've done nothing but encourage him to abandon his core values, his not mixing business and pleasure work ethic. And then there's me violating his trust when he very clearly told me he is not quite ready to move on from his awful cheating girlfriend yet, and to top it all off, because of me, Porscha is threatening to ruin his career. Poor man. I must try not to make his life any worse than I already have.

Turning to each other, we let out a sigh of relief.

'How do you feel about going into the villa? You can still back out, you know. I'll ring her and let her know you want to go home.'

I look at his handsome face.

'And I suppose they'll get me on the first flight out tomorrow?'

He nods his head.

'Is that what you want?' I ask him. 'For me to go home?'

I can barely breathe. Why am I putting him on the spot like this?

He doesn't bat an eyelid. 'No.'

'But if I don't go, the only option is to go in the villa.'

'Worst case scenario is you don't get voted off, and you win a hundred grand.'

'Well, that sounds like a no-brainer,' I say, trying to sound more cheerful about it. There's zero chance of me ever winning. 'Will I see you when I'm in there?'

'Yes. I'll be pretty much in and out the whole time. The issue is that we'd be on camera the whole time so... erm, even conversations would be difficult.'

'If only there was a secret blind spot that no one but us knew about.'

Cam looks at me with a sparkle in his eye. I can see his mind whirring. 'We'd need a code word.'

He takes my hand and leads me to the dining table. He clears stuff away, gets out a roll of paper and unfurls it. He shows me the blueprint of the villa, where the hidden camera hides are, which walls are fake and turn into secret doors and most importantly, how to switch off the microphone in the toilet while I'm in there. He swishes his finger over his iPad to give me a virtual tour of the villa.

'Don't touch anything in the villa kitchen, it's all fake,' he warns

'You're kidding,' I say. 'Don't the islanders cook their own food?'

'Nope. We cook lunch in a secret kitchen behind the false wall in the communal bedroom. It then gets delivered to them round the back of the villa. But we never show those bits. Too boring. Dinner is cooked at the production village and brought over.'

'Tell me everything.'

'The place is so big you could probably avoid everyone if you really needed to. That's the pool obviously,' he says pointing out an Olympic-sized, kidney-shaped pool on the map. 'You have to remember to take your mic pack off or it'll cost two hundred dollars to replace, and Porscha will personally come down and kick you up the fanny.'

Whaaaat?

Cam looks at my shocked face. 'You don't have that expression?' Cam seems shocked that I am shocked.

'So, anyway, that's the Tree House over there for couples wanting to get intimate. Why anyone would want to climb up there is beyond me. We have four cameras up there and two microphones.'

'How many cameras are there hidden around?'

Cam blows out his cheeks, 'I'd say seventy hidden cameras dotted around and twelve camera hides. That's the bigger cameras with operators. They catch most of the action that we show. The firepit gatherings, the bedroom scenes and the Beach Hut.'

'Beach Hut?'

'You know where the contestants go to talk to camera. So, they have more chance of getting on the final cut.'

I shudder which makes Cam laugh. 'The whole point of this show is to be on TV, Libby. You can't come on it and hide away. You have to have fun while you're in there, and let people get to know you. Let the viewers get to know you.'

'Yikes.'

'I'll tell you a secret hack that will mean you get your own bedroom and bathroom,' he says. 'Just until you settle in. Do not let on that I told you.'

The last thing I want to do is put his career at risk, but Cam assures me that he won't be working on the show next year. He can't bear the direction that Porscha is taking the show.

'Are you sure?' I ask.

'I'm so sick of her,' he says. 'It's time I set up my own company anyway.'

'With any luck, I'll be voted straight off after a few days and that'll be that. Life can go back to normal,' I tell him.

'Do you want it to go back to normal?'

My heart swells as he stops what he is doing to run a tanned hand through his hair. Christ, he is so sexy even under pressure.

'I guess not. No.'

'Okay. Good. Good.'

Things are tense.

'About earlier...' I say, the almost kiss still fresh in my mind. 'When we almost –'

The sudden crunch of gravel alerts us to my car arriving. The driver beeps the horn ruining the moment. Then the driver knocks on the door and walks straight in, ruining it even further.

Cam greets him like the professional he is while I am aghast at having to leave yet again without so much as a peck on the cheek.

We follow the driver to the car and Cam puts my near-empty bag in the boot.

Cam takes one look at me and waits for the driver to get back behind the wheel and close his door. 'Don't worry,' he says quietly. 'I've got your back. Whenever you need help in there, just say the word and I'll meet you in the blind spot. Okay?'

He shifts uneasily in front of me. 'There's erm, just one thing that I need to ask you before you leave.'

He takes out his phone and scrolls down to headshots of five muscle-mountains. 'Which three do you fancy the most?'

I must look horrified because he starts to laugh. 'You gotta pick three I'm afraid.'

'Absolutely not.'

'We'll be asking you to pick your top three favourite guys every single morning so you may as well get used to it.'

I slide onto the back seat. 'Remember. Do not let Porscha edit me to look like the slutty British villain.'

'I'll try my best. Wait,' he shouts as I close the door. 'At least tell me who's your favourite out of the five guys.'

'I've already picked my favourite, and he's not on the list,' I say, closing the door behind me.

Chapter 15

After spending a sleepless night at another villa, I wake to find that it has been turned into a hair and make-up studio with racks of clothes on wheels. People have been in and out all day, and now, after much waiting around, I stand staring at my reflection in the mirror.

'And you're sure this is the whole outfit? There isn't... you know... a bit more? It feels rather... small.'

'It's literally the smallest, mini micro, G-string monokini we've ever seen. But Porscha insisted,' says a wardrobe runner, giving me an apologetic look. I glance at the adorable floral-print shift dress she is wearing. It's the height of sophistication.

'Well, do you have a nice wrap I could put over it? Or a nice coat? I don't care about the sweltering heat.' I'm trying to keep calm. Porscha has instructed wardrobe to give me a bizarre, flesh-coloured, cross-shaped bikini made of dental floss. It is barely visible to the naked eye. I'm struggling to see it myself and I'm only a foot away from it. 'Please don't leave me like this. There must be a mesh cover I can put over this... this...' I flap my hand around, pulling at the thin rope of material that runs in a straight line from my nether regions to a collar round my neck. There's a slightly wider piece running across my chest, that just about covers my nipples. '... this outfit.'

'You have a great figure though, so at least you can carry it off.'

That doesn't really help. Not when in an hour's time I will be walking down a catwalk into the Love on the Island villa as the first ever bombshell of the series. All eyes will be on me. The introvert. The girl who has never had a successful relationship. The girl who turns invisible the moment she steps through the school gates. The girl who has been hiding her true self away for the last three years. The girl who now is hiding NOTHING, not even a camel toe. I yank at the monokini. This is ridiculous. Things could not get any worse.

Oh, wait. They can.

'What are those?' I point to a mountain of leather dog leads in the runner's arms. 'I'm not wearing a dog lead. No way.'

This is too extreme. I won't stand for it.

'They are actually made from dog leads,' she says beginning to chuckle.

'Are you walking lots of dogs?' I'm confused. I didn't see a single pet in the production village while I was there.

She holds the bundle of straps up. 'These are your sandals.'

'Sandals? For my feet?'

'Yes. They're thigh-high gladiator sandals.'

Fuck me.

'As if it isn't bad enough that my make-up has melted right off my face, and I'm wearing what is essentially a thin piece of rope tying my neck to my vulva. You're going to make me wear stripper footwear for my big entrance?'

I don't believe this. If only Porscha hadn't walked in on us, then I'd still be with Cam hanging out in perfect isolation at the villa. And we would have kissed by now. That heart-meltingly life-changing kiss that I have been cruelly denied.

The runner instructs me to sit down. 'The thing is, once these are on, it's so difficult to get them back off. All the buckle straps are at the back, see? You'll have to get one of the girls in the villa to help you.'

'Otherwise, I'm stuck in them until I'm dumped from the Island?' I joke, close to tears. Images of me having to sleep standing up in them flash into my mind.

'Yeah, pretty much.'

After a lot of complex criss-cross strapping, tutting, buckling and refastening and pulling straps tight across my thighs, I am finally helped to my feet.

'Christ Almighty. It's like wearing a pair of stilts. I'm over six feet in these. I can't even stand in them never mind walk,' I say wobbling around. The runner stands up beside me. I am now towering over her. And while my legs look like they'd belong on a giraffe, I do rather look like I charge by the hour.

'They're too high. Take them off. I'd rather go bare foot,' I bark. 'I will break a leg if I take one step outside of this villa in these strappy chopsticks. I am not some dominatrix about to go all Fifty Shades on those poor men!'

We are both startled by a loud clipping and clacking sound.

'AND CUT. That was great.'

My jaw hits the floor as two camera operators emerge from behind a hidden screen in the far corner of the room with cameras and microphone booms.

'And now if you'll follow us to the car. We're on a very tight schedule. We'll film you getting into the car and saying something like how excited you are to be going into the Love on the Island villa to cause mayhem as the first bombshell. If you could wink at camera, do a peace sign, and stick your tongue out that would be awesome.'

In a daze, I whimper, 'You mean like a slutty British villain?'

'Yes, exactly. Perfect.'

A sinking feeling sweeps through my bones. They are going to edit out all the bits where I say I'm not going to be a man-eating troublemaker and edit in all the bits that suggest I will be.

There's only one thing worse than a semi-naked dominatrix, and that's a drowned-looking semi-naked dominatrix. Halfway to the villa the sky grew dark and around half of Mexico's yearly rainfall is currently falling from the sky. We pull up outside the property and wait for the huge electric security gates to open. I look up at the giant walls hiding the villa from sight. The huge gates, locked to keep out prying paparazzi, loom high above us. The driver does about a thousand checks on a walkie talkie to confirm that yes he has the 'package' and that yes the 'package' is ready to go. The metal gates eventually slide open to allow us in.

'I can't go out in this. I will literally kill myself getting from the car to the catwalk,' I say, pointing to the rivers of mud between me and the flimsy planks of wood that have a big silver heart at the end for me to walk through. 'I won't do it. I won't.'

My runner isn't listening. My runner is talking into her headset. She is making the following noises on repeat. 'Uh huh', 'yup', 'got it', 'uh huh', 'yup' and so on. Suddenly, the rain stops, she leans over me and opens the car door.

'Go now!' she bellows. 'GO! Now, now, now! Before the rain starts again!'

After she shoves me off the seat, I am standing outside the vehicle wondering how to hop over the pools of muddy water that pave the way to the catwalk. The heat is sweltering, sending rivers of sweat down my cleavage. I wipe my forehead with the back of my arm. I blow out my cheeks. This is like an obstacle course. A movement startles me. I glance over to see some branches shaking in a nearby bush. I'm reminded that my every movement is being closely monitored and recorded.

I slap on a bright smile and take the first of what turn out to be many slips and slides. At one point I am almost doing the splits. I can hear loud gasps coming from the bush as I pick my way to the catwalk. My six-inch razor-sharp heels gather clumps of grassy mud with each step. When I finally reach the catwalk there's an audible groan of relief. I straighten up. This is so bloody weird.

I glance down once again to my outfit. My outlandish doll-sized stripper monokini. I have mud splats up my legs. My toes are filthy. And I have half the fake lawn attached to my heels.

'Wait just a second,' I say to the invisible people hiding in the bush. I hear a tutting sound and choose to ignore it. 'I'll just try to wipe some of this mud off.'

'NO TIME! WALK IN FIVE, FOUR, THREE...' The voice trails off and I obediently begin my walk of shame down the catwalk towards the big silver heart. I put one sky-scraping heel down carefully at a time. I'm almost at the heart when the sky grows dark. I scamper as best I can to the end.

I see five gorgeous couples sitting in a semi-circle by the firepit. They all have grins stuck to their faces. The show's presenter, Destiny, half woman half fringe, is looking absolutely fabulous and DRY. She announces me as the *Love on the Island* bombshell, from beneath the safety of a gazebo which is successfully covering the firepit and all the contestants. The words have barely left her lips when the heavens open yet again, and what feels like a bucket of water lands on my head knocking me clean off the catwalk.

In an instant, the downpour has magically stopped. With the help of my runner, who also got caught in the deluge, I slip and slide my way to a standing position, which is not easy in these death traps strapped to my legs.

'CUT!' Porscha bellows, striding over to me. 'WHAT ARE YOU DOING?' She doesn't even wait for me to answer. She swivels around with what looks like a smirk on her face.

'FROM THE TOP!'

Another runner comes over to help me back onto the catwalk and, between them, they wipe what mud they can, from my legs and arms. One of them flicks my wet hair from my face. I see her glance briefly at my breasts. She is trying not to look alarmed, but her eyes are telling a different story.

I look down. The monokini is all but see-through. My nipples are like two champagne corks trying to burst through.

Shitting hell.

But it isn't until she is reattaching the microphone pack onto the back of my waist, that she lets out an audible gasp.

'What is it?' I demand.

She becomes mute and shakes her head at me.

'What is it?' I hiss.

She leans in. 'Don't turn around. Whatever you do.'

'Why?'

'It looks like... I mean, I know it's mud, but it looks like you've had... just don't turn around.'

Oh my God. I'm going to have a heart attack. Cam will think I've been at the gluten again.

'ACTION!'

All the islanders are now looking at me with distraught expressions as I hobble my way over to them. My hair is soaked and hanging limply down past my shoulders. Not a beach wave in sight. Water is running down my face and pooling on my chin, to drip off like a tap. I can see their eyes are out on stalks because it looks as though I am naked. I may as well be.

The rain was cold, but it still feels bizarrely hot. I stop in front of the firepit and begin to shiver. 'Hi, I'm Libby. I'm a teacher and I like reading and Sudoku.'

Destiny looks horrified and visibly unwilling to approach me. 'What an entrance,' is all she can say. 'Libby, how does it feel to be our first *Love on the Island* bombshell?'

'Great,' I manage, my teeth chattering. I place one arm across my chest to cover my protruding nipples and the other hand over my monokini bottoms. I don't care what it looks like. I'd rather not be flashing my bits to the world. 'So great, yeah. Loving it.'

I have never regretted a decision so much in my entire life.

'So, who have you got your eye on? Anyone in particular?' She sweeps her arm across the islanders sitting around the firepit, all coupled up and immaculate looking.

Is she kidding me?

I look from one man-mountain to the next. All five of them are refusing to make eye contact with me. Two of them are inspecting their nails. How embarrassing.

'Not yet,' I say shyly. 'Maybe when I get to know them a bit better.'

'Exactly. Yeah, for sure. Yeah, Uh-huh. So, which one would you choose?' Destiny is smiling sweetly at me.

'I still feel as though I'd like to connect with them first. Find out their names and a bit about them, that kind of thing.' My legs are turning to jelly. I wish she'd just get on with the show and talk to someone else.

'One hundred per cent, for sure. Yaaaas,' she's purring and batting her lashes rapidly. She puts a finger discreetly to her earpiece then stares at me as though to say, 'CHOOSE OR DIE!'

'But if you had to choose one,' she is starting to lose patience with me.

Is this hypothetical?

'Em, that one?' I point to a man sat on the end.

'Why have you chosen Marcel?' she says, suddenly delighted.

'Erm, he's got two eyes, two arms, two legs,' I shrug, looking over at him. He is rather easy on the eye I suppose. 'And doesn't look as though he kills puppies for a living?'

This is so fudging pointless, but at least when Destiny starts laughing after a split second, where it could have gone either way, everyone joins in sniggering tentatively along.

The atmosphere is unbelievably tense for what should be a joyful welcome to the show. Marcel is not sure about everyone laughing, and says to the beautiful girl next to him, loudly enough for us all to hear, 'Don't worry, Ella. She's definitely not my type. Not in the slightest. I only have eyes for you.'

He grins to himself and lounges back on the curved seat, throwing his arm around her. She snuggles closer to him.

Everyone looks my way to see if I'll react.

As if this wasn't mortifying enough.

DING.

Ella peers down at her phone. She reads the text out loud. 'Ella. Libby has chosen your man to couple up with. You are now dumped from the island. Please collect your belongings and leave.'

Cue shocked looks, loud gasps and hands flying to mouths.

'YOU COW!' Ella bellows at me.

'AND CUT!' I see Cam racing towards me with a blanket. 'TAKE FIVE WHILE SHE DRIES OFF!' Cam barks, ignoring Porscha. 'Can we get a runner, please?'

He sweeps the blanket over me, muttering. 'Jesus Christ! You okay, Libby?' He leans right in. 'Do you need some... pineapple?' he says out the side of his mouth.

I nod quickly. 'Yes, yes please.'

Chapter 16

'Fuck me. What have they got you wearing?' Cam says, frowning, as he slides in behind the recycling bin. Luckily, I already knew about the secret door leading out from the only walk-in cupboard without cameras. It's where they will pull islanders for chats. I was able to sneak through undetected, due to the sheer uproar caused by Ella getting kicked off the show after only twenty minutes. I slid along the wall to the blind spot, my heart thudding in my chest. We are hiding behind the bin, and Cam has disabled my microphone for me. 'We only have a few minutes.'

He has been positively heroic. The way he swooped in and covered me in a blanket, issuing instructions and tut-tutting at the runners. We are crushed together. Me shivering like a drowned rat. Him looking all concerned for my mental health and well-being. I notice dark patches under his eyes. They've got that haunted look back again. The warm blue-green eyes with specks of gold, have turned to a cold grey blue. His stubble has grown a bit thicker across the jawbone so that the slight dent of the chin is no longer visible, and his hair is sticking out at odd angles. I'm not the only one who didn't get enough sleep last night.

'You okay?' he asks softly. Our bodies create a warm flow of energy as we huddle together. Like a magnet, I feel drawn to sag against him and feel his safe, strong arms wrap around me. But I can't. I grab the blanket tightly and stand a little taller.

'I didn't know that was going to happen,' I say. 'That poor girl. I feel terrible.'

'It's Porscha. She obviously chose not to share that with any of us. I'll bring it up at the next team meeting but honestly…' He sighs and I feel his breath on my cheek. 'If any of this gets too much just let me know. I'll get you out of here.'

He gives me such a concerned look that I instantly melt.

'It's okay. Really. I can handle it.'

He half smiles. 'I've put a suitcase of clothes in the dressing room for you. It was the best I could do at such short notice. I drew a pineapple on it, so you know which one it is. I think Porscha may have tampered with your other case. I imagine the outfits she's put in will be kinda like what you're almost wearing now.'

'Thank you.' I am bursting with gratitude. 'Just one more thing.' I say pointing to the backs of my thighs.

Instinctively, he crouches down, and I feel his warm fingers undo each of the buckles. If it weren't for the fear of Porscha catching us, it would be very erotic. He has an incredibly gentle touch. I literally can't breathe as he undoes the buckles around the tops of my thighs and slides the straps softly down my legs as though he were peeling down my stockings. He straightens up and we share a fond look before he puts a finger to his lips and switches the microphone back on.

He mouths, 'Good luck' to me and disappears through the kitchen door.

I wait a few seconds and go through the cupboard door into the outdoor kitchen. All the islanders are waving Ella off. She is in floods of tears and howling like a neutered cat at the injustice. She is spitting feathers and vowing to sue LoveIT TV into the, excuse my French, 'shitting ground'. When I hear her telling Destiny she can fudge right off, I seize the opportunity to scamper straight through to the 'Hello Gorgeous' dressing room and adjoining bathroom.

Again, I am so thankful that I had the virtual tour yesterday from Cam, so I have a vague idea of where I'm going. We also went over and over the blueprints so that I would know the lay of the land before coming in and the bios of all the contestants, so that I would know who I am up against.

After I've showered off all the mud, I wrap myself in a towel and go through to get ready. It's so hard knowing there's cameras everywhere. I spot the case lying under the dressing table in the centre of the room. I drag it open and exhale with relief as I pull out actual clothes made of cloth. My hand lands on a stunning dress. I'm sliding it over my head when I hear the clatter of the girls approaching. They are surprised to see me in here and gather round.

'That was so savage.'

'Yeah, like so savage.'

'One hundred per cent savage.'

'Girl, you savage.'

I stand up and pull down my dress. 'You're all just saying the same thing.'

'Because, girl, that was totally one hundred per cent savage what you did back there.'

Seriously?

It's time to make a stand and start how I mean to go on. 'I didn't know that was going to happen, did I?'

'Didn't you?'

Four sceptical faces peer back at me.

'Does the bombshell usually have any say in what happens on this show?' I argue, placing a hand on my hip. I refuse to be bullied. I came in here for... actually, I'm no longer sure what I came in here for, but I know it wasn't to be heckled by these stunning, jelly-lipped, identikit girls with their all-over tans and superb hair and nail extensions.

'Are you being funny right now?' she tuts. 'You can never tell with the British. Can you Mimi?'

'No, Amber, honey. You can't.'

Well, you can, I want to say but decide to keep quiet. I don't want my second time on camera to be me being rude. I shake my head and smile. 'I just meant...'

'We know what you meant. You came in here to find love just like the rest of us and you'll do anything to get it,' says Mimi, quite the forceful blonde. 'Including being savage.'

No, I definitely won't. It's not the *Hunger Games*.

'We've been told to get ready for a night of fireworks,' says a petite Asian-looking girl, I recognise as Amber, leafing through a hanger full of outfits. 'What's everyone wearing? Glam? Semi-glam? Mimi, where you at hun?'

'I'm going all out to catch my man's attention,' says Mimi. 'He ain't lookin' no place else tonight!'

Phew. I'm already yesterday's news.

The girls start pulling out seats, rummaging round in the wardrobes and flicking switches on hair straighteners, hair tongs and all manner of hair styling tools. Out come industrial-size make-up boxes, rolls of brushes and endless pots and pots of make-up. We have all jostled for seats at the central carousel in the dressing room to apply our 'looks' for tonight. The carousel was custom built for the show at a cost of twenty grand – Cam told me yesterday – so that we can all get round it and gossip, while the cameras can pick up everyone's faces and voices clearly. The mirrors and lights are professional standard and reveal every single flaw. I try not to flick my eyes to the camera hidden above in the Hello Gorgeous neon sign. It will be recording my every movement.

'It must be so hard to be the bombshell,' says Mimi, swishing a big fat brush over her face. 'I'm glad I'm an original. Amber, can I borrow your blusher?'

'Heck, yeah,' Amber says, handing her a paint palette so big you could paint your whole house with it. 'I'd hate to be the bombshell. Coming in, having to be all that.'

They are making me nervous. I'm not sure how they managed to bond this quick and take an active dislike to me but that's how it feels. I'm getting distinct negative energy vibes from the lot of them.

'All I had to do was walk six feet in a pool of mud and slide down to the firepit,' I joke to ease the tension. 'Nothing hard about that.'

They look at each other in disbelief. 'We meant it must be so hard having to look better than the rest of us put together.'

How ridiculous.

'I doubt I'll manage that,' I say, watching them all glam up. 'I mean look at you all. You're all gorgeous.'

Just saying the words reminds me of how I felt when Cam told me I was gorgeous. I melted inside like an ice-cream in the hot sun.

'We are, babe,' says Mimi, noticeably pleased at the compliment. 'We so freakin are! We are so freakin GORGE!'

Bit much.

'Anyway, beauty is only skin deep,' I remind her before she gets carried away with her own reflection.

'But you could still steal our guys from us,' says a small blue-haired woman. 'Is that what you're planning?'

'That's right, Binky. She could,' says Mimi. 'I'd watch your man when he's around Libby. I saw him giving her the eye.'

'I'm hardly a man-eater. Besides, you've only had your men for five minutes. You barely know them. You,' I say, pointing to the weakest-looking girl at the back. 'What's your fella's name?'

She looks shocked, like she has no idea. 'It's Germaine. Or Germanji.'

'No, Kassy. My one is called Germanji, your one is called Brid,' says Mimi.

'It's not Brid. It's Brad. He's Australian,' says Amber.

'Is he?' says Kassy.

'Not Germanji. I meant Giovanni. That's right. He's half Italian and from New Yoik. So, now who doesn't know her man?' Mimi says, her voice full of 'I told you so'.

The atmosphere has turned on a knife edge over absolutely nothing.

'Just because I can't remember who I'm coupled up with doesn't mean we don't share a deep connection,' Kassy argues back. 'Besides, I like Marcel. I might be in with a chance now because he obviously didn't like the look of Libby.'

'All I know is that I have fantasised my whole life of being on this show. It is my absolute dream to become an influencer, and if being in a couple with Giovanni is the way to make it happen, then that's what I'll do.' The girls look at Mimi smiling, until she says, 'So hands off. Everyone back-off my man. He's mine.'

'Doesn't that rather defeat the object of the game?' I ask.

The girls look at me nodding before they pounce on Mimi.

'Hang on a second, girlfriend,' says Amber. 'I am open. So don't tell me to back off anyone.'

'I am very open too,' says Binky. 'Wide open.'

I have started a whole host of bickering. I am a slutty British villain in the making, and it is all my own doing.

A phone pings while I am putting the finishing touches to my make-up. I have gone for a soft, natural, clean look. My hair is hanging in soft waves, framing my face. I've added a swipe of mascara to my already full Tatti lashes and clear gloss to my lips. I might just sweep some powder over my chin as it is looking shiny in this heat.

'I GOT A TEXT!' screams Amber, causing me to drop my pot of powder. 'CAN ALL THE LOVE ON THE ISLANDERS MEET AT THE FIREPIT?'

This causes an almighty and unnecessary kerfuffle, with all the girls leaping about squealing excitedly before they realise, they have run out of time to finish getting ready.

'What will we do? What will the boys think? Destiny needs to see us all at our best!' Mimi yells in panic.

'Libby, you haven't even started on your look yet!' Amber howls, coming at me with brushes and her massive palette. She swishes the brush over my face, smudges some sticks of foundation down my nose and starts rubbing furiously. 'Someone, do something with her hair!'

In an about turn, we are suddenly all banding together. Time pressure and a race against the clock have created an unexpected camaraderie. A fashion collective. Women supporting women. Girl power. Sisters are doing it for themselves. Buying our own flowers and holding our own hands. Because we need to look nice for our men. Who we barely know.

Another phone pings. More squeals.

'GET READY FOR FIREWORKS HASHTAG RECOUPLING HASHTAG DUMPED FROM THE ISLAND HASHTAG BOMBSHELL,' Kassy says, her voice petering out.

We all take a moment to let this digest.

'What? Another one of us is going to get dumped from the island? This is brutal. I bet it's me,' cries Binky. 'Libby's going to steal my man.'

They all turn slowly to pin me to my seat, staring at me like zombies out of a horror movie. Just then my phone pings. I gingerly open the message hoping for better news, while we all hold our breath.

I get ready to bellow it out just like we've been told to do. As soon as I see the first line the words die on my lips, and I exhale noisily instead.

It is from Porscha.

'DO NOT READ THIS OUT LOUD.' My eyes flick to the girls and back to my phone. 'Meet me in the outside kitchen food cupboard now! Do not tell anyone where you are going.'

'What does it say?' asks Mimi.

I shrug. 'Nothing.'

'It can't be nothing,' says Kassy. 'Come on, girl. What does it say?'

Under the confused gaze of the girls, I rise calmly from the carousel and leave the room in silence.

I can hear them frantically gossiping as I make my way to the outside kitchen and slip through the door marked 'PANTRY'. The light is on, highlighting the fake snack food and fake tins lining the shelves. The back wall suddenly opens and Porscha drifts in looking immaculate. I pretend to look shocked as though I had no idea about the secret door.

'Well, well, well. Don't you scrub up nicely? I wonder where you found that?' she says, looking and sounding disingenuous. I'm not sure what to say to her. Cam packed me a spectacular, orange and pink shift dress to wear and some pretty, pink matching sandals. My hair is newly straightened and spritzed to look glossy and swishy. My make-up is professionally applied because Amber is a beautician and loves a challenge. It took her under ten seconds.

'Pick Giovanni,' she says before disappearing back through the door.

I emerge from the pantry, deflated. I have my instructions. I will be stealing Mimi's man, and my actions will possibly cause her exit from the show. I'm immediately distracted by a deafening clanging sound. It's an alarm.

'Oh, my God! Where's the fire?' I yell, leaping into action. I know every fire exit and location of every extinguisher in the near vicinity. I yank the red canister from the outside kitchen wall and run onto the fake grass lawn. 'FOLLOW ME!' I scream at the contestants as glammed-up men and women emerge from opposite sides of the villa. This is basic school fire drill practice. I've done it a thousand times. 'THIS WAY PEOPLE!'

They stop briefly to glance over before choosing to completely ignore me. Instead, I see them running in the opposite direction towards to the firepit. The men islanders and women islanders instinctively run towards each other to pair up as though they've been separated by a great war and are reuniting for the first time in years.

There is no fire.

It is merely the firepit Klaxon.

I am distracted by some shaking in a nearby bush and the stifling of laughter coming from inside.

Oh, my effing word.

Feeling ridiculous, I plonk the fire extinguisher on the kitchen bench and take five to calm down. Adrenaline is charging through my veins. I need to be better than this. I take my time to wander over to the firepit because I don't want to risk falling over in my heels. And I'm in no hurry to be the cause of someone's misery.

Destiny, the presenter, indicates for me to stand back on the spot I was on earlier, leaving Marcel to sit alone on the bench with the others. I stand tall, and smooth down my dress. I take the opportunity to smile shyly at the islanders. They can't believe the transformation. This time the men are taking notice of me. They are sitting up straight. They are smiling and winking at me. They are nudging one another.

The girls are looking frostily at me before batting their eyes and smiling ferociously at their men, clinging to them like they are about to be kidnapped.

I slide my eyes along to Giovanni. He is the only man who hasn't looked at me. He is looking adoringly at his forceful blonde companion, Mimi. She is touching his face and now they are snuggling noses like an old married couple and giggling. Every now and then, he is glancing down at her bountiful cleavage and licking his lips. She crosses her well-oiled, shiny legs suggestively, and I watch mesmerised, as he instinctively reaches out a hand to run the length of it. They have such sizzling chemistry.

My soul sinks. This is going to look so bad on camera.

'Love on the Islanders,' Destiny says. 'Are you ready for your first big test? Libby, it is time to play Switcheroo. You can either keep Marcel or swap him out for one of the other guys. Which man are you going to choose?'

I avoid making eye contact with any of them and look straight to Destiny for help. I've not even had so much as a conversation with any of them due to the catastrophic downpour of rain that has been going on since my entrance. Not that any of the men came looking for me.

A huge lump forms in my throat, causing Destiny to repeat the question. 'Remember, Marcel is the guy that said he wasn't interested in you to Ella, before she got dumped. He made that quite clear, didn't he? He said, we have the quote here, 'he's not in the slightest bit interested in you', remember?'

Marcel is looking very sheepish now.

'Please make your choice,' instructs Destiny. Then a runner comes over to whisper in my ear that I am to stand for seven seconds staring straight ahead looking as though I'm worried sick, then I have to give two reasons for choosing Giovanni.

'Any reasons will do. We don't care. Then smile apologetically at Destiny and we'll pan back to Mimi. Okay? Do not move off this spot until we tell you.' The runner runs off.

Luckily for me, I have plenty of reasons to help with looking worried sick. I stand counting sheep, while staring into the middle distance, and think about my new credit card bill, my disastrous entrance, and the fact that everyone I know at home will be watching me on TV. I hear a ghostly voice floating on the air, hissing, 'Action!'.

I snap back to the task at hand. 'I, erm, I am choosing this man because he is tall, dark and handsome. And he seems like a hopeless romantic, because he says that he is writing a romantasy novel in his spare time when he's not working construction or feeding the homeless or saving blind donkeys.'

I cannot look him in the eye. I cannot. I'm sure we've all told untruths to get here but blind donkeys?

'So, erm, the man I'd like to couple up with is... Giovanni.' One quick glance tells me Giovanni is pretty fudging furious before he slaps a fake smile on his face and gets up to come over.

Mimi looks knocked for six.

Then it is my turn to be shocked because Mimi yells, 'GIOVANNI NOOOOO!'

We watch as she leaps to her feet, grabs his arm, yanks him back and kisses the sweet baby Cheeses out of him. Right in front of me.

Destiny can't decide which of us to keep an eye on. But as the kiss lengthens into an alarmingly long and uncomfortable clash of veneers, we are forced to watch Giovanni hoik Mimi's leg up so that it is practically wrapped around him. Then he really goes for it, his tongue probing her mouth, his hand almost but not quite cupping her breast, the other almost but not quite cupping her left buttock. Her hands reach for his hair and tangle themselves in it while she thrusts her pelvis at him. When they finally part, after an eternity of squelching sounds, they look dishevelled and breathless, and the other islanders all look very feckin jealous.

Like an apex-predator, she whips her head round to face me, fixing me with a triumphant look.

Fair play to her.

That was genius.

I can't help myself. I start giggling and begin a slow clap. Soon everyone joins in the slow clap with me, even Destiny.

When both Mimi and Giovanni realise what is happening, they instantly relax. Giovanni has the good grace to put Mimi down, looking embarrassed when he walks over to stand next to me at the firepit.

'I hope you're not expecting me to do the same,' I joke and after a long minute, where he works out if I'm serious, he throws his head back and laughs like a drain.

Thankfully, everyone starts laughing, even the mardy Mimi.

'Don't worry,' I say in a playful tone. 'I'll return him in one piece.'

Chapter 17

All the attention has gone straight to Giovanni's head. He looks me slowly up and down with an appreciative look on his face, which makes me immediately uncomfortable. While Porscha is instructing the crew to change camera angles, he leans over to whisper, 'I like a funny woman. And you're not bad to look at. I don't usually go for brunettes, but for you, I'd make an exception. You get me?' He looks very pleased with himself and stands with his legs apart, facing the firepit, hands clasped at his groin.

Oh my God. This empty-headed, muscle-mountain is trying to hit on me, even though his lips are still wet from slobbering over Mimi.

He winks at me, making it very clear that if I try really hard, I may be in with a slim chance. What a time to be alive!

'That's quite alright,' I whisper quickly. 'You're really not my type.'

Giovanni seems to take this as an opportunity to prove me wrong. While we are told to take five, so that Destiny can get some powder on her too-glowy face, he turns to me.

'Seriously,' he says, leaning in. 'Look at me, bro.' He flexes his biceps. 'I'm every woman's type. I'm God's young dream.'

I can't help laughing.

'I appreciate that you have an ego the size of Japan, but I hate to break it to you, some of us have deeper core values than shiny biceps. But I'm happy to play along until you are recoupled with the love of your life.'

'Who?' he says, looking genuinely baffled.

I can't decide if he has attachment issues or just a really bad memory.

'Mimi. The frozen-foreheaded girl who is staring right at us, looking like someone just drowned her newborn kitten.'

Giovanni bursts out laughing again and looks over his shoulder at Mimi, who has gone from smiling adoringly at him to stalker vibes in under six seconds. She is not loving watching the two of us do 'banter'.

Giovanni strokes his man-stubble. 'Oh yeah. She looks like she's about to scream her hair out, man. That's sick. She's a real live wire.' He blows her a kiss and Mimi instantly softens. 'I have that effect on women.'

'Oh, my God,' I'm almost choking with laughter now. 'What's with the horrendous mixed metaphors and non sequiturs? Are they forcing you to speak like that? Have they given you a script?'

Giovanni looks momentarily panicked but keeps smiling at me. 'Are you speaking English right now, bro? I have no idea what you just said to me. Are you, like, from Britain?'

My words have flown straight over his head.

'England, yes.'

'Man, that accent is so sexy. Are you, like, from London?'

'No.'

'No?' He looks taken aback.

'There are... *other* cities,' I say.

He glazes over. He has lost interest. He looks me up and down again, and then casts his gaze over to Mimi who still has her eyes trained like a sniper's rifle on both of us.

'Man. You are both smoking hot. If only there was a way the three of us could... you know.' He waggles his eyebrows at me.

I blink rapidly. 'Okay. That's enough for me. I'll leave you and Mimi to it.'

I don't care that I've been told not to move, I start walking towards the outside kitchen when Porscha barks, 'CUT!'.

She storms over to us and demands that Giovanni takes me to the terrace to 'talk'.

'But it's wet,' he complains, looking down at his chino-style shorts. Then backtracks immediately when Porscha's eyes grow wide with disbelief and looks at him as though he has suggested that he take charge of filming and directing. 'But that's okay. Can Mimi come with us too?'

Giovanni turns to wink at his forceful blonde, standing a few metres from us, hands on hips, head tilted, eyes like a psychotic prowler.

'Certainly not.' We watch Porscha stomp over to Mimi and whisper in her ear. To my surprise, Mimi's face lights up. She nods her head and immediately flies off in the direction of the main villa.

'I need a drink,' Giovanni says. 'It's pretty tense in here, huh?'

'Yep. It certainly is.'

'Want one?' he asks me. 'I'll bring it up to the terrace.'

That's the first nice thing he has managed.

'Thank you, Giovanni. That's very kind of you. I'll have...' I lean down towards my tiny microphone head. '... can you get me a pineapple juice, please?'

Giovanni heads for the outdoor kitchen.

'I'll just go to the Beach Hut first. I need to get some things off my chest,' I lie. 'I'll meet you up on the terrace.'

Once he is out of sight, I make for the blind spot via the Beach Hut, under the pretence I am going to confide my deepest thoughts to the nation. But when I get there, Mimi is coming out with a huge grin on her face. 'After you,' she says pointing to the entrance. She waits for me to go in.

Crap.

'No hard feelings?' I say to her.

'Why would there be hard feelings? It's just a game, girl. You do what you've got to do.'

'Okay, but just to be clear. I'm not interested in Giovanni. You can have him back as soon as we get a chance to swap,' I tell Mimi.

'I like that you think he's interested in you. But let me tell you, it won't be your choice. He is into me, and I will steal him off you.'

'Okay, whatever. I'm just saying there's no need. I will give him to you.'

'And I am saying I will steal him off you.'

'But you don't have to, because I am giving him to you.'

We are squabbling over him like he's a piece of meat. It's exhausting.

'He is into me. Not you,' she says huffily, stomping away.

Pointless. Such a pointless conversation.

I go into the Beach Hut and sit down wearily. Some people just have to have the last word. Luckily, I'm one of them too. I'll have to make this quick. I am hoping that Cam is making his way to the blind spot, and I am anxious to see him. I'd like to know what Porscha has planned for me and Giovanni because whatever it is, it's not happening. She wants to paint me as a villain, a homewrecker, that I'm not one of the girls. Well, we'll see about that.

'Erm, hi there.' I gulp nervously as I stare into a camera lens fixed into a wall. It is surrounded by an elaborate pink picture frame. 'I, erm, just wanted to say that I can see Giovanni is totally into Mimi, who is a lovely, lovely girl. And I would definitely not want to stand in the way of true love. Which she seems to think it is.' I am babbling because I have not thought this through. 'But to be honest he's just asked me if I'd be interested in a threesome so I'm not sure he's feeling it as much as her. That might be the Italians for you. Or maybe he's polyamorous. He loves a mixed metaphor, I know that much.' I shrug nonchalantly, run my hands down my super soft, figure-hugging dress that Cam gave me, to straighten it out. 'Anyway, we'll see what happens, but I'm sure it'll all work out for them.'

I smile sweetly to camera and slide out of there. Instead of turning right to go back to the main villa, I turn left and flatten my back to the wall inching along to the blind spot. Cam pulls me in close behind the bin and disables my microphone.

'Did you see the look Mimi was giving me?' I whisper.

'Oh man. You are going to light up our screens, Libby. Just keep being yourself and you'll be fine.'

I give him a look of relief.

'I put the fire extinguisher back by the way. Good to know you've had training.' He can barely speak for giggling.

I roll my eyes. 'Please don't air that to the world. God, everyone is going to think I'm such an idiot.'

We start giggling quietly into each other's shoulders.

'I'll try and find out what Porscha's up to, but from what I have seen, you can more than hold your own out there. You've been brilliant so far.'

It's exactly what I need to hear. Our bodies are pressed up against the wall. I can feel the firmness of his body against mine. My breasts are almost popping out of my dress. He hesitates and moves back slightly to give me more room. Our faces are an inch apart. I want to kiss him so badly. 'You better go before someone notices you're missing,' he says breaking the spell. 'By the way, you look beautiful in that dress.'

I warm at the compliment and bite my lip seductively, lost in his kind eyes, his gentle tone and his overall niceness. He feels like home. Like fun. Like nights lying on a fur rug in front of a roaring fire. Like a whole lifetime of joy just waiting for us to realise it.

'Don't look at me like that,' he whispers in my ear, before pulling away to give me a look that suggests the exact opposite. He opens his mouth to say something but thinks better of it.

There's an energy between us. He can feel it. His eyes search my face. 'Christ, Libby,' he pleads in a low voice. He steps closer and runs a hand lightly down my arm. 'We shouldn't.'

Yes, we fudging should. It's the blind spot.

The seconds tick desperately by as my heart thumps in my chest.

Here we go again. Kissing moment take three.

I reach up and pull him to me.

He smiles and blinks slowly. 'Are you sure about this?'

I can barely get the words out. 'Never been surer.'

His warm lips touch mine, tentatively at first, gently caressing, then in the next breath, he surprises me by really going for it. I match his passion and arch into him.

This is everything I imagined and more. It's like fire surging through me, liquid gold powering through my veins. He breaks off panting to give me a bewildered look.

He can feel it too.

He smiles at me before deftly switching on the microphone and disappearing into the darkness.

My heart is pounding. My lips are tingling. My head is in a complete spin. I lean back against the wall to recover. After a few seconds, I clear my throat and make my way to the terrace all flustered.

I. AM. FALLING. FOR. HIM.

I climb the slippery stairs to the terrace very carefully. I try to clear my mind of what just happened with Cam. For all it was the best kiss of my entire life, maybe I should not have kissed him. I'm a terrible person. He is trying to help me while I am trying to seduce him. He will get sacked if we are discovered. My lust for him is overriding my ability to make sensible decisions. My heart is beginning to rule my head for the first time in my life and it scares me.

I shake the thoughts away. I must concentrate on what evil thing Porscha has in store for me next. I reach the terrace to see Giovanni is waiting with our drinks. He is lounging on a daybed scattered with giant brightly covered cushions. He has arranged himself as though he is posing for a men's magazine shoot. I look at the two mocktails perched on the coffee table.

In hindsight, I'd wished we had picked a better codename than pineapple because while the fruit itself is pleasant enough, I'm not a fan of the juice. 'Thank you,' I say, sitting down on a cushion beside him. I tuck my legs underneath me and try to get into a position that is vaguely comfortable. Whoever designed this thing has obviously never had to sit on one.

Giovanni stares at me, grinning, while I wait for him to start the conversation. 'After you,' I say.

'After me, what?' he says as though I'm flirting with him.

'After you as in you can go first to talk.'

'What do you want me to say?' he asks, still grinning as though there is some hidden meaning.

'Whatever you want.'

He looks panic-stricken.

It's as though the man has never before taken part in a conversation.

I roll my eyes. 'Tell me about this novel you're writing. Does it have a feisty protagonist with a tragic character arc?

How many POVs are you writing in? Are you in first draft or is it polished and ready to go? I'm sure you'll have no end of publisher offers at the end of this show.'

I sip my drink, *urgh*, and wait for him to reply. And wait. And wait. He is struggling to think of an answer.

'Yeah man, like that was pretty dope. Sick, yeah. You get me?'

I'm a little startled, to be honest.

'Are you... are you answering the question I asked, or is this the answer to another question? One that I haven't asked?'

He looks uncomfortable.

'I was asking about your novel. You know, the one you said you're writing?'

He remains blank.

'The romantasy? The romantic fantasy?'

Nothing. There's nothing behind his eyes to suggest any hint of understanding.

It's no use. I'm going to have to administer some basic nursery-nurse style communication. I point to myself. 'I like reading books.' I point to him. 'You like writing books.'

Giovanni looks grateful. I wonder if he is nervous about all the cameras, and it is making him forget all his basic motor skills. 'You like books, yeah?' he manages, clutching for conversation. 'That's cool, bro.'

I will help him. After all, I am a teacher. Like the police, iPhone call centres and other emergency services, we are never off duty. 'Stories are essentially the building blocks of humanity. The basis of all communication.'

Now he looks petrified. 'Yeah, writing books, it's hardly like rocket surgery.'

This is such hard work. I look at his arms. He has biceps the shape of bowling balls. And they are just as shiny. 'Do you go to the gym much?'

His face lights up. 'Yeah, bro. Yeah. Like a lot.'

Another uncomfortable silence follows until I can't bear it any longer. He then leans over to me, and it looks awfully like he might be attempting to kiss me for want of nothing better to do. As his eyes close, and his lips hurtle towards mine, I jerk backwards away from him. When his lips don't find purchase, he opens one eye.

'Nice chat,' I say leaping up. 'See you around.'

Then to my horror, Giovanni yells that he is coming with me. He rolls off the bed, 'Wait,' he says. 'I wasn't going to kiss you. Please don't tell Mimi.'

Didn't I tell Cam this show is very playgroundy?

In his haste, he slips on the first step and comes tumbling down the stairs towards me like an avalanche. I turn sideways, grabbing hold of the banister, instinctively saving myself as he crashes at my feet.

'Oh my God, are you okay?' I ask. Bending down to help him. He is lying upside down in a heap, almost at the bottom of the stairs. I hope he hasn't broken anything.

Having a nurse as a sister has its perks. 'Don't move. Lie still. I'll support your head. Help!' I yell. There's an almighty thundering sound of islanders in heels click clacking towards us.

Mimi is first to arrive on the scene. 'You!' she points dramatically to me. 'What did you do? What have you done to him?' She drops to her knees to cradle his head. She puts her arm round him.

'Don't move him,' I yell. 'You might make the injury worse.'

'Don't tell me what to do,' she spits out hysterically, trying to yank him up. She is obviously not used to dealing with any sort of crisis. 'Did you do this on purpose?'

'What? No!'

'CUT!' yells Porscha. 'Giovanni, stay where you are. Or if you can, just shift around a bit to face camera three so we can get you from both angles. Mimi, you lift him up and we'll film you helping him walk to the daybeds. Then we'll do a shot of the two lovebirds getting cosy behind Libby's back. We can get some real traction going for this love triangle.'

Mimi looks thrilled at this new plot twist.

'And Libby?' We all look at Porscha as she pauses dramatically. She looks me up and down. 'How could you do this to him? Sour grapes is so not a good look.' She is shaking her head at me, but I can see a smile hovering on her lips.

Once Porscha has yelled, 'ACTION!' Mimi drops down to check on the love of her life. 'Come on Giovanni, babe. I'll help you up.'

'No,' I say to Mimi. 'Do not move him. Giovanni, where does it hurt? I'm a nurse. Well, a teacher but my sister is a nurse. I basically did all her revision for her medical exams, so I know what I'm doing.'

Giovanni smiles at me. A genuine smile.

Mimi pulls his arm. 'Come on, honey, don't listen to her. She's just jealous.' She tries to yank him up and he cries out in pain.

Everyone else is just standing around like dummies. At that moment, the heavens open and the rain comes crashing down.

Literally every single one of them ducks for cover. None of them faster than Porscha who has vanished into thin air.

There's only me and Giovanni remaining, and he's beginning to slide uncomfortably down the stairs. I swoop down to support him.

'Don't worry. I've got you.' I cradle his head against the stairs and look at his shoulders. They look wonky. 'It looks like your shoulder might be dislocated.'

'I'm coming,' yells Cam, running across the lawn. The rain is battering down, causing him to slip and slide. Two more runners appear and soon we have Giovanni on a stretcher and under a canopy at the side of the villa. The wind is howling around us.

'I'll check him over. Cam could you get a first aid kit please?' I instruct. He gives me an appreciative look and runs off. 'Get blankets, a hot honey and lemon drink and some sugar.' I order the runners. 'Giovanni, what sweets do you like?'

He looks confused.

'She means candies,' says Cam, coming up behind me with the first aid kit. 'It's good for the shock. I've radioed for a medic.'

I can't even begin to describe what a great team we make. I think it must be showing on my face because Cam keeps looking at me and biting his lip to stop smirking. I wonder if it is because he now knows what an incredible kisser I am. My cheeks are on fire every time he says anything to me.

Within minutes, I have Giovanni's sprained wrist wrapped in a bandage. I have popped his dislocated shoulder back into place and put his arm in a sling just as a precaution, and we are good to go.

Porscha makes an appearance. She throws an arm over Cam's shoulder. 'Excellent work, Cameron, darling. You are so dashing and brave.'

She looks at the rest of us as though we are lazy jobsworths. 'Back to work, people. Back to work!'

I just have time to see him bristle before she links his arm and drags him away.

Chapter 18

Giovanni and I have been instructed to go and talk to camera in case viewers are traumatised by any of the events they have seen. Apparently, helplines will flash up on TV along the bottom of the screen. It's all very sensible and I'm sure it has everything to do with Cam because he is such a great producer. And he is kind and compassionate and he is a very, very wonderful kisser.

Giovanni gushes that I have basically saved his life. I roll my eyes at camera, playing along. We joke around a bit. I say, 'Good Lord, you'll do anything to get my attention,' in a flirty manner and he says, 'I thought you were running away from me because I tried to kiss you.'

I then look awkwardly at camera because that's exactly what I was trying to do. 'And I thought you told me not to say anything in case Mimi finds out, and yet here you are telling the entire world about it.'

It's like he doesn't know how cameras work.

Once I've helped him hobble back round to the main bit of the villa, his big heavy arm weighing me down, we are greeted like war heroes. There is nothing wrong with Giovanni's ankle. He just wanted more sympathy and a more manly injury. Unfortunately for him, once the girls are fussing around him, he forgets to keep up the hobbling after only a few minutes, which has some of the men looking suspiciously at him. He is getting an awful lot of airtime and hostilities are beginning to emerge.

I spot Marcel whispering to the other guys as they all eye Giovanni being petted and stroked on the daybed by the girls. They go off to the Chill Out Zone to discuss it.

I decide, because of how massive Giovanni is, around six feet five in both height and width, and because of his sling and the need to not move his shoulder around too much, and because I'd rather have my eyes pecked out by diseased pigeons than share a bed with any of these men, to camp out in the bedroom designated for those who want to sleep alone. Primarily, it is for when couples have a lovers tiff but thanks to Cam, his hacks and his blueprint, I know that by spending the night in the Dog House as it is called, I am actually next door to the Beach Hut and therefore, the blind spot.

A siren rings out across the garden and outdoor areas indicating that it is time to go to bed. None of us have a clue what time it is. It could be seven o'clock or it could be midnight. The girls make their way towards me and we all troop back into the villa together.

While we get ready for bed, making a huge show of how we wipe our make-up off our faces and which creams we rub into our skin at night, I am secretly choosing all the floral-scented lotions and potions. I slip into a skimpy nightie that Porscha put in the case for me, obviously with attracting another man in mind. It is a complex, strappy lace number. The balcony bra makes my boobs look as though they are about to spill over the top. The silky satin baby doll material swishes against my skin and is so short it reveals the matching lace knickers underneath.

'That looks nice,' Mimi says begrudgingly. 'Hoping to get some action tonight with my man?'

I look at her upset face. She's known him for five minutes, but you'd genuinely think she cares for him.

'No. Absolutely not.' I stand in full view of the hidden camera hide, and begin my well-rehearsed speech that Cam ensured me would not be countered by Porscha. 'After such a traumatic day, for the sake of my own health and wellbeing, I'm going to take time to decompress. Therefore, I will sleep in the Dog House tonight, instead of the communal bedroom,' I say loudly and clearly. 'For the sake of my mental health and well-being.'

Mimi looks as though she's won the lottery. Her face lights up and she starts screaming. I try shushing her but she's having none of it. I'm sure once Porscha finds out she'll try to put a spanner in the works.

'I'm going to get some pineapple juice before bed. Goodnight,' I say and wave my goodbyes. None of them take any notice because the excitement levels are through the roof. This is the first night all the islanders will be sleeping together in the communal bedroom.

Binky and Kassy are beside themselves. Neither of them can remember who they are supposed to be sharing a bed with but they keep screaming with excitement every time they make eye contact in the mirror as they brush their teeth.

I slip outside and make straight for the Dog House, but at the last second I pretend to contemplate going into the Beach Hut for a heart-to-heart before standing back against the wall and sliding into the blind spot. Adrenaline immediately powers through my bloodstream. My body is literally aching to feel Cam's touch. A quiver of excitement runs down my spine at the thought.

What am I doing? What am I doing? I'm going to get caught.

Cam is there waiting. He flicks my microphone off.

Just the sight of him makes my pulse race. 'I wanted to say sorry... about kissing you earlier. I know it was wrong of me. I'd hate to get you into trouble.'

His twinkling eyes search mine. 'For the record, I knew you'd be trouble, the moment you fell off the catwalk.'

My heart starts thumping as he steps in even closer.

'I hope you don't think I'm deliberately tempting you to do something you don't want to do.'

There's a word for people like me who say the opposite of what they really mean. I give him the eyes and it appears to work.

Things have taken a very sensual turn. His eyes roam my skimpy negligée and rest on my heaving bosom. He drags his eyes back to my face. It's the most alive I have felt in my entire life. Sparks of lust shoot through me. My heart is beating so fast it's only a matter of time before it leaps from my chest, breaking a few ribs on the way, but who cares? I am living in the moment. This delicious, forbidden moment.

'I know nothing can happen between us because of the show...' I say, my voice barely a whisper.

He leans towards me. 'Well then, you should have worn a different outfit,' he murmurs in my ear. It sends a tingle down my neck.

His hand travels the length of my back, sliding down the silky material to stop just above my bottom. He presses me closer to him.

'Kiss me,' I demand.

He doesn't need asking twice. It's electrifying. There's an urgency fuelling us. It is making us brave. Making it worth the risk. As our kiss deepens, with one hand holding me firmly, Cam uses the other to cup my breast, gently rolling his thumb over my nipple, teasing it to a hard peak through the satin. A small groan rumbles from my throat as he switches to kiss my neck. It causes a delicious wave of tingles to spread across my whole body.

What seems like seconds later, a noisy Klaxon sounds, and Cam drags his warm lips up to mine for a final kiss.

'Don't forget this,' he whispers, holding up a bottle of pineapple juice. I wrinkle my nose at it, and he stifles a laugh. 'Why didn't you pick something else? Do you want to change the safe word? I mean code word. Time to go. Bedtime.'

I have never been so disappointed in my life, while his eyes are positively twinkling. I race into the Dog House, high as an A-Lister at the Oscars, jump into bed and pull the covers over me. Within minutes, the lights go out and it is safe to peel back the blanket. I lie staring at the ceiling. I touch my lips. They feel hot. My fingers trace the line of his kisses to my neck. It tingles from his touch. It is as though he has stoked a dormant fire within me, and a single flame has burst forth. It is dancing about, warming my soul. I close my eyes and picture him and breathe in deeply. I can smell him. His clean, fresh woody scent. Memories of the way he held me in his strong arms, so firm, so confident, flood my mind. The way my hands ran over his back, so broad and manly. What must it be like to feel his body on my body? I feel an ache of longing deep down. If it comes to it, I think I would have sex with him in the blind spot. Behind the bin. Up against the wall. Bin sex. Only a few feet from the nearest camera. It's so thrilling I can barely sleep.

Just as well, because literally an hour later, the Klaxon sounds again, and all the lights snap on. A runner thumps on the door and yells, 'EVENING DRESS! GET YOUR GLAD RAGS ON – FILMING IN TEN!'

I spring out of bed. I have had no sleep. I hurry to the dressing room to discover the girls are disoriented and panicking.

'What's happening?' I ask. They all look blankly back. I recall Cam telling me to beware the structure of the day, and that night will become day sometimes, and vice versa. Something about Porscha preferring to catch the islanders off-guard comes back to me.

'It's okay,' I say soothingly. 'I think it might have something to do with filming while it's not raining.' This seems to calm them down. Amber wanders over to lift my hair up.

'It looks perfect. Like you haven't even been to sleep.'

All the girls suddenly stop to check out my hair. 'I'm just lucky that I slept sitting up. I didn't want it to curl.'

'Lucky you,' she says. 'I'll do your make-up first, then mine.'

She swishes a few brushes over my face, a few licks of liner, wafts a mascara wand at my lashes, strokes my lips with a red stain and voila. I am done.

'I'm in awe. How do you do that?' I say, genuinely grateful. I look fantastic. 'Do you have a TikTok tutorial I could watch when I get out of here?' The irony is so not lost on me.

I race over to my cases to see what else Cam has packed. By mistake, I open the Porscha case and out tumbles a slutty vixen dress. I hold it up. It looks like a doggy poo bag.

'Wow, that is GORGE, babes,' coos Amber. 'Try it on.'

'No. I'd never have the confidence to wear something like this.'

I must be in Mimi's good books because I chose to sleep far away from Giovanni. She says, 'Don't be ridiculous. This dress was made for girls like you.'

'Try it on,' agrees Amber. I notice Kassy and Binky are not so keen.

I pull it this way and that, until finally I have stretched it across my body. I take a look in the mirror and my eyes nearly pop out of my head. I look as far from the real me as I have ever done. I look stunning. It is essentially plastic with cut out bits in all the right places. It has no back so I can't wear a bra.

'Here, wear these with it,' Amber flings a pair a fishnet stockings at me. 'You'll slay, babes.'

Mimi and the others are trying their best to compete, but the Klaxon sounds, and it is time to move. A phone pings. Christ Almighty, it's mine. They all look at me. It's time for me to become one of 'them'.

'I GOT A TEXT!' I yell and we all squeal with excitement. Who even am I anymore? 'ISLANDERS GET READY FOR LADIES NIGHT HASHTAG COME AND GET IT HASHTAG BEATING THEM OFF WITH A STICK.'

There's a confused silence while none of us are quite sure what to make of it.

We make our way to the firepit. The flames are in full swing, the whole villa is ablaze with neon, lit up like a nightclub. Me in my killer heels and outfit. Destiny instructs us to sit in our couples and for Mimi to stand on her own in front.

Giovanni, his arm still in a sling is looking me up and down with his tongue hanging out. 'You are so hot! So sexy! Like a hot, sexy ONLY FANS hooker nurse.'

I can't help preening under the compliment and wiggle around in my seat, flicking my hair and batting my lashes, in case Cam is watching me on a screen in one of the hides. I look seductively around for which one he might be in. I'm desperate to see him. To see what he makes of my outfit.

'Islanders,' booms Destiny from beneath her heavy fringe. It is impossible to tell whether her eyes are open or shut. 'It is time to meet your next bombshell.'

We all pretend to look confused – namely because Destiny just told us to – and the music blasts out. In walks a stunning male model. He pauses at the big love heart giving us a moment to take him in before striding confidently to the firepit. He stands with his legs even wider apart than Giovanni does. He treats us to a blindingly white smile and thousands of dollars' worth of dental surgery.

'Now, that's how to make an entrance,' I say under my breath. He takes one look at Mimi, picks her up and swings her round.

'Great to finally meet you all,' he says, putting her back down. Mimi is immediately smitten. Giovanni stiffens next to me, mumbling, 'What the fuck is going on?'

'Love on the Islanders meet...' We wait for the music to stop playing and for the camera to circle around us on a track. '... Carlton.'

We cast our eyes over him. He's tall, in perfect physical condition, has short dark hair, classic features that I would describe as captain of the football team in American high school movies-type of handsome, and he is wearing lovely shoes. If he says he's a trainee children's doctor or a vet, he's the whole package.

'Tell us about yourself, hun,' coos Destiny, clearly liking what she sees.

'I'm kinda like an introvert. I like staying home and watching movies, with a glass of wine and the candles on,' he says, causing the girls to instantly 'ooh and aah'. 'But I also like to go out clubbing, you know? Music festivals, extreme sports and travelling with a whole bunch of friends.'

So just a normal person then.

Destiny quizzes the new bombshell on who he has had his eye on, and he looks straight at me and says, 'Libby. I'm here to find my person. I'm ready to settle down and have kids.' He keeps staring at me.

I gulp.

Carlton continues on, 'After I've seen the world and climbed all six peaks in Canada. And I also have my eye on Mimi and Amber. You are all stunning. Absolutely stunning.'

'I'm afraid you can only pick one, Carlton. But I have to warn you. If you pick one of the girls tonight who is already coupled up, then that boy will be dumped from the Island. If you don't pick a girl who is not coupled up, she will also be dumped from the Island. Who are you going to choose?'

Carlton makes a right drama out of choosing. He takes so long staring at each of us in turn that I begin to feel sick with nerves. I look along the line to see the others, especially the guys, all look the same. Pale and drained. Poor Mimi is standing there like a lump of going-out-of-date cheese waiting to be picked. Seriously? What is wrong with him? She is the only girl not attached to a male. If he picks her, it would mean everyone gets to stay in the villa. Win-win.

I give myself a mental slap. This is why they do the recouplings and dumpings through the night when we are tired, weak and too vulnerable to think straight. They want to catch us off-guard and to make us cry for the camera. I look again at the guys. They look so fed up.

Hold it together Libby for goodness' sake. None of it is real anyway.

'It's so hard to choose,' Carlton says, looking longingly at Destiny. I stifle a yawn and see Amber is doing the same. Poor Mimi looks positively tearful. He looks her over again and then glances over at me and Amber.

I swear I will slap him. I will slap. He scratches his chin as though he's got all friggin day... or night. Who knows what time it is!

'You're not trying to choose an avocado,' someone yells at him. 'Just pick a frigging girl and get the fuck on with it!'

It's a few seconds before I realise it is me. *Shitting hell.* Hopefully they'll cut that bit. Thanks to some pretty intensive teacher training, it's the first time I've sworn out loud for years. I am mortified. 'I meant get the fudge on with it.'

A broad grin spreads across Carlton's face as he makes eye contact with me.

'I just love a girl with spirit,' he says in his Texan drawl. 'Come to papa.' He winks at me, and I almost throw up in my mouth. My hand flies to my lips as I retch a few times.

I shake my head vigorously. 'No, I don't think so.'

Come to papa. I mean who says that? Who?

Carlton looks to Destiny with a confused look, as if to say is this not the plan? Destiny looks astonished as though no one has ever thought to disagree.

'Well, erm...' Destiny looks about. She taps her earpiece to check it's working. 'I erm, so, Carlton. How about Mimi? You two look very cute together.'

Mimi has tears running down her cheeks. I'm very much ruining the show, but it is probably three in the morning, and I very much don't care. I just need to go back to bed and dream about how wonderful Cam is at rubbing nipples.

'CUT!' bellows Porscha. I knew that was coming. She appears before me, smoke blowing out of her ears. Cam is close behind trying not to laugh. His eyes are glassy. His hair is sticking up and he has a very sexy, sleepy look about him. 'That's the last time we get any teachers on the show,' she screams at no one in particular. 'ROLL AGAIN!'

'Could I change my mind, please, Destiny?' Carlton is asking her. 'I'll just go for Mimi instead. It'll be easier.'

Mimi looks momentarily offended until it clicks that she'll be coupled up again at last. A whole six hours or so of being single has taken its toll. She turns to Carlton and leaps into his arms, straddling his waist with her short, skinny, terrier legs. She pumps up and down a few times before he peels her off him.

'Cheers, bro,' says Giovanni who sags back into the cushion. He has been saved a dumping. He turns to me with eyes full of lust, rubbing his hands together like he's about to tuck into a Thanksgiving feast. 'Looks like it's me and you again, babe.'

'No. It really doesn't.'

Cameron comes over to the firepit and I notice he is holding something. 'We'll film from Carlton's entrance, look surprised people and then you can all go back to bed. Carlton, Mimi, places please. And action!'

Cam steps away out of shot. He has a clipboard in one hand, and a pineapple under his arm. He gives me the briefest of glances. Our eyes connect and it sets my pulse racing. I look down at my hands clamped to the edge of the seat. I must regain my composure so as not to give the game away.

It feels near impossible to control my emotions when the heart wants what the heart wants.

'So, Libby,' says Giovanni, distracting me. 'How long have you fancied Cameron?'

'Who?' I say, startled.

'Cameron, the producer?'

Fuck!!

Chapter 19

Time seems to stand still as I quickly assess my predicament. His words will have been captured on the microphone. My reaction will be recorded on camera. My mind is whizzing.

I am a teacher.

Therefore, I am resilient.

I am a quick thinker.

I am a beast when it comes to being put in impossible situations.

I weigh up all the information. Giovanni has noticed that I go to pieces every time the incredibly handsome and thoughtful, kind-eyed, mild-mannered and extremely competent producer is near. How disappointingly perceptive of him. Fortunately for me, I have four years' worth of telling bare-faced lies to school parents about their adorable little genius children under my belt.

'Giovanni, are you deflecting your own insecurities?' I say, in a concerned voice. 'Or is this because Mimi is pretending to vibe off Carlton just to make you jealous?'

I have used a simple trick of giving him a choice to make. Either choice is of no consequence to me. They simply serve to distract him from his original pursuit of the truth. It works like a charm.

'Wait. What? Is she?' His head whips round to find Mimi smiling enthusiastically at Carlton. Carlton is giving her the eye back. They both have very recent rejections in common. But right on cue, Mimi looks over her shoulder to check that Giovanni is watching her.

She smiles at him and blows him a kiss before turning back to Carlton to stroke his face.

My simple deflection is complete. Now to stoke the fire. 'You might have to put the graft in to win her back. They look like they might be catching feelings.'

'ACTION!'

Filming Carlton's entrance, us pretending to be shocked and him pretending to lay eyes on Mimi, and them being instantly smitten with each other takes only a few minutes as everyone is desperate to go back to bed.

The crew pack up their cameras at the speed of light. The islanders charge towards the main villa, and I pretend I'm going off to the outdoor kitchen to refill my water bottle. I slip through the PANTRY secret door and slide along the wall. I am beyond excited to see what Cam makes of me in this sultry outfit. I feel like sex on legs. When he kisses me, I'm going to hoik my leg up like Mimi, so that he can fully appreciate that I am wearing stockings. I'm hoping that he will slide his hand the length of my thigh, right to the top. I'm hoping that his fingers will find their way underneath the rubber dress and stroke my behind. Oh, my God, I can barely stand it any longer.

I wait a few moments, but Cameron doesn't show. We agreed that two minutes is the maximum time we can be in the blind spot without raising suspicion. The two minutes is up.

Devastated, I slip back through the secret door, into the PANTRY and hear hushed voices coming from the outdoor kitchen. I sneak a look, to see Porscha standing with her back to me, arguing with Cam.

I duck back into the PANTRY out of sight. Porscha is telling Cam to make me sleep in the same bed as Giovanni tonight. Cam is saying that he won't do it. That I have every right to choose, for the sake of my well-being and the integrity of the show. He is standing firm and will not violate his ethics.

'This show doesn't have any integrity,' spits Porscha. 'Why are you protecting the collateral? You like her. Don't you?' She sounds very jealous. 'You like her romantically.'

'No. Of course not,' says Cam, which I have to admit does pinch at my heart a little. 'From a professional point of view, she's great on camera. The public seem to love her, and she brings an extra dynamic to the show that the current contestants don't. She's different. Do I like her being on the show? Sure. Who wouldn't?'

His soothing voice calms Porscha instantly. 'Good. That's erm, well, that's good to know. It's just that if you did develop romantic feelings for anyone on the show... contestants that is... erm, there would be serious consequences.'

'I know that, Porscha. You remind me every day. I've been producing this show for two years now. You have nothing to worry about.'

Gosh, he sounds so convincing.

'You're right. I just need to keep an eye on what's what, so everything doesn't spin out of control. That production village turns into a hotbed of carnal activity at night. They forget those trailer walls are paper thin. It's just that it feels like the whole crew are bonking away behind my back. There's more action going on in the village than with the collateral on the show. We should be filming them instead!'

So, we're merely collateral instead of real people with feelings? Good to know.

Cam laughs. 'Yep, you're not wrong there.' There's a silence between them. I wish I could see what they are doing. Why are neither of them talking? 'So, don't forget we're on camera,' Cam blurts. 'And everything you say and do may be taken down and used as evidence in a court of law.' He emits a fake-sounding laugh.

Porscha clears her throat. I am imagining the worst. Her lunging at him with her perfect plumped-up pout, and hopefully, he is reminding her that the cameras are still on because he is not interested in the slightest.

'Well, if you're listening to this, you lot, keep your heads in the game,' Porscha orders. 'No more gratuitous loud bonking in the trailer park.'

I hear a cackle of a radio. It sounds like a walkie talkie. 'Roger that, boss. Message received. Over.'

Porscha laughs. 'They'll hate me even more now. You coming?'

'I, er, I have to erm, check on the...'

'Leave it until tomorrow. There's only one car left going back to the village and that's mine. Take the lift.' Porscha says sharply. 'And you can leave the pineapple here. I'm allergic.'

The next morning, I wake in the Dog House to a knocking on the door. My hopes soar at the thought it might be Cam. I had a dreadful night's sleep imagining that Porscha had him strapped to her bed. She was administering all manner of unspeakable sexual favours on him. Her plumped-up lips were sucking him dry while he was calling for my help, but I couldn't get to him because Giovanni was standing guard, towering over me like a bronze statue, his muscles rippling in the moonlight, hair flowing in the breeze.

I'm breaking into a sweat just thinking about the sexual deviancy going on in the trailer park hotbed of sin. Poor Cam. I hope she hasn't taken him hostage. The knocking continues.

'Libby, are you in there? You've slept through the Klaxon. They sent me to get you.'

My heart sinks. It's Giovanni. I pad sleepily to the door and pull it open.

'Can I grab you for a quick chat?' he asks my breasts. I am wearing the silky number.

'Sure. Which one do you want to chat to? The left or the right breast?'

'Oh, erm. Both,' he says, his eyes darting to my face. 'I mean neither of them. So, a chat, yeah?'

He's so articulate. He should write a book or something.

'What do you want to chat about?' I yawn, looking him over. He's covered in sweat. It's dripping down his arms over the copious amounts of oil he has slathered on. He is bare-chested and wearing only tight, lycra shorts that, really, look like girl's knickers. It's too much for this early in the morning. 'Have you been to the gym already?'

'No. Not yet,' he says. 'It's just so hot out there.'

He looks soaked.

'Look no sling!' he says, waving his arm in my face. 'I'm on my way to the gym. Needed to strengthen my wrist.' He starts laughing. 'In case I fail to win you over and I need it later. Wink, wink, nudge, nudge.'

I. AM. GOING. TO. VOMIT.

'Fancy a workout with me?' he asks.

Anything to get rid of him. I had enough of that last night, dreaming that Porscha was milking Cam like a goat, while they drove back to the village. I'm on the verge of saying I'd rather stick needles in my eyes when I remember everything is being recorded and Porscha will be watching. In a bid to throw her off the scent, I will pretend to take an interest in this oily buffoon.

'I'll meet you there,' I sigh. 'Give me a second to get changed.'

I make my way round the side of the huge property towards the outside gym, over by the pool area. I turn the corner and gasp, as I take it all in.

Oh, my word. It's breathtaking. It's magical. It's an explosion of colour. It's like I'm in a dream.

I catch sight of a runner in an apron laying out breakfast in the outdoor kitchen. She looks up startled as though I shouldn't have caught her in the act.

'It's incredible. It's like some sort of paradise.' I can barely take it in. I've seen the show on TV but in real life, in the bright sunshine, everything is a million times prettier, more colourful, more impressive. 'Is any of it real?' I shout over to her, pointing to the gardens bursting with tropical plants, vivid pinks, yellows, greens, blues, every colour imaginable. There are neon archways covered in flowers, palm trees dotted across neat grass lawns, fairy lights built into every surface, climbing around every tree and strung across the whole of the villa, criss-crossing above us. The deep green hedges are dotted with stunning pink flowers and trim every walkway, every wall, every balcony, every terrace.

'None of it. It's all fake,' she says. 'We have a whole team of expensive designers working round the clock for months to get everything perfect for you. Enjoy!'

I realise again just how bizarre being here is.

The outside gym is very well stocked and looks brand-spanking new. Giovanni wolf whistles as I approach. All I could find to wear was a one-piece Lycra shorts body suit in neon pink.

'At least I match the garden signs,' I say, pointing to a huge neon sign above the weights bench that says, 'Pump it, pump it real good'. I shake my head, who thinks these things up? It's one innuendo after another.

'That's my favourite,' says Giovanni pointing to a sign by the side of the pool.

It really is a wonderland of fake flowers and twinkling fairy lights.

'Love is Reel.' He waggles his eyebrows at me. 'Geddit? Reel as in social media? But it works on another level too as in real love.' He shakes his head in disbelief. 'They're so clever these *Love on the Island* dudes. They think of everything.'

I smile blankly. His parents must be so proud.

'So, Libby. I wanted to pull you for a chat.'

I pump my arms, keeping my focus on the weights in my hands.

'Because I erm, ... I have a request to make. It's er, it's about the bed situation.'

Why? I've not shown him the slightest bit of interest since I got here.

'Uh-huh?'

'I'd like you to come back to the main villa and share a bed with me.'

'Why?'

This has thrown him because he drops the heavy medicine ball he is squatting with and looks at me frowning. His mouth falls open, but words elude him.

I carry on pumping my arms to give him time to think.

He drops down onto the mat, into a perfect press-up position. Finally, after a succession of one-armed press-ups, he hits on something to say. 'Why don't we get to know each other a bit?'

I inwardly sigh. My heart is taken. This is futile but we are on camera, and while I know Cam is watching, I'd hate for people across America to think I'm not giving Giovanni a fair chance.

'Sure. Great. Lovely.' I slap on a smile. 'So, Giovanni, tell me, what's your plan after this show?'

He stops mid-press-up to answer. 'Oh, I have such a cool plan. I want to be rich and successful. And settled with the woman of my dreams. I'm so ready for marriage and kids.'

'Good for you. Raising a family is expensive. Rich and successful in what?'

'Who knows? I'm just going to go where the wind takes me, I guess, and see where I end up.'

'That's not really a plan.'

He resumes his workout. 'Well, I'll just go with the flow.'

'No, still not a plan.'

'Well, I'll just see what unfolds, you know?'

'Nope, not a plan either.'

What is he not getting?

He continues his press-ups. The heat is building as the sun beats down on us. Sweat is pouring off him as though I'm hosing him down like a beached whale.

'I'll just, like, drift on the wind, bro. See where I land.'

That is basically a repeat of his first sentence. We are simply going round in endless circles.

I could be trapped in this godawful cycle for hours. I plonk the weights down with an audible groan.

'Okay. Giovanni, I think you might have an underactive amygdala. It's stopping you from worrying about things. Anyway, good chat. See you later.'

'So, is that a yes to sleeping in my bed? Porscha kinda said I had to persuade you.'

I glare at him.

'Oh, did she?' I swivel round to stare straight into a camera hide. It's under the 'Pump me real good' sign. I noticed the sunlight reflecting off the lens as soon as I looked at it. I put my hands on my hips and go full teacher-mode. 'Well, perhaps she'd like to come and explain herself then.'

Porscha responds to my battle cry by announcing that we will all be taking part in a game. I know she is trying to have a go at me because it is called High School Drop Out.

'You'll be great at this, Libby,' Amber shrieks excitedly as we climb into a collection of obscene sexy schoolgirl outfits. When we are all ready, we take a group selfie.

I know for a fact that the giant mirror taking up the whole wall in the hallway is two-way. I stare directly into it as we pose. Mimi is doing vertical splits while hanging onto my shoulder and Amber is doing a doggy-style hump sort of thing to Binky on my other side. Her blue hair looks great against the big pink bubble gum bubble she is blowing. Kassy is doing lying down splits with me stood folding my arms unimpressed in the middle.

'This is a bit seventies, isn't it?' I say to the mirror. 'A bit sexist? A bit on the cusp as far as grooming goes?' I point to our obscenely short, pleated skirts, swinging up our backsides. We are wearing stockings and suspenders, skimpy shirts that only reach the bottom of our boobs and miniature ties. We all have our hair in pigtails. We look sexy as hell, but that is beside the point.

'I've got a good vibe with Marco but I'm going to cover my options until I've got all the feels,' announces Kassy, adjusting her skirt to make it even shorter.

'Good 'cos I'm doing Carlton but only to make Giovanni jealous. Does everyone get that?'

We all nod obediently.

'Who is Marco? Have I missed someone new coming in?' I ask.

'She means Marcel,' Amber corrects.

'I'm stuck with the tall one,' says Binky. She's barely said a word since we've been here. 'I have no idea what he's called.'

'It's Brad, hun. BRAD,' Amber says. 'And I suppose I'll get to know Henri.'

'Who?' they all ask together.

Amber sighs. 'Aren't any of you paying any attention? My one is the French guy. Henri pronounced On-ree. He's quite cute really. Although I'm definitely open if anyone asks because he seems to be hanging out with Marcel more than me. I think he might be gay.'

'Who?' I join in with them. I know full-well who everyone is. I studied hard before I came to the villa, thanks to Cam, but it's essential that I don't give the game away.

Soon, we are all standing on a padded bouncy plastic platform, girls versus boys for the High School Drop Out Challenge. There's a huge scoreboard off to the side. A seat is hanging over a large dunking pool full of water. There is a board with school subjects written on it. They range from Psychology to English to Domestic Science. I breathe a quiet sigh of relief. I might just be not so rubbish at this after all. I will stay quiet though because really, all of this is way out of my comfort zone. The heat is sweltering down on us and I'm already feeling queasy from the lack of sleep and all the stress of sneaking around to see Cam.

'Libby, you have to be our team captain,' says Kassy, looking at the girls who are all nodding.

'Thank you,' I say, genuinely quite moved at their vote of confidence. 'But honestly, I'm happy to stay quietly in the background feeding you answers. Helping with spellings. Keeping up team morale, more of a facilitator, that kind of thing. One of you should be captain.'

It's as though I didn't say anything. They all start squealing and jumping up and down, their tiny skirts flapping up to expose their tiny thong underwear. Their shirts lift up to reveal more than just a peek of under boob. The men's eyes are like dinner plates.

'Libby is team captain, and she is going to kick your asses!' Amber yells over to the men excitedly.

'Hell yeah,' joins in Mimi. 'She's a goddam mother-fuckin' teacher, that's right!'

I feel my eyes almost popping out of their sockets.

Please someone make them stop.

'She'll take you all to church, cocksuckers!' Binky, who has been as quiet as a mouse this whole time has suddenly chosen now to become a loud, foul-mouthed quiz monster.

'Question one for the team captains,' shouts out Carlton as he removes the card from the first subject on the board 'Sex Education'. As the alpha 'male' he is designated quiz master. 'How many sex positions can you get your team to demonstrate? You have thirty seconds?'

Fudging hell.

'Thirty seconds isn't very long...' I say stalling for time. The girls quickly start wrestling each other to the ground.

'Libby! Yell the position, and we'll do it!'

'Erm, missionary,' I say. I'm deeply uncomfortable with being put on the spot. The girls fling each other into position. The boys seem to be hurling each other around like rag dolls. I can barely make out what Henri is saying in his thick French accent. 'Erm, cowgirl.' I have no idea what that means but I've heard of it.

They wait for my next instruction.

'Erm, the one where... you're upside down?'

'No, name the sex position. Hurry!'

'Back to front? Would that be the Mirror Image?' I say, grasping at straws.

The buzzer sounds and the girls are not happy.

'How can you not know more than two sex positions?' Mimi yells loudly just as the buzzer stops.

I am mortified.

'The Boys have 14 and the girls have 2! The boys are the winners!' shouts Carlton. While the boys are leaping up and down, the girls swoop towards me for answers.

'Well, I erm... I haven't erm... it's not something that's really come up...' My cheeks are on fire. My sex life with Arrogant Josh was fairly non-existent on account of me wanting to get to know him more before I committed.

'Oh. My. God,' says Kassy. 'You've never...?'

'But you're old,' says Binky. 'How old are you?'

'I'm twenty-six. And I've been busy, okay? There's no shame in not being sexually adventurous.'

'There is, hun. There totally is.'

'Leave her alone. We'll do better in the next round. Come on. We're a team, remember?' shouts Amber, looking like a fierce warrior. 'Come on girls!'

Thank God, she's rescued the team morale. I go over to get dunked in the tank while Mimi peels the 'English' label off the board and reads out the question underneath. 'Rhyme as many words as you can with sock.'

Oh my word. I hope no one in the England Education Department is watching this.

Chapter 20

The questions come thick and fast, and the girls grow increasingly despondent at my lack of sexual knowledge and prowess.

'How can you seriously stand there and not be able to name strange places you've had sex? You could have just made it all up for the sake of the fucking quiz!' Kassy is livid. 'And why did you blurt out "up the bum" when you clearly fucking haven't? It wasn't even your fucking turn!'

It's true. I panicked. But in all fairness, I clearly didn't understand the question until they started shouting things like 'up a tree', 'in the meat aisle' and 'on a bike'.

I have been the only contestant to be dunked every time. I am so wet, I'm at the point of cooking to death. The heat is so intense, the steam is rising off me causing my skin to become irritated. My hair is frizzing beyond all reasonable expectations.

'Last question,' calls Carlton. The men are winning by so many that it is mathematically pointless for us to continue. The girls are now lying down on the bouncy padding. They are picking their nails, sulking and refusing to look me in the eye. 'Domestic Science. Name things that look like body parts.'

There's a huge groan from the girls. I leap to my feet, my Year Three Biology project of the human anatomy springing to mind. The boys are struggling once they have said 'eggplant' and 'huge watermelons'. They are so far in the lead they don't bother to name any more.

'Broccoli for the hair, marrow for the torso, baby carrots for arms, cherry tomatoes for elbows, oranges for knees, cucumber legs, spaghetti for ligaments, pears for feet, slices of sweet potato for eyes, peas for pupils, aubergine for the stomach, edamame beans for toes.'

On and on I go.

'Cabbage for intestines. Sweetcorn for teeth.' The buzzer goes and we have clawed back lots of points. Suddenly we are back in the game.

The girls are giving me a strange look.

'What can I say?' I tell them. 'It's a gift.'

The final round is called 'Kissing behind the Bike Shed'. The aim is for the blindfolded boys to identify who has kissed them. It looks very much like I might have to kiss one, if not all, of the boys. The girls are very excited and have perked up. Mimi nominates herself to go first. We watch as she slobbers over every single male contestant with gusto.

I have reached my limit with this game. A line must be drawn somewhere, and I feel this challenge is it. I drop to the ground in a heap.

'Count me out. I'm done. I'm not snogging any of that lot.'

I wonder what Cam is making of all this when an alarm goes off, blaring loudly from speakers all around the grounds and the runners come running over to inform us that the fire alarm has gone off, it is not a drill, and we are all to make our way to the safety point. Ironically, the safety point is the firepit. There's no way I'm going to make a fool of myself over the alarm again, so I resist the temptation to snap into teacher-mode.

There's mass confusion with Porscha bellowing, 'Which of you fuckers has set off the alarm? Who? WHO?'

We huddle together at the firepit. Islanders, runners, camera operators, kitchen staff, producers, maintenance crew and the cleaning team. There are a lot of us. They seem to be crawling out of the woodwork like ants. I'm surprised at how many people are actually on-site during the filming, half the production village it seems.

'Somebody count heads, will you?' Porscha barks. 'And where is the bloody fire anyway?'

We all sniff the air and inhale the fresh scent of olive groves wafting in from the distance and the smell of fresh paint and plastic from the villa.

'Can't we just turn that god-awful alarm off and carry on filming? Time is money people.'

The distant blare of sirens would suggest otherwise. I spot Cam on the far side from me. He looks like a man who is doing his best to ignore me. Then across the chaos, he turns to search the crowd. His gaze rests on mine with an almost tender expression, and we lock eyes. There's something about him.

There's a brightness to him.

There's a tiny hint of a smile on his lips.

Then as the islanders jostle about, I lose sight of him in the throng.

'I'll handle this,' barks Porscha as the emergency services arrive to put out the imaginary fire. 'Which one of you useless pricks can speak Spanish?'

From nowhere, Cam whispers one word in my ear and without turning around, I slip quietly away.

He is already at the blind spot waiting when I arrive. 'Were you listening to all of it?' I cringe. I'm still having visions of all the shocked faces when Carlton asked me, 'Where's the strangest place you've had sex?' and I answered with a question, 'Up the bum?' because I misheard and thought he'd said, 'Where's the strangest place TO have sex?'. Even though I tried to explain the misunderstanding many times afterwards, the damage had already been done. I think the laughing must have gone on for a full ten minutes.

'No. None of it,' Cam says trying very hard not to smile. 'Not one word.'

I roll my eyes. He heard it all.

'It was so embarrassing,' I say, burying my head in his shoulder. 'I don't suppose we could cut any of it out of the show, could we?' I look up, pleading him with my big sad eyes.

He looks thoughtful for a moment as he blows out his cheeks. 'I'll do my best but what Porscha wants, Porscha gets. It was very funny though. We all knew you'd misheard.'

I groan inwardly.

'I hate to say Porscha has a God complex, but she totally does, doesn't she?' I whisper to him. 'What am I going to do? The whole world will laugh at me.'

'She's a complete narcissist all right.' Cam is looking down at me. He's simply magnificent looking. 'It'll be okay, I promise. Ready to go back out there? I'll see if I can get you all a break while we clear up the fire brigade situation. Might take a while. With any luck they'll scrap the end of the challenge.'

'It was fortunate, the alarm going off like that,' I say. 'Were you near the fire when it went off?'

Cam gives nothing away. 'No, I was busy doing... a thing.'

I am dying to ask if the reason is because he doesn't want to see me kissing any of the boys. I wait for him to elaborate but he doesn't.

'Well, thank goodness someone sounded the alarm because I was not looking forward to having to kiss any of those boys.'

Cam's cheeks go a flattering pink colour.

'There's only one man that I'm interested in kissing,' I say, hoping he is reading between the lines.

It's the sexy schoolgirl costume. It's giving me the power of a young Brittany Spears. I casually lean back against the wall lifting one foot up to rest against it. The move causes

Cam to glance down at my stockings and short skirt. I see his eyes travel up my body taking in the skimpy skirt, the bare midriff and the ridiculously short shirt and tie that barely cover my boobs.

He blinks slowly. It all feels so wrong... yet so right. I can see his internal battle. I push off the wall towards him and in a second his mouth finds mine. His lips feel hot against mine. His hands find my skirt and slip underneath to trace the outline of my suspenders, the tops of my stockings, the delicate lace of my knickers. As our kiss deepens my hands tangle in his hair. He lifts me up as though I weigh nothing, and I instinctively wrap my legs round his waist. He holds me tight against him as we lose ourselves in frenzied passion.

He can't get enough.

I am driving him wild.

He thrusts his groin against me and almost crushes me against the wall.

'Oh, God,' he says quietly breaking off. His breathing is all over the place, as is mine. He has that feverish look again. 'What are you doing to me?'

He steps away from me. 'You'd better get back on set.' His voice is thick with reluctance.

I nod, mute with lust.

'I'll arrange a break. So that we can, erm, pull ourselves together.'

'That would be good,' I say. 'I could do with a break.' My entire body is on fire for this man.

'Go to the Tree House. I don't think any of them have discovered it yet. You might get some time alone.'

He's so thoughtful.

He kisses me lightly on the cheek before disappearing through the kitchen back door and I wonder for the millionth time how on Earth a relationship between us could work outside of this bizarre scenario. I am falling deeper and deeper for him with every interaction. The thought echoes around in my mind. After the show, what then?

I take a few deep breaths and make my way stealthily to the Beach Hut to clear up a few things on camera. Namely, the world thinking that I am a sexual deviant, just in case they choose not to cut the High School Drop Out Challenge from the show. I bump into Carlton on the way out.

'Hi,' he says. 'I thought you might be coming here. I saw you slip away earlier. They couldn't see you when they did a roll call, so I told them I saw you heading for the Beach Hut. Where have you been?'

'Oh, nowhere. Just walking around the garden to get my thoughts together.'

That was close.

'Ready to go in there?' he says, pointing to the Beach Hut entrance.

I nod.

'I just went in to say that I'd like to get to know you more,' he says. 'Especially after today. You were hilarious.'

How excruciating. My face is on fire. 'Listen, those things I said...'

He holds his hands up, laughing. 'It's okay. We were just messing with you. But you might want to clear it up with the rest of the world.'

'One hundred per cent,' I say, shaking my head with embarrassment.

He fixes me an intense look. 'I like that you're so sweet and innocent, yet so capable and... insanely hot.' He looks me appreciatively up and down while I yank self-consciously at my skirt and shirt to eke out a few extra inches of coverage. 'It's like you have no idea how sexy you are. I'd be up for stealing a chat when you come out of the Hut.'

I'm a bit caught off guard. 'Okay, yeah. Sure.'

He saunters off, so confident, so sure of himself. How do people do that?

As soon as I've finished clarifying my position on all things challenge related, I make my way to the dressing room. One look in the mirror and it is all I can do to not shriek in horror at my reflection. What a state! Hair all over in two raggedy bunches. Make-up literally smeared down my face. My nose looks sunburnt and shiny. My outfit has dried all crinkly due to the constant dunking in the water.

Binky and Kassy race in. They are wearing bikinis and looking fabulous. 'Where have you been? Quick, get changed. They are scrapping the challenge. We're going to film making mocktails, instead.'

'IN OUR COUPLES!' yells Binky. Then looks to me alarmed. 'What's my one called again?'

Because of my encyclopaedic study of the contestants, thanks to Cam, my knowledge of them is extensive. 'Marcel. Twenty-four. Likes all sport, camping and cooking vegan meals. He loves his grandmother very much because she raised him, and they have five dogs and seven cats.'

Binky looks a bit deflated.

'But he has been single for over a year, since his fiancée ran off with his dad, which triggered him to start his own business and now he is well on his way to making his first million dollars.'

She perks right up. 'I am definitely pulling him for a chat.'

'Do mine! Do mine,' squeals Kassy.

'Brad. From Australia. He likes Bush trekking, extreme sports and sewing. He has four brothers and two sisters. He is twenty-one years old and, after a dry spell of two years, he now feels ready to settle down with the girl of his dreams. Kassy, you are his exact type.'

This proves a popular move.

'Let's do Libby's make-over,' Binky yells. 'Amber! Get in here! Kassy, you do wardrobe, I'll do hair.'

Ten minutes later, my hair is up in a messy bun, my face is natural and vibrant thanks to Amber's clever make-up, and I am wearing a gorgeous bikini and matching sarong picked by Kassy from the free clothes rack our sponsor has provided. It fits me perfectly. It's colourful and eye-catching without being too revealing. We walk to the outdoor kitchen together linking arms as though we have been friends for decades. Mimi is already there draping herself over Carlton while glancing at Giovanni every few seconds.

The benches have been laid out with every kind of fruit and the shelves on the back wall are groaning under the weight of dozens of bottles of brightly coloured juices. Brad's phone pings. It's his first time. He looks like he has won the lottery.

'I GOT A TIXT!' he bellows, and we all squeal excitedly. 'LOVE OISLANDERS. IT IS TOIME TO GET FRUITY. BEST MOCKTAIL AND BEST NAME WINS,' he screeches. Everyone is leaping up and down.

'Wins what? Does it say?' I ask.

'Who cares?' yells Mimi jumping into Carlton's arms. 'It's all about the winning!'

Carlton flicks his eyes my way as though to apologise.

'Hey, Libby,' Giovanni intercepts. He has noticed Carlton looking in my direction. 'You look nice.'

'So do you,' I say out of politeness. He is wearing swimming trunks that would fit a very small child, possibly under the age of four. He has doused himself in so much oil that the first thing he picks up slips easily through his fingers, and even though I instinctively try to catch it, it crashes noisily to the floor. We have broken a glass fruit bowl and there are chunks of chopped pineapple everywhere. A voice comes across crackling out through the speakers.

'CUT! Jesus Christ, Libby. Why must everything you touch turn to shit?'

Giovanni gives me a panicked look. 'Oh my God. I'll tell Porscha it was me.' He looks positively terrified. 'She'll probably dump me from the island on the next recoupling.'

'It's okay,' I say. 'She thinks it was me. I'll take one for the team. I'm not a massive fan of pineapple anyway. Let's just crack on with the task. Name first or do you want to decide the ingredients?'

Giovanni sighs with relief and gives me a look of wonder. 'You are such a lovely person.'

I shrug. 'All teachers are. It's in our nature. What can I say?'

'YOUR TIME STARTS NOW.'

We spend a riotous forty minutes coming up with all manner of names for our mocktails. Fruit is flying everywhere. I look along the row to see all the couples taking it very seriously except us. People are racing back and forth to the juice bar, as an invisible clock ticks loudly over the speakers. The pressure is on, and I can see Giovanni getting nervous.

I put slices of kiwi on my eyes and two sticks of celery up my nose and whip my head round to ask Giovanni, 'Is this what they mean by getting fruity?'

Taken by surprise, Giovanni bursts out laughing and accidentally leans on the button for the mixer he is loading. It sends liquid flying out to splat everyone around us. I find this hilarious, as I bend over wheezing with laughter. We are drenched.

In response, he scoops up some of the mush from the bench and dumps it on my head. I then do the same but wipe it over his face. 'At least it tastes nice,' he says as we crease up laughing.

'Oh, my God,' I say, licking my fingers. 'How much sugar did you put in this thing? It's so sweet it makes me want to punch a wild boar in the face.'

Giovanni is snorting with laughter. 'Yeah. I'm gonna go outside and thump a rhino right now!'

'Wrong terrain. Wrong continent,' I say, my mind instinctively wondering if Cam is getting my reference. 'Try sub-Saharan Africa.'

Amidst the mayhem, Carlton catches my eye and gives me a shy smile. But he stands looking at me for too long. Mimi puts a hand to his cheek and turns his face away. She then turns back to roll her eyes at me.

I look back at Giovanni who is wiping his face clean while also being distracted by Mimi and her cavorting unnecessarily with Carlton.

'Pay attention, Giovanni. Let's concentrate on the task at hand. So, names for our mocktail. Which one is your favourite?'

He is chugging the rest of the sugary mocktail down like an addict. 'Which ones did we have?'

'We have narrowed it down to...' I take a deep breath and try to swallow the embarrassment. My sister, Tyrone, my friends, my distant relatives, my work colleagues will all be watching this. 'Bols Deep, Bend Over Shirley and Up the Bum... I mean, Rum. Up the Rum.' I shake my head in disbelief. 'Which do you prefer?'

I know which one I don't prefer but it seems this joke is going to run and run.

Giovanni keeps remembering the previous challenge and it sets him off giggling again. He takes a moment to mull the choices over before grinning suggestively.

'Up the Rum. It has nice imagery, plus it will always remind me of you.'

And away he goes. He can barely stand up straight. He grabs on to the bench to steady himself. When his laughter subsides, he wipes his eyes with the back of his hands and looks at me with an intense expression. 'Oh, man. No other girl has made me laugh the way you do. You're hysterical.'

'Why thank you. That's just what every woman wants to hear. That she is hysterical.'

He starts chuckling again. 'Honestly. The more I get to know you, the more I think I'm falling head over heels in love with you.'

It's as though everyone suddenly stops what they are doing to look in our direction.

Silence. Plenty and plenty of silence.

Giovanni, suddenly self-conscious, is pulling himself together and waiting desperately for me to respond.

'CUT! SET UP FOR THE BLIND TASTE AND POINTS ROUND THEN WE'LL ANNOUNCE THE WINNER.'

Chapter 21

We are given a comfort break, while the crew set up the next part of the challenge. I do hope we don't have to actually taste each other's cocktails for real. I saw Brad drop a slice of melon on the floor and casually fling it back in the blender when he thought no one was looking.

'I guess we should talk,' Giovanni says to me. He looks as shocked as I feel. I bat him away and use the reverse psychology I've trained my whole life for.

'We all know you were just joking around. Puft! No one ever means what they say in here anyway. They just think they do.'

'Yeah, bro. Totally like yeah,' he says looking bewildered. 'And like no. You know?'

Nope.

'Totally.' I scuttle away from him to find the Tree House for a quick breather. At the last second, I risk a quick visit to the blind spot, desperate to hear what Cam has made of my performance in the mocktail challenge and also, to see what he thinks of this amazing bikini I am wearing, but a runner approaches, as I hurry along.

'If you're off to the toilets, can you not wipe any of the mocktail off your hair, face or bikini, please? It's for continuity. And Porscha says don't sit down or touch anything because if you stain it, she will...erm, she will...' The runner looks down to her clipboard at some imaginary notes. She flips a page up and down searching for ways to say Porscha has threatened to karate-kick me in the throat, kill me or worse.

I stop walking. 'It's okay. I understand. I'll go back to the outdoor kitchen.'

'And just one other thing?' she says, staring down at her notes and back up to me. 'You say you don't like pineapple. Is that an allergy thing because I'm pretty sure almost everyone put some in their mocktails... but also...' she looks back down, flicks a page over scans the text. 'Didn't we see you with a bottle of pineapple juice yesterday?'

Fudge.

'Erm, yes. Yes, you did. Because I do like it. But today, I'm just not feeling the vibe. You know?'

What complete and utter bollocks. She will never buy it.

'Okay. Cool.'

She walks away as though our entire conversation made sense.

After the tasting round, which got very, very messy, most of the islanders hurry back to the villa to take showers and get ready for the evening's firepit visit from Destiny. I hang back in the outdoor kitchen in the hopes that Cam might try to contact me in some way, even though I am sticky with mocktails. I'm just about to give up when I see a downcast Mimi walking out of the PANTRY. She glances at me and looks quickly away.

'What's wrong?' I ask her quietly. 'Did you get pulled by a producer for a chat?'

She looks warily around, whispering, 'Yeah. She had the cheek to say I'm being too needy towards Giovanni.' Her voice is almost inaudible. 'She wants me to make him jealous. But how can I? Now that he's in love with you?'

'No, he isn't. He was just messing about. Probably trying to make you jealous. I'm sure he'd love it if you pulled him for a chat.'

'Really?' Mimi cheers up a bit. 'In IRL I never usually have a problem with guys. But in here, everyone is so damn gorgeous, that I feel like if we all act like divas, it can't possibly work. There's no... what do you call it?'

'There's no hierarchy,' I say, warming to the subject. It's just like being back in the classroom.

'Yeah. It's like we are all the popular kids so none of us are the popular kids, if you know what I mean?'

She has a valid point. 'I do, Mimi. You all have such an unreasonably high sense of self-importance, requiring constant and excessive adoration that it's hard for any of you to stand out sufficiently.'

Mimi nods in agreement. 'Yes, that's it.'

'And, thanks to delusional parenting, you all feel that you deserve privileges and special treatment.' I give her a sympathetic look. 'So, of course, you're all going to be easily upset at the slightest criticism or knock back.'

'Like me with Giovanni,' Mimi says.

'You might feel your self-worth plummet like a lead balloon just because he looks at someone else. I see it in class, all the time. My students are incredibly needy for attention. It makes them very hard to be around.'

Mimi is making soothing, understanding noises. 'They sound like high maintenance bitches.'

'They can be,' I say.

'How old are they? These students you teach?'

'Eight years old.'

She looks surprised. 'They start young these days, huh?'

'By the way, you can't say in IRL. It's either in real life or just IRL.' I might as well help her with sentence structure and basic semantics.

'Sure thing. Okay. Good chat. See you later.' Mimi is unsure of how to handle this information overload and bolts off back towards the bar full of mocktails and I am left alone. I look swiftly around and down at my phone. Nothing from Cam.

I've never felt more like a teacher than I have since slip-sliding through the doors of this villa, but it feels nice. After I've brushed my teeth and wiped off all the dried juice from my face, I'm just heading back from a vigorous shower when I bump slap bang into Amber.

'Thank God. You have to help me.'

'What's wrong?'

'It's Mimi.'

'What about Mimi?'

'Come see for yourself.'

I quickly throw on the Love on the Island fluffy dressing gown. Amber takes my hand and drags me down a brightly lit corridor into the main bedroom. I'd forgotten how huge it is. It's more of a light aircraft hangar than a bedroom. There are double beds as far as the eye can see. There are suggestive pieces of fruit-themed art hanging over each one. Aubergines and so on. Amber raises her arm and points down the room. Mimi is bouncing from bed to bed like a five-year-old. She's squealing nonsense, and high-fiving people who are lying in bed trying to rest.

'We're so sick of her. It was bad enough that we were up through the night. Then we were forced to wake up and 'do' breakfast even though most of us had only just had supper, and now we've just done back-to-back filming of two challenges that have basically put most of us in a sugar coma. We're just so disoriented, we have no idea of whether we're coming or going.'

Amber looks exhausted. They all look exhausted.

I watch Mimi leap on top of Carlton to twerk in his face. Then she moves onto Binky and does the same. Now, she's demanding they all hug and twiddle fingers with her. She's reaching out her arms as though she's Madonna on stage reaching down to touch fingertips with her fans. Mimi has the look of a spooked horse. I recognise a mammoth sugar rush when I see one. I hope I'm not around when she crashes.

'It's like watching a sexually incontinent puppy. But Amber, what do you want me to do about it?'

She looks at me as though it's obvious. 'You're the teacher. You tell her to stop it. She'll listen to you.'

'No, she won't. I'm not that sort of teacher.'

'What sort of teacher are you?'

The wimpy sort who is fine with children but when it comes to authority figures, does what she is told, even though she knows she is being taken advantage of. That sort.

'Please,' pleads Amber. 'Say something. She has been like this for over an hour. She's so desperate for Carlton or Giovanni or someone to find her likeable. I feel kinda sorry for her.'

She's right. Mimi will end up having a catastrophic breakdown if she carries on like this. It's just like after lunchtime when parents pack the lunch boxes full of breakfast bars, bags of sweets, chocolate bars and a token piece of fruit because they've forgotten to make anything healthy for them to eat. It makes them high as kites. Plus, it's as though she's forgotten our entire conversation from earlier about self-worth.

'MIMI,' I bellow down the room.

Everyone looks up with startled expressions.

'COME HERE!' I boom at her, amazed that she stops bouncing, climbs off the bed and walks gingerly up to me. 'Can I have a word?' I say in a low threatening tone. It works like a charm on my deranged psychopaths in Year Three. 'Outside, please.'

She nods meekly as I step aside to allow her through first. I can see everyone else breathing a sigh of relief.

Amber mouths, 'Thank you' and skips back to join the others.

We walk across the garden to the All The Feels secluded area, and sit down. 'What's going on? Are you okay?' I say, switching to my nice soft teacher voice.

I take one look at her crumpled face and instinctively throw my arms around her. She bursts into tears and starts wailing into my shoulder.

'I'm... I'm... I'm...'

Insane? A fresh stream of tears prevents me from finding out. I rub her back gently and make soothing noises.

'It's okay,' I say. 'It'll all be okay.'

Mimi straightens, trying to wipe her face with her arm. The tears keep flowing, taking her make-up with them. In that moment, she reminds me of me. I cast my mind back to Lois comforting me night after night in the aftermath of our precious mother passing away.

'Hey, don't cry,' I say to her. 'I know we're all here to find love, but you know what is much better than that?'

Mimi sniffs and shakes her head. 'No. I don't know.'

'You are surrounded by badass women who care about you. No matter what happens with the guys, we have each other, right?'

Mimi is looking at me as though I have two heads.

Lois's goodbye words come flooding back to me. 'We have each other's backs. Life is all about friendship and family, is what I'm saying. My sister told me to come in here and forget about the pressure to be popular, just be yourself and have fun getting to know people.'

Then Mimi lunges at me, scooping me into a hug. She is squeezing the life out of me and all I can see is a camera lens, hidden in a plant pot, reflecting the sun.

'So, no more bottling things up. You have friends here,' I say, keen to end the conversation. 'Friends who will listen and help.'

Mimi sniffs up the last of her tears. 'I'm just so terrified of being rejected.'

There goes the voice of our generation.

I hold her at arm's length and look her straight in the eye. 'Why? I mean, I know it's unpleasant. I have been rejected so many times from jobs, from guys, from social media. I have like NO followers but, Mimi, that's just life. What makes it feel so terrifying for you?'

She stops to think. 'I'm not sure.'

'Look, the way I see it is that every rejection is a lesson learned. I tell my class to look at it as an experiment to be a better person. We can't all get into the football team. We can't all be Head Girl. We can't all go through life winning all the time. That would be weird.'

The camera lens is still winking at me, making me conscious that all of this is potentially broadcastable.

'Erm, life is full of surprises. We just need to embrace it and be as resilient as we can. If you never try, you'll never know. And at the end of the day. You. Are. Worth. It.'

I sound like a shameful rip-off of Chris Martin if he was doing a TikTok hair commercial.

Mimi agrees. 'Libby, you are so right. No more trying to be someone I'm not. It's not a popularity contest. I am enough. No more trying to get their attention.'

It's precious moments like these that make teaching so worthwhile. Then her phone trills making us both jump.

'I GOT A TEXT!' she screams at the top of her lungs. She leaps up waving her arms in the air and runs off round the garden, bellowing for everyone to join in. I see her running into the villa screaming, 'I GOT A TEXT! I GOT A TEXT! WE WON THE CHALLENGE! WE WON IT, CARLTON!'

Well, at least I tried.

Everyone pours out of the villa with their hands over their ears. Mimi clearly did not listen to a bloody word I said. She's still waving her arms in the air even as we all stand around waiting for her to stop screaming. Thankfully she runs out of steam, and breathlessly tells us that her prize is a round of mocktails for everyone tonight.

It's immensely underwhelming. I flop down on a giant beanbag. I must go and get ready for this evening. My hair is still wet and hanging down my shoulders. It will dry naturally if I'm not careful. And I have no make-up on yet.

'Can I grab you for a quick chat?'

I look up into the earnest face of Carlton who plonks himself down next to me. For a committed loner, I haven't been pulled for a chat so much in my life, and I have to admit, it feels nice. It feels nice to be confided in and considered a confidante. It feels especially nice to be desirous and to be desired. I am experiencing a whole plethora of emotions I haven't felt in a long, long time.

'Help me,' he pleads. 'I can't take any more of her.' He points to Mimi.

'It's okay. She'll probably settle down once the twenty kilos of sugar in her system dissolves. She's just excited over the text.'

He looks unconvinced. 'She lay staring at me for over an hour this morning. Just lay there. Staring.'

'And you're sure it wasn't an absence seizure or just sleeping with her eyes open? Or meditating very deeply perhaps?'

'I wish,' he says, grinning. 'She kept sticking her tongue out at me and winking. And because we've won the challenge, they're sending us on a date.' He tuts. 'But I'd rather be with you. I think we have a good vibe. And you're naturally beautiful and funny.'

Do not get sidetracked by this charming man and his wonderful comments.

'But I bet you have a great time with Mimi. And Amber is very nice. Have you thought about getting to know her? In fact, they're all really nice.'

He ignores my advice and shuffles closer. 'You have stunning eyes.'

'Thank you. You have ... erm, a very good forehead. Nicely shaped.' Polite but not too flirty. Solid middle ground as far as compliments go.

'Who's your ideal man? What do you look for?' he says, raking a hand through his thick, dark hair and blinking slowly at me with deep, brown, come-to-bed eyes.

'Good question. Before I came here, I didn't really have a type on paper,' I say. Carlton is manspreading and running his hands lazily up and down his thighs. He's gazing at me as though I'm telling the world's most interesting story. 'But now I'm here, I've realised that I value kindness. I love a man who is thoughtful and creative.' A picture of Cam's lovely face springs into my mind. 'I love soft, light brown hair with a natural curl. He has to have eyes that you can lose yourself in for days, and that tell a story, you know?' My gaze wanders off to the middle distance. 'Eyes that swirl with the worldly colours of blue and green, and flecks of gold like the sunrise. And when he smiles, it lights you up from within, because you were the one to put it there.'

My heart flutters with the warm breeze. I can feel a smile spreading right across my face.

'Don't you mean dark brown hair and dark brown eyes?' he says, leaning in with a grin.

'No. Not at all.' I'm lost in a daze. A delicious dreamy daze.

Carlton frowns at me but I am saved by my phone pinging. I look down at the text. It says, 'Do not react. Meet me in the PANTRY.'

'Sorry, Carlton. You're a lovely guy, but I have to go. Catch you later.'

I half-run, half-walk to the outside kitchen, trying to hide my excitement. Cam must need to see me pretty badly to risk it during the day. It must have been what I said. He must know I'm talking about him. My stomach is a hive of butterflies as I smile casually to the smattering of islanders wandering around. Compared to what you see on TV, it's really quite boring when we're not all at the firepit or doing a challenge.

I feel so nervous. I hope I'm not rushing Cam into something he isn't comfortable with. The kissing and heavy petting have been escalated because of our situation – me, forever in varying provocative states of undress, and him, forever in charge with swoonworthy capability. And of course, my feelings may well have been exacerbated by the forbidden sexual chemistry.

I wander into the PANTRY in time to see the fake wall creak open. It opens tantalisingly slowly. My heart is literally in my mouth.

I shake my hair out and adopt a relaxed but flattering pose, hand on hip, shoulder slightly dropped. I am aghast to see a woman's bony, long fingers with blood red nails beckon me through.

A cold sensation sweeps over me as I slide through the gap. This is not going to be good.

'We need to check your microphone. Apparently, it is faulty,' Porscha is screwing her eyes at me. 'I have checked the logs, and it appears there are times when it doesn't pick up sound.'

Keep calm. Deep breaths. I tell myself that this is no different to being in front of the headteacher when he says he is going to observe a lesson as a matter of routine protocol, when what he means is he has heard rumours that you have lost control of the classroom.

I take the pack off and hand it over. Porscha immediately inspects it before handing it back. 'If you ever disable this pack yourself, or do something that we can't see on camera, then you are out. Do you understand me?'

I look to the floor wishing I could stand up to her but she's a very intimidating authority figure with rhino-hide and a very bitter aura.

'Who do you really fancy? What game are you playing?'

My head snaps up. 'Sorry?'

'Your top three she demands. Carlton, Giovanni and which other one?'

'Which other ones are there?' I say, trying not to sound too facetious and at the same time give the impression that I haven't been fed all of the information beforehand. 'I mean, it's hardly like we've had a chance to get to know them in any great depth.'

'Does it matter?' she says sharply. 'They're all boneheads. Just start getting to know them and pick one,' she says, wagging a finger at me. 'I'm watching you like a hawk.'

Chapter 22

Two minutes later, I'm back in the outdoor kitchen pretending that nothing happened. I might have known Porscha would be up to something. She has told me that I will be doing a hashtag secret steal along with Amber. We are not to tell the others. We will be stealing two men tonight and leaving the others 'vulnerable'. She has more or less told me that, as a result, I will be sleeping back in the big bedroom with my new partner, or else. And reading between the lines, she wants to turn everyone against me.

I see Amber marching towards me with a distraught look on her face. 'Can I grab you for a quick chat,' she says.

We walk across the fake grass, past the pool, the giant bean bags and over to a nook with a sign hanging above it, 'Cosy Cuddles'.

'We should tell them!' Amber blurts out. 'I mean no. We shouldn't. Should we? I have no idea. What should we do? Tell them or not tell them?'

'When Porscha says "vulnerable" what does she mean exactly?'

'Like they could get dumped from the island or not dumped or dumped then brought back in as a Mi Casa Su Casa, or maybe as a bombshell, or maybe brought back in on a later series. Or dumped and never, ever heard of again, like social media lepers.'

That's no help. 'Maybe we shouldn't mention it to any of them, so that they don't worry. It's not as if we actually fancy any of the guys anyway, so it hardly matters.'

Amber is looking at me wide-eyed. 'Yes, it does matter. I fancy all of them. It's *Love on the Island*, babes. You need to stay coupled up or you're out.'

Cripes Almighty. With all the hoo-hah I'd almost forgotten what I am doing here. I'm curious as to what Amber's motivation is.

'Why does staying in the villa matter if we don't meet the love of our lives?' I ask her, knowing that this conversation will get cut if it's not bickering about boys. 'Is everyone just after the prize money, do you think? Did anyone come in here to find true love?'

'Probably but one hundred grand is worth putting up with the tiredness and the insane hours, and the way you can't just get out of bed when you want, isn't it?'

'Porscha has ordered me to come back to the big bedroom tonight,' I confide sadly.

'It's not so bad. The beds are huge enough to never touch. And we could always sleep together if you want. I am so over having to lie awake for hours until the Klaxon and the lights come on. Henri and I lay staring at each other for two hours in complete silence this morning.' Amber looks tired. 'It's so weird.'

'What about the way we spend six hours a day getting ready for a one-hour evening shoot?' I add in a hushed tone. 'And the team of spies and hidden cameras everywhere we go?'

I know they'll cut that bit but I'm past caring. So far, we've had breakfast at what felt like 2pm judging by the sun high in the sky. We had a bombshell at what might have been 3am because the moon and stars were shining brightly. The alcohol isn't even real. Now they're doing hashtag steals tonight at God knows what hour. When all I really want is to spend one whole day with Cam getting to know him properly.

I'm also on the brink of getting caught. Which means getting Cam into serious trouble. He has enough on his plate without me getting him the sack. I know exactly what it's like to lose your job and have no way of paying bills or supporting yourself. The panic affects your whole physical and mental wellbeing. It's awful.

A sudden realisation dawns. 'I think I'm good to go. I've had enough of it here,' I whisper, trying to cover my microphone.

Amber gasps. 'You like, seriously, wanna leave? After only a few days?'

It feels longer. A lot longer.

'Yeah,' I say, looking around. 'It's probably best if I do go. There's no one in here that has caught my eye anyway.'

Amber looks confused. 'Does that mean someone outside of here has caught your eye?'

Oh Cheeses! Did I just say something obvious?

I gulp loudly. 'No! Absolutely not. No way. As if. Puh!'

Amber starts smirking. 'Okay. Keep your secrets then. But tell me who you are going to steal tonight. I guess it doesn't matter now anyway.'

My heart is beating fast. I need to be way more discreet than this, especially with Porscha upping her surveillance on me. 'Honestly, I have no idea. They've all just blended into one big oily muscle-mountain. What about Giovanni for you? Or Carlton? Or the other three? Poor Marcel, Henri and Brad have been glued together on the daybed hiding from Mimi.'

Amber rolls her eyes. 'She is a bit of a handful, but I'd like to get to know Giovanni more, if you don't mind? I mean, I know he says he is in love with you but... is he really? Or was that the mocktail talking?'

'Be my guest. It was definitely all those E-numbers. I suppose I could steal Carlton then. He's the only other one who has shown me any interest. We'll just have to watch out for Mimi going nuclear.'

I just pray she takes on board my advice to be resilient.

'Okay. Agreed. I guess we should start getting ready.'

One look around the Hello Gorgeous dressing room tells me something is terribly wrong. There are clothes slung over every surface, make-up brushes, pots, bottles, tubes, big orange foundation sticks abandoned on the central getting ready station, hair pieces hanging over the mirrors and the air is heavily scented with sickly sweet sprays and perfumes.

'OMG. What has happened here?' Amber gasps. 'We've been ransacked.' Then she immediately inhales a sharp breath as Mimi stands in the doorway looking like a pantomime version of herself. Tears are streaming down her face, mascara smudging her eyes, two gashes of bright red blusher smearing her cheeks and sticky gloss highlighting already puffed-up lips.

'Help,' she squeaks, before launching herself trembling into Amber's arms. 'Help me.'

I immediately leap into action, fearing the worst – a catastrophic mental breakdown. 'Come and sit down,' I say gently. 'Tell us what's wrong. What happened to you?' I guide her to one of the stools and crouch down before her.

'It's Carlton,' she sniffs. 'He doesn't seem excited about our date tonight. I think he...' She bursts into a fresh stream of sobbing. 'I don't think he fancies me -hee -heee,' she wails, putting her head in her hands.

I take a moment to understand what she's saying. Where is her resilience? There has to be more to it than that. 'And you're this upset because?'

Mimi looks up at me, a look of annoyance briefly flits across her streaked face. 'Because when I spoke to him, he said he could... he could...'

Amber begins to massage her shoulders. 'Let it out, babes. Let it all out.'

'He said he could take or leave it. He said he wasn't bothered what we do for a date. I think he has his eye on someone EEH-EEH – EH - EH... else.'

Oh.

'Who could it be?' she asks us. 'Who?'

'Don't you like any of the others?' I say, trying to understand the extreme heartbreak on display *and* the lack of mathematical prowess. There are only four other women in the villa. Two of whom are stood right in front of her. It's not that hard to work out.

'I do,' she says, wiping her eyes dry. 'Giovanni. It's always been him.'

Amber gives me a brief guilty look. 'It's still early days, Mimi. I mean, it's totally normal for us all to pass the guys around as we get to know them. I barely know who is with who, we've swapped so many times. Who cares who we couple up with at the beginning, right?'

Who is with whom, but I'll keep quiet.

Mimi sniffs up her tears and digests what Amber is saying. 'Yeah. Cool. But just promise me that neither of you will go for Giovanni or Carlton.'

She is staring at us with pleading eyes.

PING.

We look at Amber as her phone flashes. 'Oh, shit.' She looks at me and opens the message. 'I GOT A TEXT!' she bellows. We follow her through the villa, out to the garden where everyone has come running to hear what awaits us.

'Islanders, it is date night in the villa hashtag look your best, hashtag dinner for two, hashtag secret steal.'

My heart sinks as they all jump up and down excitedly trying to work out what is going to happen.

Four hours later, and we are dressed to kill. The girls have gone all out for glamour and spindly heels. Our hair and make-up is perfect. We have all bonded over the secret to effective contouring and making your eyes pop. The atmosphere is electric with excitement. Only, Amber and I have to play it cool, and we are not altogether comfortable with the deception.

We make our way to the outdoor kitchen to meet the boys. We can hear them singing and shouting at each other and when we get there, they unexpectedly serenade us. They shuffle into formation and Henri, who I've barely had time to notice before, starts singing. He has a deliciously velvet voice and we are mesmerised. He's amazing. The other boys join in with a mixed degree of harmonies and they do a simple dance routine for us.

The girls squeal as though the Backstreet Boys have reformed and are thirty years younger. They seem smitten with the boys who, I suspect, have been elevated a notch up the heartthrob scale. When the song comes to an end, Henri's phone pings.

'LOV EELANDAIRS. MAKE YOUR VAZE TO ZEE FURPEET. EEZ TIME TO DO ZEE ULTIMOOT STILL.'

'What's he saying?' shouts Mimi. 'I can't understand a bloody word.'

Henri looks hurt which gives Kassy the immediate hump. 'Leave him alone, Mimi. I'd like to see you speaking French. He's doing his best. Just because we can't understand him doesn't mean you have to say it out loud.' She turns to Henri. 'DOES IT, ON-REE? YOU SPEAK THE GOOD ENGLISH. YES?'

Well, he certainly speaks better English than you, I think feeling sorry for him. Mimi looks affronted as we follow the boys to the firepit. The girl-power from earlier is evaporating like steam into the warm night breeze. We are surrounded by twinkling lights. The pool area looks amazing, lit from underneath. All of the flowerbeds are ablaze with lights of every colour. It is a brilliant feat of engineering and certainly helps us to feel like we are on another planet. Far, far away from the ordinary world. Where people behave in a rational manner. Where cares and worries are more than just simply about hair and make-up. I also have no idea what time it is or what day it is. I'm starting to forget how long I've been in here and where I came from.

Henri is lagging behind on the way to the firepit. 'Hey,' I say. 'You are a brilliant singer. Thank you so much for doing that. Did it take you long to practise?'

Henri breaks into a huge smile. 'Sank you, Libbee. Yes. Two dayz.'

Because I'm a teacher and therefore it's in my nature to show off any linguistic skills I may have, no matter how poor, I say, 'Je vous en prie.'

Henri's eyes light up. 'Tu parles francais?'

'No,' I say. 'But I'd love to learn. Life is a learning journey as I always say.'

He gives me an appreciative smile as we take our places. Music is piped through the speakers to announce the arrival of the goddess that is Destiny. We all watch her surreal, slow-motion entrance down the catwalk, through the massive silver heart, hair gleaming, tiny dress swishing around her slight, orange frame, huge unmoving fringe curled under to perfection, until she comes to a stop in front of the roaring firepit.

'Islanders, tonight we have a special surprise for you. Carlton and Mimi are going on a date!'

This is not news. Mimi has been squawking about it non-stop all day to the point that I'm pretty sure we all just want them to disappear and get on with it.

She repeats herself, 'Carlton and Mimi are GOING ON A DATE! YAAAAY!!'

We dutifully yay along with her. A movement along the bench where we are sat in a semicircle attracts my attention. It is Carlton. He is looking at me, and at the mention of going on a date, he rolls his eyes. Then, to my horror, Destiny catches him and turns her gaze to me as though I'm somehow complicit.

'Unless...' Destiny says. 'Unless someone secretly steals him away!'

Cue gasping and looking at each other as though we are shocked to our cores.

'Libby and Amber, please come and stand with me. As you know, tonight each of you must steal a man.'

We get up and I daren't look back at Mimi, who is whispering furiously with Binky and Kassy about how sly we are in not telling them. We turn to face the remaining islanders. To be honest, I can barely be bothered. I'm only interested in one man on this whole continent, and he's forbidden fruit.

My thoughts drift to Cam and I can't help wondering where he is. Is he watching me right now? Is he hidden somewhere in the villa or is he back at the production village listening to the crew bonking away? My heart flutters when I think of how, if I wasn't in here, I could be hiding in his trailer, or we could be in a holding villa. He would be chaperoning me and showing me the delights that Mexico has to offer while I lap it up eager to learn. I snap out of it.

I shouldn't be here.

It's just crossing my mind to announce that I'm withdrawing from the show, when Destiny barks at us, 'LADIES! Choose a man to steal. Who is your secret lover?'

Amber leaps straight in. 'I choose this man because he seems very sensitive and gives me a good vibe. He caught my eye from the start, and I'd like to get to know him more. I choose Giovanni.'

Giovanni looks pleasantly shocked. He gives me a look that is almost an apology. As though I would have picked him.

'I'm sorry you've missed out, Libby. Better luck next time,' he says cockily as he takes his place next to Amber. He gives her a cheeky wink.

Now they all think I fancy him. It's so childish. I will make my shock announcement.

Destiny booms, 'Ooh burn! Well, that's Libby told. Libby, how are you going to get revenge on Giovanni? He clearly thinks you still have the hots for him. Who are you going to steal to make him jealous?'

Everyone is looking at me. 'Erm, the thing is. I'm not sure I want to choose anyone because I think I'd like to leave the...'

'You can only choose one! CHOOSE NOW! WHO IS IT?' Destiny has a wild look about her and because I have a penchant for knee-jerk reactions around authority figures, I swiftly look across all of the islanders.

Mimi is looking desperately at me not to steal Carlton.

Carlton is almost begging me with his eyes to steal him, steal him real good. But if I go there, the can of worms will be horrendous.

I look at Henri and he smiles shyly back. 'Henri,' I blurt without thinking. 'I choose Henri.'

'Why?' says Destiny sounding annoyed. 'You forgot to tell us why first, and then the drum roll off-camera and the long stare into the middle distance and then the reveal.' She is speaking to me like I am in Year Three. She is trying to teacher-talk at me.

'Because he is French,' I say defiantly. 'And he is a great singer.'

'CUT!' says Porscha, stomping towards us. 'Do it again from the top. Libby, for Christ sakes, try and get it right this time, or we'll be up all night filming. It's not hard. Two reasons, stare into space and then reveal. Okay?'

She swaps catty looks with Destiny. This is so embarrassing. It's not even as if I have won the sympathy of my fellow islanders, because Kassy is looking as though I have just announced that I will also be taking her kidneys as well as her man. Binky is clinging to her Aussie hunk and Mimi is stroking Carlton's stubble and mouthing 'thank you' to me. Carlton has not taken his angry gaze off me since the announcement. I am in so much trouble now.

Amber gives me an understanding look, as Destiny takes her place to reshoot the scene. We do the big reveal and Henri looks suitably delighted when I choose him. I sigh in relief that it is all over.

'Islanders. We have two new couples. Libby and Henri, Amber and Giovanni. You will join Carlton and Mimi on a throuples dinner date.'

We all cheer and act excited, whooping and oohing.

'I've always wanted to be in a throuple,' yells Giovanni, causing us to laugh politely.

Destiny smiles broadly at us before swivelling around to face the others sitting by the firepit. 'Binky, Kassy, Brad and

Marcel...' Destiny powers down as she stares blankly into space. We wait for her to jolt back into action. She looks from one to the other. 'You are all now dumped from the island. Please pack your bags.'

What?

The silence that follows is sickening. None of us can believe it. We look at one another in confusion. This has got to be a joke. They can't do that to people. It's too cruel.

Binky bursts into noisy sobs as Kassy throws her arms around her. I run over to offer comfort, but Kassy looks up, her eyes full of furious tears.

'THIS IS BULLSHIT!' she screams. 'TOTAL BULL-SHIT.' She looks around at our shocked faces before screwing her eyes at me. 'YOU!' she points. 'HOW CAN YOU STEAL MY MAN WHEN YOU AREN'T EVEN INTERESTED IN HIM?'

She has the attention of every single person. You can hear a pin drop.

'This whole show is fixed. It's a complete con. I saw you kissing someone behind the villa.' Kassy stands up and waves her hand in my face. 'THAT'S RIGHT. I SAW YOU. YOU WERE KISSING A MAN. AND IT SURE AS HECK WASN'T ANY OF THESE GUYS!'

Chapter 23

We are all frozen to the spot. I look Kassy in the eye and try to brazen it out. 'Are you sure it was me?' I look around with a confused expression to see if anyone could believe such a tale. 'This isn't sour grapes because I chose Henri, is it? I can understand you're mad at me, Kassy, but this accusation has come at rather a very convenient time, hasn't it? Besides, there's no way I knew you would be dumped or else I wouldn't have chosen him.'

Henri frowns at me. I'm not exactly helping myself.

'I didn't mean it like that. You're very nice, Henri. We'd all love a chance to get to know you.'

I feel dreadful deflecting the truth, but it is essential I sow the seeds of doubt. It's fine me getting axed from the show but not fine if Porscha does some digging – even a light scratch on the surface – and finds out the mystery man is Cam. I'm certain she would sack him rather than let him be with a woman who wasn't her.

'I see. So, you would have chosen MY Brad? What a traitor!' Binky yells at me. She too is excessively livid at being dumped from the island and is acting as though it is all my fault.

How am I enemy number one all of a sudden?

'KEEP ROLLING,' shouts Porscha running towards us with her head turned at a sharp angle towards a nearby bush. 'This is pure car crash. Stay on Kassy, and then keep switching between her and Libby.'

Two camera operators, dressed in black like a pair of snipers, peep out from behind the bush giving Porscha a thumbs-up as she passes by, one hand to her earpiece, the other pointing here, there and everywhere. 'Good. Camera five and six,you stay with Carlton and Giovanni. Twelve, you stay on Henri and, camera eleven, you pan out to the whole group. Can we get aerial in here pronto? Move it, people. Move it!'

So much is happening right now. I scan the scene. Destiny is smoking a cigarette and talking to one of the assistant producers in hushed mumbles. They keep peering over at me and then quickly back to each other. Porscha is running from bush to bush to make sure the snipers know who their targets are. Runners are fiddling with lights and big furry microphone booms. And Kassy and Binky are openly sobbing. Brad and Marcel are having their backs slapped and doing manly 'bro' hugs with fist bumping and promises of seeing each other on the outside.

'I need my vape back,' Kassy yells to one of the runners. 'Then I'm going to the Beach Hut to tell the whole world what a fucking fix this all is.'

'I'll come with you,' agrees Binky. 'It's an absolute fucking disgrace. You all should be ashamed of yourselves. Treating us like easy meat.' She sweeps a furious glare around the area while all the runners and producers do an excellent job of professionally ignoring her. She spots Destiny sucking away on her ciggie. 'Unless, Destiny, hun. Is there any chance I'll get picked to come back on as a bombshell?'

Destiny throws a sympathetic glance towards her and shrugs.

'I will go to the Beach Hut too.' We see Mimi, not one to be left out, wading into the slanging match. She puts her hand on her hip. 'After all, she nearly chose Carlton, and it could have been me being dumped. I'm so traumatised right now.'

'I didn't nearly choose Carlton!' I say. 'You specifically told me to leave him out of this, so that you could have him.'

Oops.

It is now Carlton's turn to look livid. He yells to Mimi, 'You deliberately ruined my chance of happiness with Libby just for your own selfish gain?'

Mimi visibly gulps. She has lost her words. Then she looks at me. 'She didn't want to steal you anyway. She said she wasn't interested in any of you. You're all just one big oily muscle-mountain to her.'

All the men turn to stare at me.

'No. Of course you're not all one big oily muscle-mountain.' I blow my cheeks out. I'm never going to come out of this in a good light. 'I think you'll find that I've been taken way out of context. The truth is, I think I should be the one to leave the...'

'STOP TALKING! STOP IT,' cuts in Porscha. 'Libby, with me. NOW!'

I immediately do as I am told.

'JUST TELL US THE TRUTH,' yells Kassy as we pass her. 'WHICH ONE OF THEM WERE YOU SNOGGING BEHIND THE BINS?'

Oh Christ.

Apart from anything, the truth sounds far from classy. I am mortified.

The men look at each other with blank expressions before the denials and accusations begin.

Porscha all but manhandles me over to the PANTRY and through the secret door into the safe space. Before she has a chance to say anything, Cam bursts through the door. We trade looks.

'Cameron,' Porscha says with almost a sad tone. 'I think it's better if I deal with this alone. Woman to woman.'

'But I want to explain. It wasn't Libby's...'

'LEAVE US!' Porscha yells at him. 'I said I'll deal with it. You get back to make sure all the carnage is captured on film. I want tears, tantrums, meltdowns and everyone to take turns in the Beach Hut. We need to really capitalise on this situation. I want maximum emotional collapse. Get Kassy to reveal she was catching real feelings for Henri. Get him to say that he is devastated that Libby broke them up. And poke that trauma of Binky's. The one where her last boyfriend ran off with her dad. Or is that Brad? Poke something.' She gives him a sharp look. 'Don't just stand there. Do your job.'

Cam ignores her.

Suddenly Porscha's walkie talkie goes ballistic with people yelling that they need instructions as though she's ordered a military airstrike. While she's distracted, Cam smiles at me.

'Are you okay?' he says gently. He lifts his arm as though to comfort me, before thinking better of it.

I nod slowly. 'Yes, thanks. I think it's probably better if I leave the villa. I seem to be causing a lot of trouble.'

'Are you sure?' he says, giving me a tender look.

'Yes. I'm sure.' I give him a shy smile. I hope he realises I am giving up the show to spend my last few days with him.

'Well, you've certainly been a big hit on the show,' he says. 'You're really something special. You don't just light up the screen.'

My heart skips a beat.

'And you know, you could go on to win it.'

'Cam,' I say, my voice barely audible. 'That's not the reason I came here.'

Instantly, he gets my drift.

'DON'T MIND ME, WILL YOU?' screams Porscha, causing us to jump. 'Cam, back to work. NOW! Unless you'd like to admit to something? Or maybe Libby has something she wants to get off her enormous chest?'

It sounds like a threat. There's no way I can drop him in it. I will take our secret to the grave. It was in the blind spot.

It's Kassy's word against mine. An upstanding member of the teaching community.

Cam shakes his head, sighing heavily and gives me one last look, his face a mask of fury. He keeps his voice calm and even. 'Porscha, Libby has formally requested to leave the show. Libby, you can go collect your things. I will meet you at the entrance. See you soon.'

I watch him leave.

Porscha reaches out, yanking at my microphone pack and switching it off. 'Now, listen to me. This... this crush that you have developed for a member of MY staff is not happening. You understand me? IT. IS. NOT. HAPPENING.'

My heart is hammering in my chest. She is bloody terrifying. I'm so sick of being bullied by authority figures like her. And to play with people's lives as though they mean nothing? I feel anger beginning to boil away deep inside me and from somewhere, I find my voice.

'No, Porscha. It is happening. I will leave this villa, and the show, and then I will be doing whatever the hell I want to do. And if that is to get to know a member of your staff after filming has finished then I will!' I stand folding my arms in defiance. My blood pressure must be sky high as adrenalin whooshes round my body.

She leans in, towering over me. My vow to leave the show and run off into the sunset with Cam is not landing well.

'I'll tell you what is going to happen. There's no way you are leaving this villa. You will stay in here where I can keep an eye on you. You are going to go back out there, and act all surprised at Kassy's outburst. Kassy is going to admit she made the whole thing up about seeing you kissing someone who is not in the villa. She will point the finger at Carlton. Mimi will become hysterical. That will reignite the whole love triangle which, by the way, has fizzled out now with your ridiculous crush on Cameron.' She shakes her head at me, throwing up her arms in frustration. 'Such an inconvenience. We had to re-edit a whole episode.'

My jaw drops to the floor. It sounds awfully scripted to me. And she hasn't listened to a word I've said.

'I want to see you flirt with Carlton in front of Mimi to make her jealous. She will provide some much-needed entertainment for the nation, and you will play the part of the callous British villain. Which is why we flew you all the way to Mexico in the first place.'

I stand tall. 'No. I won't do it. I'm leaving.'

I'd like to see her try to stop me.

'Okay. If you leave the show, then I will fire Cameron.'

What?

Porscha looks deadly serious. 'Not just that. I'll badmouth him to all the networks. He'll never get another job in TV production. And it'll be all your fault.'

Porscha looks at me with daggers in her eyes.

'You wouldn't.'

She raises her eyebrows. She totally would.

'If I so much as suspect that you are communicating with him in secret, I will sack him and I will edit this show to make sure neither of you ever work again. You're a teacher, right? Who will hire you after they've seen you cussing live on TV and sleeping with every single guy in here? We go out to over ten million viewers. Including the UK.'

I gulp. 'But that's not true. I never swear. Well, just that once. And I'd never sleep with anyone, especially not on TV.' I'm starting to panic now. I've seen the show. I've seen how misrepresented they can make the islanders seem. I'd be just another bitter islander that no one would believe because the damage would be done. There's no smoke without fire.

We lock eyes. Hers are hard and full of mal-intent. Mine are full of panic and worry for mine and Cam's professional futures. I feel faint and reach out to steady myself.

'You have ten seconds to decide,' Porscha says coldly. 'Are you in? Or out?'

I am struggling to know what to say. 'So, let me be clear. You are threatening to ruin my career if I leave the show?'

'Correct.'

'And you are threatening to ruin Cam's career if I have anything to do with him, romantically or not?'

'Correct. You are not to encourage him with this childish crush you have developed. Do you not think we see this all of the time? He is a nice guy. Why get him fired just because of some unrequited feelings you have for him. Poor man. Such a shame for him to suffer because of your selfishness.'

'That isn't... that's not how it... you're wrong. You can't do this. You can't blackmail us like this.'

'I can and I am. You signed all your rights away before you came here. It's all in the small print,' Porscha lets out a bored sigh. 'Your time is up. In or out?'

Oh my God. I feel so confused. I wish my sister was here. All of a sudden, I yearn to be back home. Back at home with her and Tyrone, laughing and joking, hanging out, watching films. My simple, safe life.

'What if I leave quietly? I leave tonight. I don't see Cam ever again. He keeps his job, and nobody's careers get damaged?' I plead.

'Don't try to haggle with me and stop telling me how to do my job. We've had double the viewing figures since you appeared on screen with your ridiculous and pathetic carrying on. For some reason, the public seem to like your car crash approach to life.'

Oh God. Has the whole world been laughing at me?

Porscha flicks her shiny mane of red hair over shoulder and leans towards me. 'I'll spell it out for you. More viewers means more sponsorship. More sponsorship means more money. More money means another series. Simple. Now answer the fucking question. In or out?'

I lower my head. Every instinct inside me is to fight back but this seems like an impossible situation. The gamble that I leave, and she ruins our careers, is too high a risk. I need more time to assess the situation to find a proper solution.

'I'm in,' I say, looking her square in the eye. 'But you have to promise not to sack Cam. None of this is his fault. He hasn't done anything wrong. You're right. I tried to approach him... but he never... he's very professional. There's nothing going on between us.'

Porscha tries to weigh up whether I'm telling the truth. It will suit her to imagine that I came onto Cam, and that he is not interested in me.

'Done. I don't want to see you two within a mile of each other. Is that clear? Now, slap a smile on it because you have a hunky French man to drool over. I expect you to make

Carlton and Giovanni jealous but not a word to Amber or Mimi. Not that they'd figure it out, the empty-headed bimbos.'

I feel sick.

'And by the way, you will be sleeping in the communal bedroom with the others from now on. No more being a hermit. It's time to be a team player.'

Chapter 24

As soon as Porscha hands me back the microphone pack and leaves, I burst into tears. I smother the microphone to disguise my noisy sobs.

I feel powerless.

My tears are barely dry when I hear an almighty commotion outside. Everyone seems to be arguing with everyone else.

I wipe my face with a nearby tea towel and step cautiously outside. All the islanders are shouting while the two girls and two boys in the throes of being dumped on national TV drag their cases to the huge heart. They are being forced to go back the way they came, minus the huge hopeful smiles they arrived with.

Amber looks distraught. Mimi looks bewildered while Kassy and Binky are forcing smiles onto their tear-streaked faces as though they have clearly been ordered to battle through it.

'EVERYONE CALM THE FUCK DOWN,' bellows Porscha. 'I think you're all forgetting this is a game. A FUN game to win one hundred thousand dollars. ONE. HUNDRED. THOUSAND. FREAKING. DOLLARS. Can we all remember that, please?'

There's a fresh burst of tears from Kassy. 'I wanted to win so much.'

'And you still might,' Porscha says, an evil tilt at the corner of her lips threatening to lift that tight smile of hers. Binky and Kassy brighten almost immediately throwing her an optimistic look.

'It's a game,' Porscha repeats. 'Anything could happen.'

We all take a moment to digest this new information.

'Is she saying they will both come back to the villa?' whispers Amber to me.

'I hope so,' I whisper back. 'I really hope so.'

The mood instantly lifts. The boys start high-fiving and 'bro-ing' like mad. Suddenly we are air-kissing, and we are lifelong survivors, in it together like The Squid Game or World War Two.

'We'll never forget you. Hope to see you very soon,' Binky is yelling forcefully over her shoulder. 'I've had the best time ever. Let's keep in touch. Best friends for life.'

'Me too,' croaks Kassy. She's done so much angry yelling and screaming that her voice is knackered. 'It's been the greatest time of my entire life. I'm so sad to leave you all but at the same time I'm so happy. I miss my...'

We wait for her to think of something.

'I really miss my dog.'

This provides a much-needed excuse for us to ooh and aah and console her and request that she gives her pooch big hugs from us, because even though we all know she doesn't own a pet, we would want it to know we care if she did. She gives me a hard look on the way out, which pinches at my conscience.

'See you soon,' she says almost under her breath. 'I know what I saw.'

Another stab to my conscience.

We wave them all off and look baffled at one another as the remaining six of us make our way back to the firepit. None of us know what is happening.

'SO, WHO IS READY FOR THEIR ROMANTIC DATE?' bellows Destiny, emerging suddenly from behind a bush, causing Mimi to scream with fright.

The warm breeze lifts Destiny's fringe, like the flaps on a Boeing 747, to give us a rare glimpse of what lies beneath. She is looking wild-eyed and positively coked up to the eyeballs. It is very clear that we'd all forgotten she was still here, and that we would be required to do more filming. My soul droops at the thought of going on a date. Henri looks over at me with an almost apologetic smile and shrugs his shoulders.

'Are the four islanders who just left really out out or will they be coming back in in?' I ask Destiny who looks expressionlessly back with a nonchalant shrug.

'FIREPIT!' Porscha yells.

We gather round the firepit so that Destiny can bring some energy to our flat and demoralised demeanour. 'Islanders. You three couples will be happy to know that your dates will be voted on by the public.'

This is news to us.

'And the couple voted to have the most chemistry during the date will spend a saucy night in the Romantic Hideaway. YAAAS!' Destiny yells, encouraging us to get excited and start waving our arms around as we sit there.

My mind switches instantly to panic mode while the cheering goes on around me. This is the same Romantic Hideaway that Cam showed me on the virtual tour. The room with walls and floor covered in fur for maximum comfort, whichever way you choose to have sex, upside down or back to front. The room with the love swing hanging from the ceiling and the suggestive objets d'art placed on the bubble-gum pink shelves. The room with the sex toy cupboard where Cam hid a massive blue rubber vibrator with flat batteries because he was too busy having fun with me, he forgot to replace them.

Right, I have a game plan. And the game plan is to have the worst date humanly possible, resulting in the fewest public votes.

Henri turns to look at me with his shyly confident smile and whispers, 'Zee French make zee best lovers. I will make sure we win.' He taps the side of his nose.

Not on my watch we won't.

We are glued to Destiny as she reveals what type of date we are going on. 'We asked the public what type of dinner date they wanted to send you all on. They had to choose between a romantic three-course candlelit dinner al fresco on the beach.'

We all cheer.

'Or a romantic picnic by torchlight in the wild beating heart of the Yucatan jungle.'

We let out a less enthusiastic cheer.

'Or a romantic time potholing down a nearby haunted mineshaft with a packed lunch and a bag of crisps.'

Silence. And plenty of it.

'And the public voted for…' She touches her earpiece and proceeds to stand staring into space for a count of ten seconds, rather like an AI robot powering down.

We are all quite spooked when she jerks back to life and reveals where we are going.

Twenty minutes later, we are dragging ourselves back to the main villa. Morale is at an all-time low.

'The public must really hate you,' says Mimi giving me a sympathetic look as we make our way from the firepit back to the main villa.

'Or they hate all of us,' I say, trying to counter the argument. 'What makes you think it's just me?'

She stops to put a hand on her hip, tilting her head. 'Purleese, girl. You've done nothing but get people dumped from the villa since you got here and you've like, stolen every man you can get your hands on.'

'Not true,' I say. 'Besides, the public might be genuinely interested in Mayan industrial history.'

'At least we won't get eaten by tigers,' says Amber, trying to look on the bright side. 'I'm not sure I could cope in the jungle when it's dark. I hate the dark so much.'

The thought of my recent trek into the jungle with Cam makes me smile. 'Wrong continent. Right terrain.' I say almost to myself. 'Although, I'm fairly certain it will be even darker down the pothole.'

Ambers bursts into tears. 'I can't do this. I'm off to the Beach Hut to tell the world about my dark phobia.'

Mimi tuts. 'How convenient. I have a fear of rope, but do you hear me bleating on about it?'

It takes all of five seconds before she runs after Amber. 'Amber, honey. Babe. I'm here for you. Let's do the Hut together.'

I stare after them.

Porscha will make extra sure that I won't be seeing Cam while I am in the villa. My heart droops at the thought. He is the only thing about being in the villa that sparks joy. Everyone in here, with their flip-flopping allegiance, seems to have a hidden agenda and would gladly throw me under a bus to win the one-hundred-thousand-dollar prize money.

When Amber and Mimi return from currying favour with the nation, we go to the dressing room to take our make-up off, and discuss the shock of tonight's events.

'I think we'll see them again. And even if we don't, then I'm sure they'll have a great time on the outside,' mulls Mimi. 'I bet they come back in as Casa girls. Maybe the boys will come back in too, but to be honest they didn't exactly rock my world. I can't even remember their names.'

I shake my head in despair.

'Giovanni told me that he heard Carlton telling Henri that he was going to say that he's open to having conversations with all three of us. He doesn't want to tie himself to one girl as it is still early days,' Amber says as she wipes off her heavy foundation and bright pink lip gloss. She looks innocently over to Mimi. 'I think it's only fair that I talk to him if he pulls me for a chat.'

'Girl, why would you say that to me? You know I have my eyes on Giovanni and Carlton.'

'Hold on, girl. You can't claim all the guys and expect us not to give them a chance. Carlton is clearly not into you. He made a strategic decision.'

I'm immediately suspicious. It would be just like Porscha to force us girls into a war over the boys.

'For your information, Carlton told me that he wants us to be coupled up because he is sick of Libby leading him on and then dumping him at the last minute. I wouldn't call that strategic, would you?'

'That is literally the very definition of strategic. Isn't it, Libby?' says Amber.

'Divide and conquer, they call it,' I say.

They eye me dubiously.

'What is?' Amber says, looking a bit guilty.

'What we're doing. They have us bickering like schoolchildren when really what we need to do is learn to trust each other and unite against them.'

Amber stops vigorously moisturising and Mimi puts down her face wipes, as the penny drops.

'What's the plan?' Amber asks, coming in close.

'I say we sleep in separate beds tonight. Make a point. If those boys think they can play us for fools, they have another think coming.'

I hold my breath and wait to see how this idea lands. I will do anything not to share a bed with Henri.

'Agreed,' says Amber.

'Totally,' says Mimi. 'Although I might start off in bed with Carlton, touch his weiner and then when he gets excited, I will sneak off to the spare bed. I might even give him a full hand job just to make sure he picks me to couple up with.'

What is she not getting?

'No. That's not what we're trying to do. In fact, it's the opposite of what we are trying to do, Mimi,' I say sternly. 'Do not give Carlton or anyone else a hand job. We are trying to play it cool so that they know we are not to be manipulated.'

Mimi looks disappointed. 'Okay, then.' She stands up to reveal that she is wearing a highly provocative skimpy, black, lace negligée with cut-out bits and a balcony bra that is all but throwing her breasts in our faces. She twirls round so that we can see there is nothing at the back. Whatever string is between her butt cheeks is firmly hidden or invisible.

'What are you wearing?' gasps Amber, her eyes popping out of her head. 'I thought we were doing the opposite of whatever you are doing?'

'I'm showing the boys what they are missing. Isn't that the plan?'

'Well, if you're doing that, then I will too,' says Amber rooting through her case and pulling out slips of lace and thongs. 'Got it.' She holds up a tiny leopard print see-through mesh onesie the size of a baby's sock and stretches it out.

'You do you,' I say wearily. With no Cam to impress, I couldn't care less. 'I'm going to wear the least attractive nightwear I can find.'

I lay my case down flat and open it up. There lying neatly folded on the top is a t-shirt with a picture of one solitary pineapple hanging from a plant with a caption 'Hang in there'. I stare at it before gingerly picking it up. I hold it close. 'I'll wear this.'

Cam is sending me a message; I just know he is.

A few minutes later, after Mimi has doused herself with sickly sweet perfume, we stand admiring ourselves in the floor length mirror. Amber and Mimi look spectacular, like Victoria's Secret models.

'It feels as though you both should be wearing wings, killer heels and carrying whips,' I giggle.

'And I like your choice of outfit,' says Amber. 'It's very statement. Very elderly woman in a care home.'

We all start laughing at my oversized 'Hang in there' t-shirt over baggy striped pyjama bottoms, also two sizes too big. Only my neck is visible.

'Now, stick to the plan,' I tell them. 'Nobody is getting a blow job. Not on my watch.'

We get a slow clap from the three boys as we enter the huge bedroom and parade down the central aisle between all the beds. The boys are whooping and cheering, especially at Amber and Mimi who do look absolutely stunning. They both make an extravagant show of walking like catwalk models, arms swinging and every few steps they stop and twirl to show off their amazing figures. Henri looks gutted when I come through the door dressed like his grandad. Then as we pass by and make our way down to the bottom three beds and get in them, the cocky, self-assured expectation rapidly disappears from their faces. Suddenly the whooping turns into moaning and huffing.

None of us have a clue what time it is, but the lights go off very suddenly, and before I know it, the boys are all snoring their heads off.

Living the dream is utterly exhausting.

Chapter 25

'Who in their right mind votes for potholing down a haunted mineshaft?' Giovanni says as we all climb into our harnesses the next day. We were woken at the crack of dawn to drive two hours through the jungle. We stopped off at a virtually abandoned roadside café for the toilets and breakfast, which was a plate of huevos ahogados which we were told was 'drowned eggs'. They were delicious but probably not what we should have eaten on such a bumpy ride.

'Zeez costumes are very, very unsexy,' says Henri, pointing to our regulation baggy boilersuits.

'It's cruel is what it is. Cruel,' says Amber looking genuinely upset. 'And these safety boots. I wouldn't be seen dead in these IRL.'

She must think we're all part of an elaborate hallucination.

'I'm covered in mosquito bites,' complains Mimi, regretting having tried to roll her boilersuit up into a short playsuit.

'They are getting everywhere,' shrieks Giovanni, swatting at his arms and legs. 'I'm sure they're inside my suit.'

I take out my trusty insect repellent and spray everyone down. I pass Mimi some lint doused in ointment for her to dab on her bites to calm them down.

While they all try to give me a grateful smile, they look miserable. The instructors, who look haggard and genuinely surprised that anyone in their right mind has booked this tour, explain that the mine is haunted with the souls of over two hundred miners who lost their lives digging for precious metals.

This deflates the mood even more.

While one of them starts to unload what looks like enough rope to circumnavigate the Earth at least twice, the other explains that his forty years as a search and rescue team leader makes him the ideal expert for a mission like this.

'I'm not going down there,' says Mimi, looking from the rings of rope to the dark entrance to the mineshaft. 'Oh my God! What was that?'

'What was what?' shrieks Amber.

'That,' Mimi yells. 'I saw a shadow. A ghost!'

'That's it. I'm not going in either. I hate the dark,' says Amber. 'I can't deal with it. I just can't.'

Both girls look genuinely terrified.

As I look at the boys and camera crew, it is very clear that no one is looking forward to this activity. I can't believe I'm about to do this, but someone is going to have to do a pep talk about facing your fear and the great benefits that result from personal challenge.

'Erm, listen,' I get off to a shaky start. It's difficult to find what the potential benefits might be of exploring a haunted mineshaft that looks about to collapse around us the moment we step foot inside. 'I'm sure it's perfectly safe. Come on, guys. We've got this. We can do it.'

'Yes, it is safe,' says the expert. 'This is why we have fitted each of you with an extra harness in case of a fall. You have a headlight in your helmets in case of power failure from the generator. You have no oxygen but try not to breathe heavily when you are down there. Take some spare rope as there are lots of unexplored shafts. Do not go in them or you might not come out. Always watch where you put your feet in case of snakes. And you have flares in case communications fail with the above ground team.'

I notice he is not wearing a harness himself. 'Are you coming down with us?' I ask hopefully.

'Jesus, no. Definitely not.'

'So, one of you will stay up here and only one of you will go down the mine with us?' I need clarity because I can feel my blood pressure getting high.

'No.'

This causes everyone to start looking at each other in panic. Even the camera crew start mumbling about not getting paid enough.

'We have a man down there already,' he says quickly changing his tune. 'He's a good man,' he adds, as though we are all worrying over nothing. 'He will secure the wooden beams and clear the rubble so that you can enter the forbidden chamber.' He crosses himself three times as though he is doing something ungodly. He shouts down the shaft and after it echoes a number of times, somebody eventually answers. It sounds very far down.

Oh, my word. This is not good.

'Ready?' he says.

'Was that our safety briefing?' I ask, shocked. 'Who has done the risk assessment on this? Who is designated first aider? Who has the emergency comms device? Is there a GPS tracker on all of our suits? Where is the designated meeting point, both below ground and above ground, should any of us get lost? What is the procedure in the event of a medical emergency?'

Everyone is staring at me in a hopeful manner. Perhaps we can avoid going down on health and safety grounds. However, the instructors look as though they are willing me to shut the fudge up. I am making everyone more nervous. And for the sake of great television and a big financial payout for the potholing experts, we must go down this hole in the ground.

'Ready?' he asks again. We all nod glumly. 'Let's go.'

After what can only be described as an appalling descent, involving Mimi breaking not one but two of her Shellac nails, Henri almost plunging to his death, Amber screaming all the way down and Giovanni bursting into tears, we all reach the bottom in one piece and set off to find the ancient Mayan relics that none of us give a single shit about.

'It feels like we have been walking for hours,' complains Mimi. 'It's dark and wet and horrible. And it's freezing down here. What's romantic about this?'

'It feels like we have been listening to your whinge-fest for hours too,' says Carlton sounding fed up.

We are deep within the mine and can barely make each other out. We are wearing thick padded gloves as the rock surface is jagged and slimy to touch in places where water is dripping down. Every few minutes, the instructor demands that we each call out our names by way of regular head count. Giovanni, recovered from the initial shock, has already played a practical joke on us and didn't say his name which caused mass-fretting. Our nerves are wound tight to snapping.

'We stop here to admire early Mayan digging tools,' says the instructor as we emerge into a poorly lit cavern.

Amber sniffs up tears behind me. She has been quietly crying since we set off. Giovanni is quick to comfort her. In the dim light, he puts a reassuring arm around her shoulders and hugs her in close. 'I've got you.'

It's very sweet.

'I wish someone had me,' moans Mimi, looking at Carlton. He has been stuck to Henri like glue, ever since Henri said he recently served for eight years in the French Territorial Army. At least we all feel a little safer. 'Oh my God, I'm going to die down here! I'm going to die, aren't I?' she suddenly shrieks.

'We're almost there. Air very thin,' says the instructor, sniffing the air loudly. He's almost invisible to us.

'My anxiety is through the roof!' Mimi bellows, clearly at the end of her tether. She is breathing very rapidly. She will breathe herself into a panic attack if she is not careful.

'Look at me,' I say firmly. I reach out to hold her by the arms. 'You have to control your breathing. The air is thin. You need to take deep calm breaths. They will send the right signals to your brain that you are okay, and everything is fine.'

Mimi looks scared to death. She shakes her head, 'But it's not fine. We are miles beneath the ground with tons of heavy rock above us. We are lost because we have been walking for hours and the instructor has no idea where we are going!'

The atmosphere suddenly shifts up a notch to major panic mode.

'Is that true?' cries Amber.

We could all do with some reassurance around now, but the instructor is slow to react. It serves as a tipping point. Mimi starts convulsing.

'I can't breathe. I can't breathe. I'm going to die. And it's all my fault. I wanted to come on this stupid programme to find love. But now I'm going to die instead. Crushed to death in this horrible orange boilersuit. The last thing

I'll ever get to wear,' she sobs. 'It's hideous. I'm so embarrassed.'

'Look at me, Mimi. Look at me. Keep looking at me.'

She tries to focus on my face, her eyes wild with fright. I make a snap decision not to tell her that the colour of her boilersuit should be the least of her worries because I hear a hissing sound that is definitely not a tyre deflating.

'Breathe,' I say, taking a deep breath in myself. 'In... and... out. In and ... out.'

The islanders gather around us, and we all start breathing slowly together until Mimi gets her breath under control.

The instructor holds out a flask of strong-smelling coffee. 'Have this. Calm you down.' He passes around six cups and gently pours a dark-coloured substance into each one. Steam rises with each pour, and we take it gratefully. We huddle together around a big torch that reflects off the rock to make the cavern even eerier than before. The slightest movement causes shadows to dance around the formations.

We sip the coffee. It's very sour-tasting and bitter but it seems to have an immediate soothing effect on all of us.

Carlton copies Giovanni and puts his arm around Mimi. He gives her what looks like a genuine smile. He catches me looking, and to my surprise, smiles at me too. I'm pleased he has stopped being so angry with me. Maybe it was seeing

Mimi in that ludicrously sexy negligée last night that has changed his mind about her propensity to moan on and her near-psychotic tendencies.

'Ah,' says the instructor, shining the light towards the cavern wall. 'There it is.'

We gaze at the rock in awe. There are paintings and markings. They are thousands of years old.

'That's the best thing I've ever seen,' whispers Amber.

We are quick to agree. They are magnificent.

'It's like those stick men are talking to me,' adds Giovanni, his eyes like saucers. 'Can you hear them?'

We listen to the breeze whispering to us. The images seem to be moving as the torchlight dances around.

I feel lightheaded. I sniff the coffee. 'What's in this coffee? I ask the instructor.

He shrugs.

'Whatever it is, it's got me as high as the Eiffel Tower,' laughs Henri, holding his cup out for a top up.

Oh, my God. No wonder we've all calmed down.

'I need a wee,' Mimi says, sagging against Carlton. 'I feel faint. I'm seeing things. I'm seeing ghosts all over the place. And those eggs are repeating on me. Where's the nearest toilet?' Her high-pitched squeak ricochets off every surface.

A voice comes from the darkness. 'If you need the toilet, you'll have to go back to the surface.'

My nerves are on end because I could have sworn that was Cam's voice. This drink is more potent than I thought. I nearly spit it out as he comes into view. He steps out from behind one of the camera crew who I'd totally forgotten were following stealthily behind in silence. My jaw is on the floor as they all start begging to go back to the surface with Mimi. Suddenly, all of the islanders need the toilet.

Like a drill sergeant, I listen to Cam bark orders to the crew, instructing the guide to take us all back to the surface by the quickest route possible. There's a huge cheer which causes some rubble to fall around us.

'Yes,' says the guide lowering his voice. 'We go now. Before the ghosts come back.'

As we make our way back along the pitch-black tunnels, I fall back so that I can walk with Cam. He has instructed the crew to switch off the cameras, pack them into the bags and buddy the islanders to make sure we get to the surface before the shaft falls down around our ears.

'I can't believe it's you,' I whisper, turning off my microphone. 'I just can't believe it.' I'm so overwhelmed to see him, or possibly a bit high as only lame repetitions are forthcoming. 'I just can't believe it. I. Just. Can't. Believe. IT.'

He looks sideways at me and, in the dim light, I see his eyes crinkle.

'How are you?' he whispers back. 'As soon as I saw you hadn't left the villa, I suspected Porscha had done something. She's refusing to speak to me. I came to find out if you're okay. And you're not... not in some sort of hostage situation.'

I nod quickly. 'You've come to rescue me?'

Cam puts a finger to his lips. One of the crew has turned round. 'Okay back there, boss?'

'Sure thing, buddy. We should be at the shaft entrance any minute now,' Cam says in response. This has the bonus of causing much relief and excitement.

Cam leans over to whisper in my ear. 'Do you still want to leave the villa?'

'Yes. Definitely.'

'When we get to the top, pretend you feel sick.'

'Okay. Why?'

'Trust me. I have a plan.'

I let out a huge sigh of relief. 'You do? I can't believe you'd come all this way down here for me.'

'I'd do anything for you,' he says quietly as we reach the entrance to the shaft. His eyes are twinkling in the torchlight.

My heart soars. That's the most romantic thing anyone has ever said to me. 'I can't let you risk your job for me. What if you get caught?' I whisper back.

'You're worth the risk.'

He is looking so intensely at me it's all I can do not to tell him that I love him. That I've fallen head over heels madly in love with him. He's so kind. So thoughtful. So funny. So heroic. So great to be with. I can't imagine being with anyone as perfect for me as he is. He gently strokes my cheek, and he looks about to say something when suddenly, a gust of stale air whistles through the tunnel, causing an ethereal shrieking sound.

'GHOSTS! I CAN SEE THE GHOSTS!' Mimi screams.

She's right. I can make out figures swirling around us. Huge twirls of something catching the light and disappearing.

'OH MY GOD!' Carlton is yelling. 'GHOSTS!'

I almost leap into Cam's arms. He clutches me to him as I hide my head in his solid chest.

'C'est de la poussière. Du calme! Du calme!' Henri is yelling.

'It's dust!' translates Cam, much to everyone's relief. 'It's just dust.'

Dust clouds swish around us forming shapes in the darkness. It is very, very scary. When we all take a moment to process, I lift my head from Cam's chest. I am still enclosed in his tight grip and my heart is thumping wildly. I inhale his scent. The lemon and woody aroma is a welcome distraction as I rest my face against him. I close my eyes to hear the beat of his heart. I feel the heat of his body.

'Two questions,' I whisper. 'One. Are you wearing body armour? And two. How many languages can you speak?'

His cleverness and unexpected talents are an enormous aphrodisiac, and I am inappropriately aroused considering our unique and terrifying circumstances thirty feet below the Mexican jungle in an abandoned mineshaft.

Cam tries not to giggle and tells me with his eyes that we are still trying to maintain a professional distance for the sake of the rescue mission.

'Put these on,' instructs the guide once we are safely at the base of the shaft. 'We will lift you up one by one. Check each other like at the beginning.'

'But I can barely see,' moans Mimi. 'What am I supposed to be checking?'

The instructor rolls his eyes and points to his metal carabiner loops and yanks on one of them. 'You no check properly, you die. Very simple.'

'I'll buddy On-Ree,' says Carlton quickly. 'Mimi, might be best if the instructor checks your harness.'

While everyone gets busy pulling at flaps and checking buckles are tight and secure, Cam turns to me. 'Let's get you checked over.'

In the darkness, my senses are awfully heightened because Cam is very much like a heroic action figure. His eyes meet mine and in slow motion he reaches for me, gently pulling each fastening. With each tug I find myself inching closer to him until we are only a few inches apart. The last buckle is by my pelvis. He gives it a strong tug. I feel that sexual chemistry swirling up from inside me. It's all I can do to keep a straight face. It is essential we do not draw any unwanted attention.

'It's not as fun as ziplining into the cenote,' he murmurs. It causes me to think back to the image of Cam getting out of the water like a Greek god, water dripping over his every muscle. I wonder if he is picturing me in my tiny two-shoelaces bikini.

When it's my turn, I linger on Cam's shoulders as I reach up to check the buckles. He reaches out to steady me, placing his hands gently on my waist. It causes electric sparks to shoot through me. Without taking my eyes from his, I slide my fingers lightly down his arms to check his body harness and clips. I hear him take a sharp intake of breath as I deliberately run my fingers slowly over his stomach and round to his lower back.

I want him. I want him real bad. My breathing is all over the place. It doesn't help that the air is so thin down here and making me feel woozy and lightheaded.

'Are you okay?' he asks. 'The air is so thin down here.'

The moment we lock eyes I realise it isn't the air. It's him. It's all him. He has such a dizzying effect on me.

Giovanni flicks me a quick confused look. I am instantly reminded that discretion is key. I step quickly back from Cam. 'So, erm, right. That's you checked and ready to go.'

When we eventually get to the surface, the team are in various states of well-being, gasping for fresh air, running into the jungle for the toilet – a designated clearing of mud - and piling into any truck they can, keen to get the hell out of here. Amid the chaos, Cam instructs the crew to stick with the islanders and travel back together.

'Tell Amber that you are feeling sick and are going to the toilet.'

I do as he says and run over to Amber as she's getting in the truck with Giovanni. 'Listen,' I say. 'I'm not feeling great. You go ahead and I'll hitch a lift back with one of the instructors. I think I'm going to be sick.'

Giovanni gives me a sceptical look.

'It'll be the eggs,' Amber said. 'And the ghosts. I've thrown up twice already.'

I pretend to retch, and Giovanni quickly slams the door shut. 'Okay. See ya!'

The truck roars to life and sets off. This causes a chain reaction with people bellowing names out, and instructions to 'GET A MOVE ON!'. Kit bags are flung haphazardly into the back of trucks and engines are violently revved as though we are fleeing a terrible earthquake.

When the convoy has left in a cloud of dust, I look at Cam, confused. Where is our transport? Why are we not fleeing with the others?

'It seems as though we are stranded in the middle of the jungle. Are we stranded in the middle of the jungle? What sort of rescue plan do you call this?' I squeak.

I don't care how good-looking he is, this is not a good plan. I look around at the dense jungle, the trees looming above us. The entrance to the mineshaft is making serious whooing noises and I can hear myself getting hysterical. 'What were you thinking? Are they coming back for us? How will we get out of here?'

Cam stands looking at me in amusement. It causes me to stop jabbering. His eyes move from mine to peer over my shoulder. He has a massive grin on his face.

'Oh man. I don't think I will ever get used to this.'

'To what?' I say, twisting round to see what he is looking at. My eyes nearly pop out of my head as I see a ghostly figure walking towards me. It has my face, my hair, my body. I steady myself on Cam and he is quick to throw his arm around me. I feel so light-headed and, for a second, think I am imagining it.

'Hi sis. Fancy meeting you here,' says Lois.

Chapter 26

We throw our arms around one another. It feels so good to hold her. I breathe her in, as I have been doing my entire life. Her energy becomes my energy. She squeezes me even harder and whispers, 'I've missed you so much.'

She takes one look into my eyes and says, 'You have questions. Me too.'

'We have to go,' says Cam. 'You can fill each other in on the way.'

Lois and I hold hands as we race through the clearing to the jeep that Cam has parked up. We set off immediately, both of us huddled in the back while Cam drives. He has to twist in his seat to reverse out. It's very tricky, so Lois and I wait before we launch into our mammoth Q and A. It gives me a chance to fully appreciated what excellent bone structure he has. The light bounces off his hair, his lashes and his impeccably shaped eyebrows. His DNA is truly magnificent. Like Angelina Jolie and her famously symmetrical face, Cam must be the world's only other human being to have such symmetry. There's nothing you would change about his face. It is all perfect. He is simply breathtaking. And he is willing to risk everything... just for me. How have I managed to land someone so magnificent, so courageous and so downright brill –

'Stop it. Put your stalker eyes away. You're being way too much,' Lois leans in to hiss.

This makes me blush even harder. Sisters! She's only been with me five blinking seconds and already she's criticising. I start giggling because of course, she's completely right. I'm like a giddy teen with a horrendous crush on a kind-hearted global singing superstar. When we swerve onto the dusty road track, Cam rams the vehicle into first and we race off. Every now and again, I catch his eye in the mirror causing me to blush, blink and clear my throat.

'How are you here?' I ask Lois. 'How come you're with Cam? What is happening?' I am so disoriented.

'Cam rang me as your next of kin to say you were leaving the villa. But I was already here at the airport because you had sent me a message,' she says. 'Anyway, we were waiting for you to leave the villa, but you never turned up. And the airline lost my luggage.' She rolls her eyes and does that throwing up her hands thing I do.

'What message?'

'The message. The one we planned before you left.'

'I have no idea what you mean.'

'You sent me the Chris Martin message.' Lois is frowning at me. 'You said in episode three "If you never know, you'll never try" line which is clearly code.'

'Code for what?'

Cam catches my eye in the mirror. I can't tell whether he thinks we are both insane, or whether it is just my sister that he thinks has lost the plot. I throw him a weak smile and try to get to the bottom of why my sister has flown thirteen thousand miles across the planet because she thinks I am incapable of toughing something out.

'The code that you need me to come and...' she lowers her voice. '... fix you.'

It's no use. I start howling with laughter. 'Oh, my word. Lois, you are such a bad liar. You have always wanted to come to Mexico, and you have been desperate to go on Love on the Island since the show started! Please don't use me as an excuse.'

Lois is the picture of guilt.

'Okay. I really wanted a holiday. But honestly, I do think you need rescuing from yourself because I am not kidding you, sis, that whole 'up your bum' thing still has me roaring with laughter. Poor Tyrone pranged his car on a lamp post, he was so busy laughing. Three days it took for him to eventually stop. You're an actual meme and you're trending on TikTok.'

Cam snorts with laughter. 'Sorry. I'm not laughing. I just got some... dust up my nose.'

I tut loudly. He's not the worst liar in the car.

'I appreciate you've come all this way but,' I say sadly, 'I can't leave the show yet. Porscha has threatened to...' I stop talking unsure I should be revealing this to Cam.

'What has she threatened to do?' Lois asks, shuffling closer and taking my hand. 'Is she bullying you?'

I avoid making eye contact with Cam in the mirror.

'No. I mean, yes. Kind of. But it's complicated.'

'Just leave. You've been on the show. You've fulfilled the contract criteria. Tyrone has been over it at work and all the lawyers say you can leave without any repercussions.'

My sister's face softens at the mention of Tyrone. 'Ah, tell him thanks,' I say. 'I miss him. I bet he's so jealous you flew out here without him.'

Lois grins. 'He's here! He's at the hotel. We've brought our engagement holiday forward. As in we've put it on the credit card. And those bastards owe me so many holidays, it's a joke. So, we'll drop you at the villa, pack your stuff up and we'll get you out of there. We'll stay on for two weeks and have a lovely holiday together!'

'I wish I could, but it's not that simple.'

'It is. Just stand up to this Porscha person. It's about time you learned to stand up for yourself.'

'I know. You're right,' I say in hushed tones. 'But I... can't. I have to go back and finish the show.'

Lois looks confused and leans over to Cam. 'I thought you said Libby was desperate to leave?'

'She's blackmailing you, isn't she?' says Cam, his voice flat. 'It's about me. She's forcing you to stay and is using me as bait.'

I nod. 'Sorry. She said she'd badmouth you to everyone in the industry and you'd never work in TV again. She also said she'd edit me to look really bad, and I'd never get another teaching job.'

'Oh my God. What a nasty bitch.' Lois turns to me. 'Give me your boilersuit and your hairband. And your muddy boots.'

'You can't be serious.'

She practically yanks the suit from my body. 'Hell, yeah, I am. I came all this way to make sure you are okay. I'm not going to let her get away with this.' Lois has steam coming out of her ears. 'I'll go in there and give her a piece of my mind. Your mind. I'll give her a piece of our mind.'

'How did you get to be so fiery? Anyway, it won't work. She'll still sack Cam and she'll turn a whole nation against me, and we'll both lose out.'

'Not if we get a proper plan together,' says Cam. 'I'm not a producer for nothing. Being creative with the truth is what I do.'

'We have approximately three minutes,' I say. 'There's no time to come up with a plan.'

'Okay. How about this?' Lois says to Cam, wiping some mud onto her cheeks and hair. 'I swap with Libby for one night to buy you and her some time to figure all this out?'

'That is a terrible idea,' I say.

Oh, how the tables have turned.

'Cam, will I get to meet Destiny?' Lois says, ignoring me completely. 'Is she as awesome as she comes across on screen? Is she really that orange in real life?'

'Lois, you can't pretend to be me just to go on the show.'

We all take a beat to let the irony sink in.

'Libby, let me do this. I swear nobody will notice.'

'I suppose it would be good to have the night to think about what to do,' I say, looking at Cam. 'What do you think?'

It appears Cam doesn't need to think twice about it.

'Hide under that blanket while I drop Lois off with the others. I can see them just up ahead. When all the trucks pull up outside the villa, Lois, you jump out.'

'Don't worry, sis. I've got this. Cam has told me about the blind spot and the secret meetings.' She waggles her eyebrows at me. 'Cam, meet me tomorrow morning. Oh, my God. I'm so excited. I'm going to be on telly!'

'That was such a fast emotional turnaround even for you, Lois. Rage to excited in less than a minute.'

'It's my trauma training. We learn to move on quickly. I never dwell on the past.'

Within minutes, we have pulled up outside the villa. I am safely hidden on the back seat of the jeep with a bag on top of me. I whisper to Lois, 'On a scale of one to ten how nervous are you?'

'About fifty-three,' she giggles. 'But I can't wait! See you soon. Give my love to Ty!' She slams the car door shut. A few seconds later, I hear Amber and Mimi yelling my name and, it all seems so surreal, as I hear Lois yelling back to them. The voices fade and Cam drives away.

After a short while, the jeep pulls over to a stop. 'The coast is clear. You can come out now. The hotel is in the opposite direction of the production village so we should be good.'

I climb into the front seat. Cam looks at me with those kind eyes of his. 'Thank you. Thank you for trying to protect me, Libby. I really appreciate it. But honestly, you don't have to. Porscha can do what she likes. I'm not threatened by her. I have a solid reputation as one of the good guys in this biz. Whereas she doesn't.'

'Oh. Right.'

'The only thing that does bother me is that she could hurt your career… and you.'

'Oh. Right.' My face is on literal fire. My cheeks are burning again. He could fry an egg on them.

'Listen,' he says, looking down at his hands on the steering wheel. 'I know I said that I wasn't ready for anything. But… I've fallen for you.'

'Oh.' And there goes that invisible force pulling me towards him.

Where are my words? Where? Where?

'I've never met anyone who makes me feel so… I just want to spend every minute of every single day with you.' He dares to look at me. 'I'm so excited when I'm around you.' He twists in his seat and gently cups my face. He looks lovingly into my eyes. 'I just feel like anything's possible. I don't care that we have an ocean between us.'

I can feel myself welling up. Tears are about to spill. I am so full of joy that I am going to burst.

'But I'd need to take things real slow.' He looks shyly at me.

He's so cute. Incredibly cool and handsome but also so, so cute. How is that even possible?

'Slowly,' I say.

'Sorry?'

Oh, look. I've found my words. 'It should be "take things slowly". It's an adverb.'

He raises his hand to smother a laugh.

'Sorry. I don't know why I do that. It's like a compulsive disorder.'

Why am I actively putting him off me? It's the gluten all over again.

'Oh, man. Am I going to regret this?' Cam asks, his head flopping onto the steering wheel. I can see he is dying to laugh.

'Yes,' I confirm. 'Yes, you probably will. In fact, I'm certain of it.'

Cam revs up the jeep and we head off to meet Tyrone at the hotel. 'I like you, Libby. I like you a lot. You make me laugh so much. I haven't been happy for so long. It kinda feels like... like you were sent to me.'

'Like we were meant to meet at this moment in our lives?'

He nods. 'Pretty much.'

'Perhaps you felt you'd lost something that you couldn't replace but now...'

'Are you Coldplaying me?'

'Yes. Sorry.'

'Okay. How insane are you exactly?'

'Insane enough. Let's just leave it at that.'

He puts his hand over mine and pulls a reassuring cross-eyed crazy face. 'Fine by me.'

I. AM. FLOATING. ON AIR.

Chapter 27

Once the excitement at seeing Tyrone in the hotel has worn off, we get to work like we're planning Mission Impossible 27. He wasn't entirely pleased that Lois, his fiancée, has gone into the *Love on the Island* villa and is keen to switch me back in.

'I knew she wanted to go on that show. I knew it,' he says with a good-natured but exasperated sigh.

'Believe me, there's no competition. She loves you unconditionally. She's obsessed. You have zero worries, Ty. She will not be interested in any of those boys.'

'And you'll be able to see her on camera immediately, rather than two days later when the episodes are aired,' says Cam setting up his monitors and laptop. He clicks a few buttons, and the villa comes into view from twelve different angles.

'That's so cool,' says Tyrone. 'Show me Lois.'

Cam zooms in to hear Lois talking to Amber and Mimi. All six islanders are still loitering by the jeeps and SUVs that brought them back from the haunted mineshaft. They all look dusty and fed up, except Lois.

'You have the same smile,' says Cam.

'Hey bro, don't even go there. You want to try living with them. It is so weird at times, especially when for a split second I'm not sure which one is which.'

'I'm the tidy one. She's the messy twin. Where's the problem?' I joke with Tyrone. I guess he must find it difficult at times. 'Don't worry. I will move out eventually, I suppose.'

Tyrone is quick to apologise. 'Hey no, Libs. That's not what I meant. I have no problem with it. If anything, you're much easier to live with than Lois.'

'I'm not bossy like she is,' I say.

'Or as indecisive,' he adds. Who could forget Lois's nightly forty-minute doom-scrolling to choose what to watch?

'And while I'm a much better cook, Lois knows how to suture wounds and make slings out of old shirts so...'

'She'll make me a great wife,' he says with a dreamy look in his eye.

Cam is pretending not to listen to us. Which is fine by me because it almost sounds like an interview for me being ideal girlfriend material for him. Although, part of me hopes to have Cam look like that about me some day.

I snap out of the fantasy to concentrate on the screen. Lois is mimicking my every move expertly, and looking like she is enjoying it. 'So, back to the plan.' I look at them both. 'Two things. How do we play Porscha at her own game, so that I can leave the villa on my terms without all the backstabbing and blackmail? And how do we switch Lois back out tomorrow without anyone seeing?'

'I'm not a lawyer for nothing,' Tyrone says. 'Backstabbing and blackmail are practically in the job description. Wait. What is happening?'

We watch the screens as the islanders are herded to the firepit to stand in front of it. They look bedraggled. And there, sitting round the firepit are ten very glamorous and attractive NEW Love on the Islanders. They are grinning away as though they know a secret the others don't. Destiny springs out from behind the bush with a gleeful pose.

'Old islanders, meet the NEW islanders!' she says, laughing. 'Look at the state of you all.' She starts laughing hard and encourages the new islanders to laugh along. I can see runners off camera waving their hands and yelling 'Laugh harder!' and 'Keep it going!'. The old islanders look confused as hell.

'Porscha has brought the new islanders in early to catch them out,' Cam sighs. 'Christ, I'm sick of her going behind my back all the time.'

PING.

Lois has a text. She looks about to burst with excitement. 'I GOT A TEXT!'

'She's always wanted to do that,' says Tyrone.

'Destiny, Destiny! I got a text,' Lois yells. 'Destiny, I think you are amazing.'

'Read it out then,' says Destiny in a patient tone.

'I love you by the way,' Lois tells her. 'You're the best presenter. And we all love you in England. You're totally famous over there.'

Destiny perks up. 'Well, let's hope all the UK viewers get voting for you to stay in the villa, Libby. Now, honey, how about that text. What does it say?'

'Old islanders. Get ready to fight for your place in the villa hashtag bring it on, hashtag best self, hashtag anything goes. Oh my God, is this for real?' Lois asks. 'What does it even mean?'

'It means, old islanders, that tonight you are going to have to earn your place here and seduce one of the new islanders into letting you stay.' Destiny has a huge grin plastered to her face. 'You'll be pulling out all the stops. Get your party piece ready!'

The camera pans out to the cocky-looking newbies sat looking like the cat that got the cream and then the worried glances of the oldies. Only Lois seems remotely up for it. The others all look increasingly deflated.

Tyrone groans. 'God, she'll love flirting up a storm in there. She better not do her party piece with any of them.'

Cam pulls a yikes face at me behind his back, and I try not to laugh. Lois will love doing her party piece on TV.

'Get your glad rags on. Party starts in one hour!' bellows Destiny.

'CUT!' yells Porscha making a beeline for Destiny who whips out two vapes and hands her one. They start chugging away like lab rats while all the islanders make their way over to the main villa.

'Look at the muscles on that one!' cries Tyrone. 'And Jesus, look at him. He looks like an aftershave model. I'm sure he's been on TV.'

'She'll be fine,' I say.

'It's not her I'm worried about,' he jokes. 'Lois will eat them all alive.'

We watch them all pile into the dressing room. It looks chaotic. New bodies, new cases full of outfits, and shoes scattered everywhere. They are jostling for space and the oldies are changing out of their boilersuits, as Lois subtly looks around for my case full of clothes. Cam and I trade worried glances.

'Did you tell her about the pineapple case?'

'No, did you?'

Cam shakes his head. At that moment, on screen, a runner enters dragging two ginormous suitcases.

'Hey Libby, your luggage finally arrived,' he says, dragging two familiar cases over to her. We see relief spread over her face as she thanks him and immediately pops them open.

'At least she has clothes to wear, and all the new people will draw attention away from her,' I say to Tyrone.

Cam interrupts, 'Sorry folks, I need to go back to the production village, pronto, before Porscha gets suspicious.'

'I'll help you pack this lot up,' I offer.

Tyrone says he is going to bed to sleep off the jetlag. 'We'll get a plan together when I wake up.'

'I'll show you your room before I head off,' says Cam to me. 'You're booked in under a false name. Ty says their luggage didn't arrive either, so I'll chase it up when I get a moment. I'll bring some stuff over later because I'm afraid your back-up case is in the villa.'

We leave Tyrone and head out into the hotel corridor. 'I really appreciate everything that you're doing for us,' I say once we arrive at my room, a few doors down from Tyrone and Lois's room.

'It also means that you have to stay in your room tonight I'm afraid. The show is aired every night, and the locals know that we are somewhere in this area, so you'll be spotted immediately if you go out. Especially as you are so like your sister to look at.' Cam shakes his head. 'It's so.... bizarre.'

'Shame. My one night of freedom and I'm stuck here.'

Cam's cheeks redden. 'I could always keep you company. I'm dropping some stuff off anyway... I mean, if you want to. It's fine if you're too tired.'

'I'd love to. It'll be nice to show you my normal side,' I say pulling a funny face. 'Let me know what time you'll be coming by so that I have time to hide the cauldron and the love potions.'

'Planning to put me under your spell?' He's matching my crazy and I like it. 'No need. I'm all yours. See you later.'

I close the door behind him and sag to the floor. I'm out. I'm out of the villa and I have a date with Cam tonight.

Tonight. My emotions are swirling around inside me. I love him. I absolutely love and adore him.

I run a hot, soapy bath. The hotel has provided a large selection of toiletries and smellies that I am going to take full advantage of. Even in this heat, I think it will be the only thing to calm me down. My heart feels like butterfly wings buzzing in my chest. The last week has been insane. It isn't until I relax into the luxurious bubbles that I realise how intense being on camera 24/7 has been. But that is nothing compared to falling head over heels in love.

Three hours later, I answer the door to Cam. 'Tyrone is still sleeping. I texted to ask if he'd like to join us for a bite to eat later,' he blurts.

'Great. Thank you. Come in,' I say, trying not to sound stiff and awkward. I smell amazing, and the fluffy white robe looks good against my tan, my hair is hanging in shiny loose curls, and because I'm devoid of any make-up, I am using extreme shyness as blusher.

'You look... clean,' he says coyly. 'I brought you these.' He thrusts a bunch of wildflowers at me. They are gorgeous. I inhale the scent.

'Thank you so much. Erm, drink?'

'What do you have?' He sounds as nervous as me.

Good point. 'I could rustle up some water from the bathroom tap.'

He starts laughing. 'I also brought this.' He produces a bottle of chilled white wine. 'I thought we might order room service. Are you hungry?'

My eyes light up. He really is my dream man. I get a wave of scented woody spice as he passes me to pick up the menu from the side table in the hotel room. We go outside onto the balcony and take in the expanse of wild jungle before us. It stretches for miles in all directions. Miles and miles of uninterrupted thick green wilderness set against a setting sun. There are two chairs and a small round table facing out over the jungle.

The heat hits me instantly.

'If it's too hot we can always go back inside,' he says, looking back into the room where there is a massive king-size bed and very little else. He clears his throat. 'I'm sorry, I didn't mean...'

'It's fine. I didn't think you did,' I say hastily. 'Besides, I wouldn't ... not on a first... or even a second... never. No. Not never. But eventually, maybe.'

I'm not sure where I'm going with this. Am I telling him he'll be waiting a very long time to get into my knickers? Possibly decades? My cheeks flame. 'Sorry. I know we agreed to take things slowly. I'm just so nervous.'

We lock eyes and I see relief spread across his face. 'Thank Christ. Me too. I've been a wreck all afternoon.'

'Really?'

'I got changed at least four times.' He shakes his head. 'I never was any good at dating.'

'What a relief. I'm positively awful. I might spill wine over you on purpose, just to get it out of the way.'

Cam chuckles. 'Okay, but only if you let me trip over and break something expensive.'

'Fine, be my guest. I'm not keen on that lamp. Let's consider this a good date if neither of us leave in tears, in debt or in an ambulance.'

'Deal. Although, I'm sure you're way better at dating than I am. You're smart, funny...'

'I'll have to ask you to stop there,' I say abruptly. 'I will not be held accountable for my actions if you insist on showering me with compliments in this ridiculous manner.'

Cam bursts out laughing, reaching out his hand to brush a wisp of hair from my eyes. My heart stops beating for a full second as he leans towards me and plants a light kiss on my lips. They tingle at his touch, making me long for him to do it again.

'You're looking at me that way again,' he says hoarsely. He cups my face and draws me in, this time his kiss is longer, deeper and growing more passionate by the second. My whole body feels on fire at his touch. I respond by running my hands through his soft hair and down his back, causing him to let out a low moan of desire. He pulls me closer to cover my neck in sweet kisses that send electricity shooting through my body.

We kiss for hours. The sun has set. The sky is bright with stars by the time we come up for air.

'I want you,' I say, when I can bear it no longer. His eyes mirror my own lust and desire as he slowly loosens the belt of my dressing gown. He slides it slowly from my shoulders. It falls to the floor, and the look on his face sends a crackle of electricity shooting up my spine.

It's time.

Chapter 28

'I'm not even going to ask how long you've been watching me sleep,' says Cam, opening one eye. A huge grin spreads across his face. 'How is it morning already?'

'Best night of my life,' I gush. 'Who knew it could be like that? Best. Ever. EVER. Night. Ever.'

My whole body is on maximum alert. Every nerve ending. Every fibre. Every muscle aches. Even muscles I had no idea about. I have butterflies upon butterflies upon butterflies flitting about in my stomach.

'I hope you... enjoyed the...' Is calling it love-making too much after a first time? 'Erm, the... encounter as much as I did. I mean... how was it for you?'

Are there TikTok tutorials on appropriate pillow talk? Because I feel this sounds more like a straw poll for Uber.

'And would you consider doing it... again? Perhaps?'

Yes, I sound needy. Yes, I sound desperate. But yes, he's fucking amazing so who cares?

Cam rolls over and leans up on one elbow. He flicks the sheet off my chest in one smooth movement and places his lips on the nearest nipple. A frenzy of delicious sparks ignites somewhere deep in my soul. He trails a lazy hand down my body to between my legs. He lifts his head to look lustfully into my eyes, 'Honey, the problem is never going to be me not wanting to make love to you.'

He slips his fingers inside causing me to moan softly. I want him so badly.

'Oh my God,' I say with a gasp. He's circling something down there which is causing me to throb like an engine. A pulsating heat is radiating out all over my body. 'Again. Do that again.'

'Do what?' he says playfully, his eyes are sparkling as he disappears under the covers to spread my legs wide.

An hour later, we are in the corridor outside my room. 'So, we appear to have ignored everything we said to each other about taking things slowly,' Cam says, as we make our way to Tyrone's room to set up the surveillance and hatch our plan to switch me back out for Lois and to get me dumped from the island without getting Cam sacked in the process.

'Uh-huh,' I say, happily.

'And you're sure you're okay? I mean, it's a big deal and all.'

'I'm fine. Better than fine. I am so unbelievably fine, it's unbelievable.'

I'm twenty-six. I can handle it. Even though I feel like I'm going to explode with excitement. I am desperate to tell Lois EVERYTHING. Cam and I have been making love. LOVE. His words. And we made love three times. Four if you count what just happened.

'And you're sure you want to keep this,' he flicks his finger between us, 'under wraps until you're out and we can figure out how to be together?'

I nod. We agreed to keep our fledgling relationship under wraps for now. It's too early days to be telling people that we have amazing, off-the-charts sexual chemistry. It's too early to say that all I can think about is him, how lost I become when he touches me, or how my heart melts the moment he looks into my eyes.

'Absolutely. Let's keep this professional until we get a solid plan together. I'd hate for you to become too distracted,' I say, gazing lovingly at him. 'By the way, you look utterly gorgeous this morning.'

He gives my hand a sneaky squeeze and pulls me to him. He leans over to place a light kiss on my cheek.

I snap to attention just as Tyrone opens the door. He welcomes us in and gives Cam a hand setting everything up.

Tyrone keeps flicking subtle glances between me and Cam but saying nothing. Then Tyrone starts trying to hide a smirk every time he looks at me.

Seriously? It can't be that obvious.

'So, you guys have fun last night?' he asks while setting up the monitors. 'What did you do?'

What didn't we do?

'Did you come up with a plan? Or were you too busy?' Tyrone says, managing to keep a straight face. The game is up. We managed to hide our secret relationship for almost a minute.

Cam goes bright red and is the very picture of guilt.

'We discussed a few things,' I say in a guilty tone, while scrapping about in my sex-fuzzled brain for something concrete to give him.

There was very little discussion going on last night. Very little. I may have asked if Cam needed some water one time when he emerged from beneath the sheets looking utterly exhausted. Apparently, I am one of those women who can have multiple orgasms, one after the other. But I am also one of those women, he said, who becomes wildly insatiable when not fully serviced. Who knew?

'Great. What's our next step?' Tyrone says switching to efficient lawyer mode.

Now it's my turn to go bright red.

'We established a good solid foundation for going forward,' Cam says diplomatically. 'Okay. Let's see what is going on inside the villa.'

He has executed a perfect deflection to spare my blushes.

We watch Lois interacting with all the islanders. Cam rewinds footage of last night and they listen to me ooh and aah about how gorgeous my sister looks, and how friendly and open she is being with them all. She's an expert at flirting that's for sure. Then we watch Lois perform her much talked of party piece.

Tyrone groans as we watch Lois undress one of the fellas with such speed and efficiency that, when she steps back to reveal him wearing a mankini made entirely of bandages, everybody gasps as though she is a real magician. She's even had time to fold his clothes and places them carefully in his outstretched arms.

The islanders love it, and Lois gets lots of claps and praise.

I'm in no hurry to go back to the villa. I could stay in bed with Cam instead, doing all manner of exotic things for days on end.

'Lois is enjoying herself way too much for my liking,' says Tyrone. We watch her being pulled for a chat by a very hot muscle-mountain who is clearly impressed with her skill set. 'How fast can we airlift her out of there?'

'Cam can smuggle me back in during one of the next outings. But how do we get Porscha to change her mind about me being on the show?'

'Simple,' says Tyrone. 'She's jealous of Cam with other women, right?'

We listen to Tyrone outline a perfectly plausible yet quite ridiculous plan that involves Cam spending too much time alone with Porscha.

'No. He shouldn't be doing that,' I say. 'It's too haphazard. Too reliant on external variables.'

I have developed a sudden jealous streak.

'Well, the alternative is you do it,' says Tyrone. 'Make sure you couple up with one of the guys in the villa to take the heat off Cam.'

'No,' says Cam. 'Too obvious.'

Maybe he has suddenly developed a jealous streak too.

'Are you going to veto any suggestion that involves you not being with each other?' Tyrone asks. He's gone full barrister mode.

'No.' And yes.

'Is there something going on that I should be aware of?' he probes, his shoulders starting to shake.

'No. Of course not,' I say.

'Are you sure?' He's finding himself increasingly hilarious. 'You two are behaving like loved-up teenagers,' says Tyrone, sounding like a father figure.

Cam is studying the keyboard while I am studying my lovely, pedicured toenails.

'We do need to agree on something,' says Tyrone. 'I would like my fiancée back so that we can enjoy our holiday together, rather than me watching her enjoy the holiday on her own.'

He's right.

Cam has engineered it so that Lois is going on a date with one of the new guys. The date is a romantic candlelit picnic on the beach at sunset. When Lois needs to go to the nearby makeshift toilet cabin, I will be waiting inside ready to switch clothes. I've had to study what hair and make-up she is doing and, thanks to Cam, she is bringing the lipstick with her in her purse. It should work.

'Ready?' Cam asks. 'If it all goes to plan, we should have you out of there in under two days.'

'Great. And I'll come back to this hotel once I'm out?'

'Correct. I'll be waiting for you,' he says. His eyes have not stopped sparkling since our... let's just call it our date night. We seem to have ignited a fire in each other. He is all glorious flames, burning brightly and I appear to be shining like the sun every time I look at myself in the mirror. Gone is the grey, lifeless, haunted look that we both wore.

'I'll do my best.' I feel empowered and strong, like a proper boss-lady as I make my way stealthily to Cam's SUV.

'Wait,' calls Tyrone, running towards us. 'I was watching the live footage. Porscha just pulled Giovanni and told him to dump Amber so they can throw her out. Then she told Mimi to dump Carlton so that she can steal one of the new guys, but really, Porscha told Destiny, it's so that she can throw Mimi out too. She says "Libby" is becoming too popular and she wants to get rid of any allies. She paired you, with a guy called Eugene.'

Cam looks at me smiling. 'It is totally playgroundy, isn't it?'

'Nobody does playgroundy like teachers,' I smirk. 'It's time to play her at her own game.'

'Good luck in there,' says Tyrone, trotting back towards the hotel.

'I'll keep feeding you information once you're in, seeing as Porscha seems to be changing her mind every two minutes,' Cam says with a note of exasperation. 'We need a new code word for the blind spot.'

'How about every time I say, 'Fix you'? As in let me fix you a drink or something like that?'

Cam is smirking again. 'Nope. I feel like you want me to enable this obsession of yours with fixing people through the medium of song. It's very troubling.'

I start laughing. He's bang on the money.

'Okay. How about I say Canadians do it better and then you come running?'

'That's more like it.' Cam revs up the engine and off we go. I am studying the top-secret notes that Cam is given each day by Porscha and the rest of the team. They scribble down options for changing the narrative to create surprises and shocks. If it weren't playing with real people's emotions, it would be quite clever really.

'These are really good. It's like reading a film script.'

'Please don't pretend that you didn't sneak a look all those times, when I left them lying around.'

'I swear I didn't. I have a real problem with that kind of thing. I think it's because I'm a teacher. We're like bloodhounds when it comes to pupils lying. We know all the tells. And we're like socially conditioned to follow orders.'

'You're going to really struggle with this plan then. It basically involves you going around lying to everyone,' Cam chuckles.

'No. It involves me going around planting seeds of doubt. There's a huge difference.'

'Well, if it gets too much, you know what to do.'

'Thanks. It's good to know you have my back in there.'

'We make a good team, don't we?' he says, taking his eyes from the road to quickly glance over.

After only a week in his presence I feel like the best version of myself. And even better, I feel like this is only the beginning.

'I had a thought,' he says as we trundle along a back road towards the beach where Lois will be having her date. 'A way for us to be together. After you leave the villa.'

Play it cool, Libby. Play it cool. Do not yell or scream or let him know you have been imagining yourself in wedding dresses all morning.

'Would you consider...?' he says but before he gets a chance to finish, his phone rings. The Bluetooth picks it up. Cam puts a finger to his lips.

'Hello?'

'Cam, it's me, Graeme. Listen, I need to tell you something. It's about the cameras and the accidental blind spot. I wasn't going to tell you, but something came up.'

'What came up?'

'I er, it's sort of... well, the camera that was supposed to cover that spot was rigged up a metre away covering the actual blind spot in the PANTRY. It's the only camera that Porscha doesn't know about, and we didn't tell her because she'd have a fit. But our team caught her threatening poor Libby so many times. It's really upset them.' There's some crackling as the reception breaks. 'Boss, we also have her on camera blackmailing you and Libby. We don't know what to do.'

Cam looks at me. 'Bring me that footage pronto. Tell no one.' He clicks off the call. 'Looks like we have our secret weapon.'

Chapter 29

Cam drives the car off the main beach road, onto a dirt track and cuts the engine. We are set back just enough that we can still see the sun twinkling off the sea as pelicans dive for fish. It's a hugely serene and romantic spot enclosed by jungle. 'We'll be a good distance from the crew and your sister here. But we'll have to go on foot the rest of the way once it is time to do the switch. You go back to... Christ, what's he called?'

I flick through Cam's notes. 'Eugene. He's twenty-seven years old. He's a dental nurse. He is a single father to a cute puppy called Floppy and he loves boats. He spends a lot of time in the gym when he's not hanging out with Floppy.'

Cam looks impressed.

'I have a class of over thirty children every year. I have to get to know them inside out or else they play you like a cheap fiddle. Speaking of which,' I say, flipping the notes over. 'This new guy Winston will be perfect for Amber.'

'Would you miss going back to England if I asked you to stay here with me?' Cam says with an earnest expression. 'It's just that I wondered if you want to... no pressure, but I just thought that it would be good if we...'

'Yes.'

'You don't know what I'm going to ask,' he says, smiling. Sparkles of joy radiating from his face.

'It's still a yes.'

He's just about to lean in and kiss me when we hear the rumbling of cars going past from our hiding spot behind a dense thicket of trees and vegetation. Cam checks his phone. 'It's them. They're setting up and filming in twenty. We should give them at least half an hour before we approach.'

'Half an hour sounds about right,' I say, licking my lips. Cam watches my tongue, so I slow down the movement and give him the look he has come to fear.

'Oh no,' he says. 'Don't look at me like that.'

I reach out my hand to stroke his thigh.

'No. Not happening,' he says laughing. His eyes are telling a completely different story.

I swirl my fingertips lightly around his crotch area, teasing him so that he hardens inside his denim shorts.

'You're terrible,' he says, looking at me awestruck. He visibly gulps and looks about to check that we are completely secluded.

Without taking my eyes from his, I slowly unzip his shorts. His breaths are coming short and sharp.

'I'd like to give you something to remember me by,' I say huskily.

Cam makes a choked sound in response, nodding his head vigorously. 'Yes. Yes. Definitely. Oh, God, yes,' he manages to say just before my lips make sweet contact.

Cam is sitting in a complete daze. It was all over very quickly due to the *unusual circumstances* he says. 'I've never been so turned on in my entire life. That was insane.' He looks over at me with dark, enticing lovey-dovey eyes. His pupils are greatly dilated, and I am thrilled at his response. I feel like a powerful, wanton woman, firmly in control of her sexuality.

'Let's rescue my sister,' I say, getting quietly out of the car. We make our way along the beach front, following the sound of the waves crashing. We step over brambles and duck under tree branches. The forest is alive with creatures making noises.

'It's incredible,' I whisper to him. 'It's such a spiritual feeling to be here surrounded by mother nature, and the intricate synergy between all of these plants and insects and animals. I feel so small in comparison. It really is wondrous, don't you think?'

Cam is still giving me goo-goo eyes. At that moment a snapping sound nearby causes us to stop. The snapping is followed by a popping sound and a whistle. I look up and there above us in the tree is the cutest-looking family of monkeys sitting watching us. Next to them are the most brightly coloured birds I've ever seen, tapping away at the branch.

'Mating calls,' says Cam. I mean, he would know all about that, wouldn't he? 'Quick look, a flying squirrel.'

'This place is magnificent. I wish I'd trained to be a conservationist rather than a teacher. Imagine if this was your classroom? Imagine if you could show future generations what we're losing if we don't change our ways.'

I'm not sure what I've said but Cam is positively bursting to tell me something.

'What? What is it?' I whisper.

He shakes his head. 'I'll tell you when this is all over.'

A few more steps and we reach the spot where they have already put up a makeshift toilet cabin. Cam silently points to it, and we make our way over and cram inside. It seems like an eternity of trying not to kiss each other in the name of being professional before the door creaks open and we see Lois standing grinning at us.

'Christ Almighty, if I have to hear one more word about that bloody puppy getting stuck in the blinds...'

She stops whispering to take us both in. Her eyes dart back and forth, observing and assessing our body language in a split second. And without saying a word her mouth forms an 'O' as she does an embarrassing pantomime wink at us.

My cheeks burn and when I look at Cam, he is equally unnerved. She's even worse than Tyrone.

'Say no more,' she says, holding up her hand as though to stop us divulging our huge secret, even though the first two people we come across have figured it out immediately.

'I'm so pleased for you,' she whispers in my ear as she hugs me close. She reaches into her bag and pulls out the red lipstick she is wearing.

Cam steps outside while we swap clothes. Once we emerge, Cam indicates that we need to move fast and before I have time to say anything, he swoops in and places a light kiss on my lips. 'See you soon,' he mouths. We part ways. Me, heart thumping deliciously as I walk towards the sea, and them, scurrying back to the hidden car.

'Hi, I'm back,' I say, approaching Eugene. He is talking to one of the camera crew.

'Hi. They said we can have me talk briefly about what type of woman I'm attracted to, and then we can head back before it gets too dark. Apparently, there are jaguars here that hunt at night.' He looks petrified.

We are instructed to sit facing the sunset while they do a shot of us from behind. Eugene is staring longingly at the sea with a faraway look in his eye. 'Floppy would love this. She loves a good sunset over the open ocean. She can sit and watch me fishing for hours and hours without a word of complaint.'

'She sounds like your ideal woman.'

'She is. She absolutely is.'

'So, your ideal type is someone very like your dog?'

'Yes.'

He's such a red flag.

'So, ideally you're after a woman who is good at cocking a leg, sniffing gates and licking herself in public?'

I'm not helping myself here, but Cam has got me high as a kite with his sheer loveliness. I am experiencing huge cravings for him. He has been gone less than twenty minutes and my body aches for him. On the plus side, no one has noticed that I am not Lois.

We travel back to the villa in eery silence. All of us are watching out for animals that accidentally stray onto the road. Porscha's male assistant, River, is driving and our runner is up front. It's time to start putting Tyrone's plan into action.

'Eugene, what do you think of Destiny? She's awesome, right?'

'Perfect, yeah. The whole package. Those bangs. So cool.'

'I'm not surprised she's with Cameron. They make a very cute couple.'

River twists briefly in his seat before turning his eyes back to the road. It is getting very dark.

'Who is Cameron? Was he a bombshell?' Eugene asks.

'No. He's one of the executive producers. I saw him and Destiny making out. I thought it was common knowledge. Please don't say anything.'

'No. Of course not. He's a helluva lucky dude to pull her.'

'And Mimi has said she's open. Did you know that she volunteers at an animal rescue centre? She's mad about pets, especially dogs.'

His eyebrows shoot up in the dim light of the car. 'Really? She never mentioned it.'

'No, she wouldn't. She keeps the obsession quiet. You won't mention it to her, will you?'

'No. Floppy could do with a strong female figure in her life. I'll definitely pull Mimi for a chat. She'll love hearing about the time Floppy got stuck in the blinds.'

'She definitely will. Oh, and one more thing. Can you let Winston know that Amber is totally ready to make a commitment? Porscha asked me to tell him, but I forgot. He needs to pick her at the recoupling tonight.'

'Sure thing. And should we choose each other?' he asks politely.

'I really think you and Mimi are a match made in heaven. You've got the same puppy vibe going on. Choose her.'

And the first of many seeds is sown.

Once we arrive, the crew get out and film us entering the villa not holding hands. I walk straight to the Beach Hut to deliver my pre-arranged speech that Cam wrote, before heading over to the outdoor kitchen to hang out with the girls who are huddled around the bar. It doesn't take me long to slot right back into where I left off, except for pretending I've already met the new girls, and pretending not to know that Porscha has given both Amber and Mimi conflicting instructions. I'm enjoying reconnecting with them. My little escape has reinvigorated me. I'm ready to have some fun playing Porscha at her own game. It's time to fight back against the bullies.

'Bubbles?' I ask the girls as I stand behind the kitchen bench busying myself with fake prosecco bottles and when I bend over to get some glasses, I sneakily reach down to my microphone pack and switch it off.

'So, you really didn't connect with Eugene, babes?' asks Mimi in her silky voice.

'No. Mainly because he is vibing off someone else in here. Vibing big time.' I give her the eye.

Mimi looks interested. 'Who me? He likes me?'

'One hundred percent.'

'Hey, Amber, Eugene told me that Winston told all the guys that he is ready to make a commitment and settle down with you. I guess you two have really hit it off. I knew you would.'

Amber looks surprised. 'Really? Oh, okay then. I guess that changes things.'

'Things were discussed,' I say, trying to hint that we have a new set of instructions. 'Ahead of tonight's recoupling.' I mouth the word 'Porscha' as I hand them a glass each.

Amber and Mimi are getting my drift and raise their eyebrows subtly to let me know they know that I know.

Job almost done. One more person to tackle. Right on cue, my phone pings.

'Meet me in the PANTRY. NOW!'

I put the phone back in my pocket and switch my mic back on.

'Is that a text?' Amber asks.

'Probably just confirming my top three picks before the firepit. Back soon.'

I make my way to the PANTRY just in time to see Porscha slide out from behind the secret door. She looks furious.

'Your mic pack. Give it here! Have you fiddled with it?'

'No,' I say, handing it over. It's all I can do not to smirk. 'You look tired,' I say. 'Is everything okay?'

Her beady eyes bore holes into mine.

'I guess it must be exhausting being on call 24/7. It's bound to have an effect on your skin and hair.'

Porscha self-consciously pats her hair. 'I don't know what you're talking about. Anyway. Eugene is picking you tonight.' She stands back expecting me to argue.

'Fine. We really like each other. I think we can go all the way to win this. The public seem to adore me, and Eugene is your typical squeaky clean boy-next-door. We make the perfect couple. Besides, I am really into his vibe now. He's going to steal a kiss from me later round the firepit in front of Destiny. What do you think?'

Porscha is looking stunned. 'But I thought you hated... anyway. Whatever.' I can see her mind whirring. She is despising this new development. 'At least it will stop you obsessing over Cameron. He's way out of your league.'

I pretend to look confused. 'Honestly, there's nothing going on there. He told me he was in a relationship anyway, so there's no point fancying him.'

I feel a stab of guilt at what I'm doing because she genuinely looks hurt.

'I know,' she says abruptly. 'I heard it from someone else. Who cares anyway? I was never that interested but he should have come clean and not led me to believe it was you he was interested in. Men!' she says, throwing her hands up in exasperation. 'Do not touch that microphone! I'm still watching you.' She turns at the last moment. 'And if you think a Brit is going to win this show, you have another think coming. Just go out there and do as you are told.'

'Oh, just one last thing,' I say to her. She can't believe the audacity. I pull out my phone and open the email attachment that Cam has just sent through. I hold it up so that she can see herself blackmailing me to stay on the show and threatening to ruin Cam's career.

Her face drains of colour. She nods silently, holds up her hands and disappears backwards through the door.

And my work here is done.

As we gather round the firepit, Mimi, Amber and I on one side of Destiny and Giovanni, Henri and Carlton stand on the other.

'New islanders, it is time to make your decision. Out with the old, or in with the new?' she says dramatically. As the sombre music is piped out from the loudspeakers, we watch Destiny zone out once more and the camera operators slide the camera back round to the new islanders. They have all been instructed to look like their lives are hanging in the balance.

First up is Eugene. 'I'm choosing this girl because she has a kind heart, and she rescues animals for a living in her spare time as a hobby. She's someone that I can see being a great stepmom to my fur baby.'

Don't get me started, I'm not even going there.

'If she was a dog she'd be a Chow Chow. The girl I'd like to couple up with is...'

Mimi and Amber are exchanging confused looks. Out of the corner of my eye I can see Porscha hovering by the camera operator. She is pressing her earpiece and looking at her notes. She nearly has a kitten when he says Mimi's name. I swing my eyes back to see Mimi scream with excitement as she leapfrogs the firepit to get to Eugene. She reminds me of the flying squirrel I saw earlier. She clamps onto him until it becomes embarrassing for everyone involved.

Destiny is quick to move on to the next contestant which greatly vexes Porscha, by the way she is staring at her. I can see the Cameron rumours may have driven a wedge between them. When Amber gets picked by Winston, and two of the new girls opt to pick Giovanni and Carlton, it's time to say goodbye to the remaining islanders.

Over half of the new islanders burst into noisy tears.

'CUT!' yells Porscha charging towards us. 'What is going on? Why are you all picking the wrong islanders? Where the bloody hell is Cam?'

Destiny takes the opportunity to power down while the islanders start accusing one another of being two-faced traitors and race over to Porscha to beg her not to dump them from the island.

Amid the chaos, Porscha swivels round to point at me. 'You. It's you, isn't it?'

I smile serenely back with a shrug.

I will leave karma to do the rest.

Chapter 30

Two days later, the four of us are sitting at the Mexican restaurant in the village with a banquet of delicious-looking, authentic dishes in front of us. Onions, peppers, strips of meat and strips of vegetables are hissing and sizzling from hot plates. Bowls of tacos, nachos, guacamole and glasses of spicy beer weigh the table down. Me and Lois are glammed up to the eyeballs in fabulous make-up and hair pieces. We are wearing two of the showstopper outfits I chose back in London, and we are wearing killer heels which make us almost as tall as our partners. Their eyes almost popped out of their heads when we walked into the hotel bar to meet them.

Lois has told us all about her time in the villa. 'Libby, you could have warned me though. It's one thing seeing them on screen but in real life… they're all so much…'

'Better looking?' I say.

'Yes! And…'

'Taller?'

'Christ, yes. And they all have such...'

'Perfect white teeth?'

'Uh-huh, and don't get me started on how...'

'Ripped they all are?' I nod back.

'Insanely ripped.'

Cam asks Tyrone, 'Are they always like this?'

He gives Cam a sympathetic look. 'Always, mate. Always finishing each other's sentences.'

'Speaking of which,' Lois turns suddenly towards me. 'Now that you've got all those interviews to do and you've been offered a sponsorship deal for those children's charities, you're not going to be able to fly back with us, are you? How long will you have to stay here for?'

'Well,' I say, feeling about to burst with joy. 'I've decided after the TV and magazine interviews and photoshoots, that I am obliged to do, thanks to you not reading the small print, to go travelling for a few weeks. Mexico, island hopping round the Caribbean and then over to Miami. Then there's a few wrap parties to attend and some *Love on the Island* functions for sponsors. And after that, I'm meeting Cam in San Francisco.'

Cam takes my hand across the table. He faces Lois and Tyrone, 'I've asked Libby to stay with me in the States for a while.'

'Then we'll see what happens after that,' I say, my cheeks colouring.

Lois takes my other hand, tears springing to her eyes. 'I'm so happy for you, sis. It sounds exactly what you need right now.' A smile spreads across her face. 'I'll let you have her for a few months, okay?' Lois looks at Cam. 'Then I want her back. Deal?'

Cam smiles softly at me.

I am taken. My heart belongs to him and his to mine.

Our future is an exciting adventure about to happen.

'Oh, I almost forgot,' I say. 'Cam, what happened with the results on the show today?'

Cam takes a swig of spicy beer and wipes his lips with his napkin. 'The public voted unanimously for a recoupling and chose those two couples to stay in the final.'

He's smiling broadly.

'It's Mimi and Carlton and Amber and Giovanni, isn't it?' I say hopefully.

Cam nods. 'One of the couples will definitely go on to win it next week.'

I'm so pleased for them. And while I didn't win the prize money myself, I feel that I came out of the villa an absolute winner, with a prize beyond my wildest dreams.

After dinner, Cam and I go for a barefoot moonlit walk along the beach. The sand is like soft powder beneath our toes. The sea laps gently beside us. I'm in a short floaty dress and Cam has rolled up his trouser legs. His hand feels firm in mine, like he never wants to let go.

He gives me an adoring look. 'I'm going to miss you while you're gone. I'm falling in love with you, Libby. I'm crazy about you.'

'I fell in love with you the moment I heard your dreamy Canadian accent,' I say, swooning at how lucky I am.

He frowns playfully. 'You thought it was American.'

'I beg to differ.'

Although he is completely in the right.

He leans towards me. 'I fell in love with you the moment you said that wheat bloats you.'

'Well, I fell more in love with you when you confessed to being a failed vegan.'

To be fair, he hasn't given me much to work with as far as faults go.

'And I with you,' he says trying not to laugh. 'When I heard you...'

'If you say, "up the bum" I'm leaving.'

He starts sniggering, 'Honestly, there's so much to choose from but I'll go with when I heard you telling Chap 3 to choke on her own vomit. We've all been wanting to say that to her for months. But none of us had the guts.'

He stops laughing to give me a serious look. 'Libby, you are my ideal woman. I've never met anyone like you. You're funny, you're smart, you're adventurous and spontaneous...'

'What did I say about showering me with compliments?' I say in a teasing voice. All we are missing is fireworks, but at that moment we see a shooting star streak across the night sky.

'Make a wish,' he says.

'Way ahead of you,' I say, pulling him down to the warm sand.

'You're giving me that look,' he says hoarsely, the energy between us becoming instantly charged. A white-hot surge of electricity shoots through me as I place my hand on his chest. His heart is racing too.

'Kiss me.'

He doesn't need asking twice.

The End.

About the Author

Jo Lyons spent years working in Turkey as a holiday rep, in the Alpes at a ski resort, in the south of France at a vineyard trying not to put them out of business before eventually ending up in Spain as a teacher. She thought she'd put her fairly adequate skills of 'getting on with people' to good use, but on her way to The Hague, she became terribly distracted by a DJ and motherhood. Twenty of her best, frozen-foreheaded years flew by before she suddenly remembered her previous ambition for world peace and politics... oh yes, and to write a book.

You can sign up to her newsletter and visit her website at

www.jolyonsauthor.com

Twitter: @J0Lyons

Instagram: @Hinnywhowrites

Facebook: @JoLyons

Acknowledgments

So many writer and reader friends helped me get this book to publication. Huge thanks to all of them: Jayne, Jess, Julia, Farrah, Cristal, Amanda, (my beloved writing coven) Alice, Nicky, Nichelle, Kim, Keith, Claire, Cara, Joanna, John, Wez, Helen, Deb, Genize, Shauna, Mrs B, Mags, Paula, Shelley, Maria, Waneens, Linds and my sisters, aunties and cousins and my niece Gabs who read all the terrible first drafts and encourage me to keep going.

And a special thanks to all my fabulous readers who take the time to get in touch, pass the books on to their friends and post lovely comments on social media. I could not do any of this without them. Lastly, huge thanks to my wonderful family. I have the funniest husband and sons anyone could wish for. They support and encourage me throughout all of the ups and downs. I have enormous respect for anyone who sets out to write a book and gets to the end without wanting to hurl themselves off the nearest cliff. Be nice to writers – we are ALL in varying states of emotional collapse.

Benidorm, actually

"Ladies and Gentlemen, we will shortly be arriving in Alicante. Please ensure your big lips and heavy eyebrows are securely fastened, your eyelashes are stowed in the upright position and your leg tattoos are clearly visible for landing."

Connie Cooper's classical music career is at a dead-end. She's singing cheap covers to a sea of bald heads and the nearest she has been to a romantic relationship in years is watching the Bridgerton buttocks scene on a continuous loop.

The last thing she needs is to be on a flight to Benidorm with strict instructions to impress the boss of Jezebel Music. But as she tries to keep up with support band, The Dollz, and the constant flashmob dancing, the going out in less than you'd wear on the beach and their obsession with the promiscuous bearded-Nuns in the villa next door, the boss seems less and less impressed. The clock is ticking. She's meant to be finding her voice, not finding his brooding good-looks irresistibly attractive...

Printed in Great Britain
by Amazon

37824278R00229